THE BIONICS

Alicia Michaels

Crimson Tree Publishing

The Bionics

Cover Design by: Marya Heiman

Typography by: Courtney Nuckels

Daddy. If it weren't for you sitting me down in front of the Star Wars movies growing up, I might not have been enough of a nerd to come up with this story. Sorry I could never get into Star Trek.
I'd like to thank my friends and critique partners R.K. Ryals and Carly Fall for not laughing in my face when I approached you about giving me your opinions on a story about half human, half robot people and for your honesty and willingness to beta read at the drop of a hat.

PART ONE:
THE BIONICS
(Blythe Sol)

ONE

BLYTHE SOL AND DAX JANNER
DALLAS, TEXAS
AUGUST 15, 4010
4:00 AM

I AM AWAKENED BY MY INTERNAL ALARM SYSTEM AND ALL I WANT IS to ignore it. I want to turn it off, roll over, and go back to sleep. The impulse to burrow beneath my thin, scratchy blanket, and ignore the world outside the house I have taken shelter in is strong.

Unfortunately, my internal alarm doesn't work that way and won't shut the hell up until I'm on my feet with my eyes open. I have the feeling that my alarm—which should only be heard by me—has also awakened Dog. I'm wondering if it emits one of those high-pitched screeches only dogs can hear. The furry bastard is licking my face with his hot tongue before I've even finished rubbing the sleep from my eye. I pet him on the head absently and stand, stretching the fatigue out of my human limbs.

I'm still not used to reconciling my human half with the robotic additions gifted to me by the Healing Hands department of the Restoration Project. It's especially jarring first thing in the morning—half of my body takes longer to wake up than the rest. Eventually, I am able to stand and give Dog a proper 'good morning'. The wiry mutt looks up at me expectantly, his tongue hanging out of the corner of his mouth. His tail swishes from side to side until I go over to my pack and fish out a few strips of beef jerky. I still don't know what breed he is. Medium sized with ginger-colored fur, he looks to be a mix of Irish terrier and God knows what. He reminds me a lot of myself, a mishmash of different things: black, white, girl, robot. We're both a conundrum.

Dog leaps up onto his hind legs and spins in a circle for the treat, bringing a smile to my face as he always does. I have very few reasons to smile these days. It's the only reason I keep the fur ball around, despite the fact that my situation isn't exactly ideal for keeping a pet.

The muted mumbling of the television from the next room lets me know Dax is awake and watching the news. I also smell food, which means he's making breakfast. Rifling through my pack, I find a clean shirt and replace it with the one I slept in. I've only brought one pair of pants with me, so I'm glad they're my most comfortable brown suede. I pull on a pair of heavy wool socks and my boots before reaching for my jacket. It's heavy with all the odds and ends I keep in the many pockets lining the front, but it's warm and functional.

I grab the small pouch containing my toiletry items and walk into the bathroom, mentally thanking Dax for letting me take the big bedroom. While the house has been cleared of all furniture—with the exception of a beat-up couch in the living room and the bed I slept in last night—the power and water still run, as well as the heat. I fill my hands with water from the faucet and splash it over the dirty mirror, using the sleeve of my jacket to wipe a clean spot big enough for me to see myself. Opening the bag, I take my time with the essential grooming: brush my teeth, splash my face with water, and comb my shoulder-length, dark brown hair into a ponytail. Once that's done, I brace my hands on the sink and stare at myself in the mirror.

I keep looking for that girl who had dreams of joining the Army and the ranks of the Military Police, of riding around on one of those sleek hover bikes and pinning one of their gleaming, silver badges to my shirt. Of being a hero, the kind of person people could look up to and trust. Like my father.

At only nineteen years old, I have lost most of my optimism; that girl is gone. I am now the antithesis of everything she once believed in. Sure, I look the same: caramel-colored skin halfway between my mother's white and father's black, brown eyes, beauty spot just beneath my left eye. Yet everything about me has changed, and it has absolutely nothing to do with the Restoration Project's accessories. With a sigh, I reach into the bag for my contact lens case.

The single, glass lens stings like a bitch on contact and will hurt for hours after I put it in. But, it protects my bionic eye from the police scanners and keeps me safe while I'm walking the streets with Dax. There is no protection for my robotic arm, except for the polyurethane glove the Professor constructed for me to wear over it. It looks like my other hand and seals over the skin right above my elbow, where the titanium and gadgetry end and I begin. It repels water, is heat and cold resistant and, more importantly, keeps me looking like the other normies.

After a minute or two, the excruciating pain in my left eye fades to an annoying throb. By lunchtime, it'll be an irritating itch and by the time I'm ready to take it off, I'll have gotten used to it. I slip my digital watch on and grab my bag before returning to the master bedroom, throwing it into my pack. Rolling my blanket up, I slide that in there as well.

4:20 am. Better get a move on.

Dog sits near the door on his haunches, waiting patiently for me to open it. As soon as I do, he's rushing to the living room to greet Dax, who's sitting on the couch in front of the television. The sleek sofa is the only piece of furniture left in the room. The remnants of the family that once occupied are scattered across the floor. Broken photo frames, forgotten children's toys, and articles of clothing tell the story of a family recently terrorized by the Military Police. The television is working just fine though, even if it isn't one of those sensory-stimulating models they have in the big cities that are still standing. Those babies have picture so colorful and sound so realistic that you'd swear the actors of your favorite shows were right there in your living room. You can smell what the TV chefs are cooking, as well as the fabric softener in commercials full of smiling people and soft towels. I step over a broken vase and dodge a disembodied baby doll head, dodging the debris scattered around the room like landmines until I reach the kitchen.

Dax has, in his usual fashion, made the most of what we found when coming upon this house the night before. He's located and cleaned a few pans, plates, cups, and utensils and raided the fridge.

"Fresh eggs?" I ask as I dig into the pan he's left on the stove. The eggs are still warm and are mixed with bits of Dax's rationed beef jerky. "Potatoes?" I scoop some of those onto my plate too, eyeing the orange concoction in a glass pitcher on the counter with awe. "Is this real orange juice?"

"The house couldn't have been vacant for more than a few days before we showed up," Dax says from where he sat on the couch, glued to the news. "The expiration date on that orange juice was for a week from now. And the potatoes aren't real, but the eggs are, so eat up."

We fall into silence again as I sink down onto the sofa beside him, sitting my glass on the floor between my feet. I dig into my eggs and groan aloud with ecstasy. It's been months since I've eaten real eggs. Despite the beef jerky, which is an odd mix, I wolf it down pretty quickly, content to let Dax finish watching the broadcast in peace.

Silence between Dax and me is comfortable, which is good because I'm not much for conversation unless I have something to talk about. Dax knows this about me and understands that my silence isn't always a bad thing. After I'm done eating, I glance at him out of the corner of my eye. He is reclined against the back of the couch, his long legs spread with Dog resting between them. His smooth, brown skin is offset by dark, midnight black hair buzzed close to his head and twinkling brown eyes.

Dax is a great, hulking beast of a man, broad in all the places that count, but as warm and charming as they come. He and I are only a few years apart in age—he's nearing his twenty-first birthday—and I always wonder what our lives would be like if we'd met before the nuclear blasts that hit several major cities in the United States and changed our lives forever. Would we have ever met? Would we be friends? More than friends?

I often tease him that if he didn't have titanium ribs and a set of robotic legs, he could be on one of those electronic billboards in the city, posing in his underwear. Dax always laughs at me, but I think it's true. Then I think what a shame it is that guys like Dax can't be models. They can't be anything but dead or in hiding.

Him finding me two years ago was one of the best things that ever happened to me, because it saved my life—*he* saved my life. He turns to me and smiles, and I smile back. Besides Dog, he's the only one that can make me do that.

"Ready, B?" he asks, reaching for the remote and turning off the television at the height of President Drummond's speech. The image of our brown-haired, blue-eyed national leader disappears, and I am relieved to be free of his deceptive gaze. "I think I've had enough of that asshole to last me all week. How 'bout you?"

I snort as I stand and sling my pack over my shoulders. "I don't know why you watch that garbage. All they do is fill the airwaves with his messages and his voice. If you're not careful, you'll become one of his mindless drones. You're already part robot, so you're halfway there."

Dax laughs and stands, pulling on his blue-jean, fur-lined jacket. I always joke that it makes him look like one of those old-fashioned pilots they have photos of in the museums. He pulls a skullcap over his head, and I dig mine out before stuffing my ponytail in it and covering my ears. I have gotten used to bundling up every morning before starting out. Ever since the burning out of the ozone layer, and our nation's pitiful attempts at constructing a synthetic replacement that left our planet in even worse shape, the weather is unpredictable. While August used to be the hottest month of the year in the state of Texas, today we will more than likely find ourselves tramping through snow.

I stare up at the smooth, white exterior of the house with its round windows and clear, glass roof. It's a beautiful house—this is one of the few areas in the state not affected by nuclear war—but too conspicuous for us to use as a hideout in the future, so I tell Dax we should burn it. If the MPs should come back looking for more of our kind, our fingerprints and hair fibers will be everywhere. We can't leave any hint of our presence in this house or neighborhood and since we can't use it as a hideout, we'll burn this beautiful place to the ground.

He finds a gas can in the garage and goes back inside. Dog and I stand on the brown, withered grass out front and wait for him to come out. By the time we set out on our way, the house is lighting up from the inside with orange flames, soon to be no more than a pile of smoldering ash. We really kick it into high gear then, putting as much distance between us and the house as possible before the fire department shows up.

As we walk, I reach into one of my many pockets and pull out a pair of gloves. They don't offer much protection from the cold, and I technically only need one since my bionic hand feels nothing. But I wear them both because for one hand, they're better than nothing, and if I'm going to wear one, I might as well wear the other to keep from looking suspicious. It's a beautiful morning, even if the sun hasn't come up yet. A few stars remain in the sky, and that pretty mix of pale blue, orange, and pink has just started to spill out over the horizon.

It is now 5:00 am..

We're making good time, although I dread going back to headquarters empty-handed. Coming back with even one refugee would be worth it, but at this point, it seems like too much to hope for. We've been in Dallas for five days now, combing various neighborhoods for signs of life or people in hiding.

"Do you think there's anyone left in this neighborhood?" I ask Dax as we walk. I am keeping a sharp eye on our surroundings, counting on my bionic eye to give me readings on any nearby signs of life. It's picking up the body-heat signatures of me, Dax, Dog, and a rabbit hopping past us across the street, but nothing else. It's got our environment's temperature read at thirty degrees, and is telling me there's a seventy-five percent chance of sleet and freezing rain tonight.

Dax shrugs. He is looking for signs of life too,

even though he knows I'm more likely to spot them first. "I doubt it," he says. "Looks like we got the short end of the stick this mission. MPs likely raided the entire 'hood."

I nod in agreement but don't say anything else. With the house in that condition and still standing, it was more than likely that an arrest had been made, just like Dax said. Some poor soul had been imprisoned before we had a chance to get there and save them, along with who knew how many others on the block. Typically, when these neighborhood raids happen, entire streets get cleaned out as people like me are arrested and their families are punished for harboring them. I shudder at the thought of what is being done to them.

"We can't change what happened at that house," Dax says, and I know he's sensed the direction of my thoughts. He knows I tend to take these things personally. "We save the people we can, B," he reminds me, repeating the age-old mantra of the Professor. I know he's right, but I still can't help it. Seeing that house reminded me of my own childhood home... of kneeling on the front lawn, surrounded by MPs in their gleaming white armor. Of staring down the barrel of a gun and waiting for death. That was the last time I ever laid eyes on my family.

I never will again.

"There are plenty of houses down this street to check," I say, quickly changing the subject. "Hopefully, I'll get a readout and we don't have to go back to Jenica empty-handed."

Really, I don't give a flying fuck about Jenica, but

I need an excuse to voice my desperation at needing to find someone... anyone.

Dax glances at his watch. "We have a few hours before the hovercraft makes its rounds. Let's get moving."

By noon, I am discouraged, cranky, hungry, and ready to go back to headquarters. Not a soul exists in this abandoned neighborhood. Either Jenica's intel was wrong, or the people we've come to find are long gone, probably incarcerated, dead, or holed up someplace else.

We're standing on the corner of what was once a busy intersection, in front of a row of hollowed-out storefronts. We've walked for hours toward the rendezvous point—a section of town long since abandoned for the newer, more modern houses, offices, and shopping centers. Soon, bulldozers will take out what remains here, and gleaming, towering, white buildings will replace the ones we stand in front of now.

I lean against a storefront window beside Dax, watching Dog run around in circles and try to catch the snowflakes that have been falling for about an hour now. He's an ugly little mutt, but he's mine. Well, ours. Dog is just as much Dax's as he is mine. I glance at my watch just as the humming sound of the hovercraft reaches my ears.

"On time as always," Dax says with a snort. "Do you think she schedules and times her bathroom breaks?"

I cut him a glance out of the corner of my eye.

"Jenica? Yeah, I could see that. Urination scheduled for five o'clock pm."

Dax's guffaws become full-fledged laughs as the large, oblong shadow of the hovercraft blots out the meager light of the sun. I picture Jenica in the cockpit with her black, waist-length, bone-straight ponytail and sharp features. Dax and I have a running joke going about that ponytail. We are both of the opinion that it holds her face up. No way are her eyes really that narrow and sharp, or her cheekbones so well defined. Technically, this only applies to half of her face, as the other half is made of titanium, but still.

The hovercraft lowers over us and the hatch opens, releasing the ladder for us to climb in. Our pilot and team leader, Jenica Swan, is waiting, along with the six other members of our crew. Her starched, black jumpsuit is spotless as usual, not a crease out of place or a speck of lint to be found. Her boots are polished to a high and glossy sheen. I don't think she's got a single split end in that sleek ponytail.

Dax and I slide into our seats in the front row, directly behind Jenica, and buckle our harnesses. One look over my shoulder reveals the rest of our crew and the bedraggled group of refugees they've found. I nod in greeting to the crewmembers and try to smile encouragingly at the dozen or so people they rescued. I know what they're feeling, and realize many of them have been through what I've been through. My eyes lock with a girl no older than me, with smooth, cocoa-colored skin. Her eyes are dark and wide and her hands are shaking. I don't see any machinery, so I wonder if she has bionic organs of some kind. There are others there too, family members of those with more obvious hardware, but this girl is alone, and something tells me she's one of us. Then I wonder if she's lost her family like I have, since none of the other rescued people have her dark skin or luscious features.

I want to encourage her, to tell her I know where she's been and that we're here to help; that she's safe now. But none of those words come and I turn away from her, closing my eyes against her pain. It is too much for me, reminding me of things I'd rather forget.

Ignoring Dax's concerned look, I gaze out at the now-moving horizon over Jenica's shoulder. We make fun of her, but that is one dedicated member of the Resistance. She's also one hell of a pilot. I often wonder about Jenica's past and why she's as hardened as she is. I've never known a child to be born that way. Something had to have happened, but behind the machinery that takes up most of one side of her head and face, I can't find a clue. She's as hard as ever, and I wish I could be more like her. She doesn't seem to care when we come back empty-handed. I, on the other hand, can't stop thinking about it.

Seeing that empty, trashed house in Dallas brings back so many memories, and I can't help but think of my own family. Those thoughts bring an acidic taste to my mouth. I turn toward the window, stare at the moving clouds beside me, and wonder if that taste will ever go away.

Sometime during the flight, I nod off. I can't fight the fatigue, combined with the gentle movement of the hovercraft when they combine to sedate me. As my eyes slide shut, my father's face appears, blotting out the velvety darkness of dreamless sleep.

"I want you to have this," he says as we sit together at our kitchen table. He slides something across the stainless-steel surface toward me. His eyes—dark brown like mine—crinkle at the corners when he smiles, turning the hardened face of a soldier into the loving expression of a dad. When he pulls his hand away, his gleaming, metal Lieutenant Colonel's rank pin is resting on the table next to my coffee cup.

Eyebrows wrinkled, I reach down to pick it up, turning it over in my palm and studying it. "Your pin? But, don't you want to keep this?"

He shrugs, leaning on his elbows against the table. "I have plenty of things around here that remind me of my time in the service," he replies. "This is special, though."

Running my thumb over the pin, I smile. "I remember the day you got pinned," I tell him. "They had that big ceremony and Mom wore that red dress."

His smile widened at the memory. "She always looks so pretty in that one. I'll never forget the sense of pride and accomplishment I felt when she was given that pin to place on my lapel. It was a promotion fifteen years coming, something I'd worked so hard for."

"You were my hero that day," I admit. "That was the day I decided I wanted to be just like you when I grew up. That was eight years ago, and I still feel the same way. You're still my hero, Dad."

His eyes get a little watery, and he reaches out to grab my newly attached titanium hand. Even though I can't feel his touch, my fingers wrap around his, reacting to the stimulation. "I want you to keep that pin as a reminder, Blythe," he says, his voice growing hoarse. "I may not always be around to remind you—"

I laugh, shaking my head. I can't imagine a world without him in it. "Don't you know? Heroes never die."

He laughs with me, swiping at the tear forming in the corner of one eye. It wasn't until he was gone that I understood why he cried that day as he tilted my chin up with one hand and stared into my eyes.

"I want you to remember to always stand up for what's right," he says, serious again. "No matter the cost, Blythe. In the end, no matter what you've lost in the fight, justice will always prevail and the good will outshine the bad. Sometimes... sometimes, it takes a while for it to happen, but I believe that it can. Do you understand?"

I am suddenly jolted awake as a baby begins crying in the back of the hovercraft. The mother of one of the refugees rocks and shushes the infant, but I'm already losing my hold on the dream, and my father's face has retreated back into my memories.

"Hey," Dax whispers, watching me closely with worry in his gaze. "Are you all right?"

Running a hand through my hair, I take a deep breath and release it. "I'm fine," I lie, resting my head against the back of the seat once more.

Do you understand?

My father's words come back to me now, causing me to reach up and caress the rank pin I keep attached to the collar of my jacket. I swallow past the lump in my throat and try as hard as I can, but in the end, I just can't. Standing up for what was right didn't do him any favors, and in the past two years, it hasn't done much for me either. I lay awake some nights and wonder just how far he meant a person should take this whole standing tall thing. Until they'd lost everyone they ever loved? Until they were so fucked up in the head they could never properly love anyone ever again? Until they lost hope, and all passion for the cause they stood for in the first place?

I'm sorry, Daddy, I thought, turning to stare out the window again. *I just don't understand.*

TWO

I AM GRATEFUL WHEN JENICA LOWERS THE HOVERCRAFT OVER THE painted landscape of Nevada. After two years away from my hometown in Georgia, the rusty walls of Red Rock Canyon look more and more like home every day. Calm sweeps over me as we hurtle along through the canyon, shaded from the stifling Nevada heat by the mountains jutting up from the ground. While we encountered snow in Texas, the state of Nevada and its desert stretching away from bustling Las Vegas, is still hot as hell. In fact, global warming and our ruined ozone layer have rendered it even hotter.

Everyone is glad we didn't encounter the MPs, especially with the scared and likely malnourished refugees in the back of our craft. We are all capable of fighting when necessary, but our Resistance is a peaceful one and we try not to kill when we don't have to.

The round, steel portal carved into the side of the canyon opens to allow us entrance, and we are soon hurtling through the dim metal tube that leads to

Resistance Headquarters... and home.

As we shoot out the other end of the tube, the citadel that was built into the red mountains as a haven for our kind comes into view. Jenica dodges other crafts and steers us toward Hexley Hall, the living quarters of all children and family members of refugees. There are so many of them that Hexley Hall is filled to over capacity. These people will likely have to share space with some of our other residents until construction is finished next door on Regent Hall. For now, I'm sure they are just happy to have a place to lay their heads without fear of arrest or execution.

Jenica lands the craft on the lawn of Hexley Hall and unbuckles her harness, turning toward the scared people huddled toward the back of the aircraft.

"All refugees come to the front of the craft, where I will document you and pass you on to the matron of Hexley Hall, Milica Brady. She will see you all settled into your quarters and provided with whatever necessities you were unable to bring with you."

"What about the others?" a voice calls from the back of the craft. I whip around in my seat to put a face to the masculine voice. From behind the others appears a head of blond hair, a broad pair of shoulders, and deep blue eyes that lodge my heart in my throat. The refugees part to reveal him and I can only stare, slack-jawed. He is as large and wide as Dax, with smooth skin and features chiseled from stone. His brow is furrowed over eyes narrowed on Jenica. I look across the aisle to find Dax staring at me quizzically, and then back at the stranger.

"Excuse me?" Jenica asks, her tone sharp. "What others?"

"When do we help them? The other Bionics stuck out there?"

Jenica's jaw hardens and her hardware hums as she narrows both eyes, human and machine. "We don't use that term here," she says, referring to President Drummond's nickname for us. The Bionics, they call us—humans modified by government equipment. They created us and now they hate us, fear us, force us to go into hiding to protect ourselves and our families. Because Jenica's hardware isn't as easily hidden as mine is, I know the term is especially sensitive for her, thought it doesn't really bother me. In fact, most of us use the term in reference to each other and others like us. It's being called a Bionic by outsiders that put some of us on edge. It's the implication that we are not human because of our modifications.

"I'm sorry," the stranger says, running long, slender fingers through his hair. "I didn't mean it that way."

Jenica nods once, but I can tell she's still not fond of him. She's not fond of anyone who speaks out of turn. "I am sure you didn't. You should be more careful about throwing that word around. As far as the other *victims* goes, that is not your concern Mr...." She looks up at him pointedly, pen poised over her clipboard, human eyebrow raised.

"Gage," he answers. "Gage Bronson."

Jenica writes something in her neat, precise scrawl. "Mr. Bronson, rest easy. The very capable field soldiers you see in front of you are working hard every day to rescue those of *our* kind that need it."

Gage doesn't miss Jenica's emphasis on 'our kind'; it's obvious by the pulling of muscles around his mouth and the flash of defiance in his eyes. He swivels those eyes toward me, and I am frozen in his stare, unable to look away. We look at each other just long enough for me to notice that there's a rim of silvery gray around the outside of his blue irises before I tear my gaze from him, embarrassed. Gage doesn't say anything else to Jenica, but he has definitely made his presence known, and I'm officially curious.

What is he doing here? He's obviously not one of us; he looks like he belongs in one of the metropolitan areas, those unaffected by nuclear war or radiation. He has none of the desperation in his eyes that most of us carry in our fight to stay alive. There's determination there, though, and I can't help but admire that.

Jenica motions the refugees forward, and they step up one at a time to register. I wait patiently in my seat as she records their names and other stats, including their bionic parts. When Jenica gets to the dark-skinned girl I locked eyes with earlier, she answers that her skin has been genetically modified to have the hardness and durability of Kevlar. I see Dax's eyebrows shoot up, and several of our other crew members whistle and murmur to each other. A girl with skin made of Kevlar would be an amazing addition to our team. She says her name is Yasmine Zambrano, and I make a mental note to remember it.

When she gets to Gage, he, of course, lists no

bionic appendages, confirming what I suspected. What he does next, though, blows me away. He reaches down and picks up a little girl—one I hadn't seen before now—and holds her against his chest.

"Agata Schwenke," he says. "Seven years old. Bionic spinal cord and bionically engineered left brain."

If Yasmine's revelation was enough to stun everyone, this was definitely one to blow that right out of the water. I stare into the soulful, wide eyes of little Agata and see intelligence there. Part of her cerebrum—the segment that computes logic, math, and speech—has been bionically enhanced. Agata is more than likely smarter than everyone on this craft. The Professor will want to study her for sure.

Gage and Agata are last, and Jenica leads them all toward the opening and ladder, where they climb down and are met by Milica Brady. I watch from my window as the matron greets them and them motions them toward the open doors of the hangar, Jenica's notes in her hand. As they disappear, I wonder about Gage and the little girl. Is Agata his sister? His daughter? Whoever she is, I can't help but think him brave for bringing her here. If the Military Police ever found out he had been here or helped a Bionic escape, he would receive the death penalty. She must be someone important if he braved coming to the very center of the Resistance to save her.

Jenica boards the hovercraft again, and my thoughts leave Gage and little Agata. I will seek them out later, but decide for now to think about a hot meal and my warm bed.

"I don't trust him."

I already know who Dax is talking about, but I don't want to let on that Gage has been popping in and out of my thoughts since I clapped eyes on him earlier, despite my attempts at changing the direction of my thoughts. Clad in only a bra and clean pair of pants after a shower, I'm rifling through my dresser for a shirt. Dax is reclining on my bed, his hair still damp from his own shower, his long legs propped up on my footboard. He's watching me get dressed, but I take my time. I have no reason to be a prude around Dax; he's seen a lot more of me than just my bra. Not on purpose, but that's just kind of the way things are when you share a bathroom with a girl but don't know how to knock.

"Who's that?" I mumble distractedly.

I turn to face him, and Dax purses his lips and tilts his head. "Yeah, okay, like you haven't been thinking about him?"

My cheeks get hot, and I tug on the hem of my shirt. "What? I have not! I mean... you know..."

Dax grins. "Relax, Blythe, I just meant that I know you're curious about him and that little girl. A bionic left brain? It's unheard of."

I turn toward my mirror, plucking the uncomfortable contact lens from my eye with a relieved sigh.

"The Professor is going to love that one," I say as I blink a few times, allowing my robotic eye to focus on my reflection. It gives me a reading of all my vitals and I blush when I realize my heart rate has spiked during our conversation about Gage. I let my wavy, damp hair down and run my fingers through it, feeling much more like myself now that I'm in my room, showered, and wearing clean clothes.

"Ready?" I ask.

Dax leaves his reclined position on my bed and stands, his head nearly scraping the low ceiling of my room. I'm lucky enough that I don't have to share quarters with anyone, but Dax might as well be my roommate since he's always here. He drops his pilot's jacket over a chair and removes his sweater, revealing a gray, sleeveless undershirt that showcases his barrel-wide chest and powerful arms. I roll my eyes at the sight; now the girls will be mooning at him over dinner and asking me to introduce them to him when he's not looking.

"What?" he asks with a shrug at my annoyed expression. "I'm hot."

Fucking perfect.

"Let's go," he says, patting his empty belly. The sound of his titanium ribs echoes in his chest and the clanking of his footsteps are heavy. He's taken off his boots and is walking barefoot, his prosthetics peeking out from under the cuffs in his cargo pants. The titanium echoes on the floor as we walk, falling in with the other members of our team who are leaving their rooms for the dining hall. Mosley Hall is a mishmash of outcasts, half-human/half-robots, who have all shed their disguises. Titanium gleams everywhere as the sound of hardware echoes from the walls. Eyes glow, cogs whiz and whir, and I feel more at home surrounded by these sights and sounds than I do anywhere else. Energy levels are high, and it seems Dax and I are the only ones who have come back empty-handed from our mission.

Olivia McNabb, a spunky blonde with bionic adrenal glands and a titanium right hand runs up beside me in a blur. Anytime I feel a rush of air whipping around or past me, I always look for Olivia. Her enhanced adrenal glands give her an extra boost of adrenaline, lending her lightning quick speed and reflexes. She's removed her polyurethane glove and uses her robotic hand to push her messy bangs back from her face.

"Hey, how'd it go out there?"

Dax shrugs but cuts his eyes at me. I feel concern emanating from him, and I know he's wondering about how I'm feeling after staying in that trashed house. It's something we do while on missions, but nobody knows better than him how hard it is for me to be reminded of a past I'd rather forget. It feels even worse when we don't get there in time to save the people we are there to save.

"No MPs, no Bios," he answers simply as we leave Mosley Hall and cross the arcade toward the dining hall, which is situated right at the center of Restoration Resistance Headquarters. The grass beneath our feet and the blue sky and clouds overhead are synthetic, but I appreciate them. The Professor created the program to give us a sense of still living in the outside world. Without the changing weather, we'd just be living in a gigantic hole carved into the side of a mountain. I appreciate the normalcy of rain or snow every now and then. It follows the patterns of the seasons—at least, the seasons we used to have before the ruined ozone layer—so for now, we've got a balmy summer evening and a slight chance of rain.

"That's too bad," Olivia answers. She turns to me with an impish smile, and I already know what's going to come out of her mouth next. "You get a good look at that Gage guy?"

I keep my gaze straight ahead, avoiding both their stares. I can't afford to let them know I still can't get those blue-gray eyes out of my head.

"Yeah," I answer as calmly as I can. "What about him?"

Olivia rolls her eyes. "Okay, play dumb. I'm just going to go ahead and say it. He's freakin' hot."

Dax frowns, and I see the corners of his mouth tense. I laugh at him, which only draws his dark, hawkish gaze toward me. I shrug.

"How does it feel to have to share the henhouse with another rooster?" I quip.

Dax doesn't answer, but his lips tighten and I think he's about to blow a gasket.

"Dax doesn't trust him," I offer, filling in the silence.

"Really? Seems all right to me."

"Olivia, if you would think past how fast you can spread your legs for this prick, you might actually see the truth."

Olivia flips Dax the bird with her bionic hand. "Fuck you, Janner."

She's pretending to be mad, but her wide grin says it all. Olivia is the Resistance Headquarters' slut and everybody knows it. She and Dax have been friends with benefits for a while now, but I pretend not to know about it. For some reason, the thought of my best friend and the neighborhood hoe getting it on fills my mouth with bitter bile; it's not exactly a topic of conversation I want to pursue.

"Come on, you two, use your heads," Dax continues, stopping just outside the doors of the dining hall. "How many Normals do we have running around the place?"

"You mean besides Gage?" Olivia asks.

Dax nods once.

"Not that many other than the family members of the other Bios," she answers. "Oh, well, and the Professor, but he doesn't count. He's practically one of us."

"Exactly. There's a reason we don't let them in. We have no idea what he wants or why he's here."

"He's a family member too. He's protecting the little girl," I argue. As soon as the words are out, I regret them. Dax is staring at me as if he'd like to shake some sense into me. Deep down, I know he's right and I should be suspicious of Gage. After all, there's a reason we are here. "Look, I just don't think we should be crucifying this guy just because he stood up to Jenica, or because he's not a Bio. There are other people here just like him who have brought their children, siblings, or parents to try to escape the MPs. You know the penalty for harboring a Bio is death in some states. This guy has nowhere else to go."

"We don't know what kind of connections he might have or what kind of information he might be feeding someone on the outside," Dax argues, dropping his voice to a harsh whisper as a few more of our team and some of the refugees walk past us and into the building. "We have managed to stay hidden for years and letting this guy in could prove to be our most fatal error."

"Well, what do you suggest we do about it, Captain-Fucking-Know-It-All? The Professor never turns anybody away unless they give good reason. So far as I can tell, all he's done is rescue a little girl," Olivia challenges, her hands on her round hips. Dax's jaw ticks, and I know he's about three seconds away from smashing her face in... that is, he would he if she were a guy... and if he could catch her first.

"Don't you have someone you could be screwing right now?" Dax counters.

Olivia sways her hips and bats her eyelashes. "You offering, baby?"

"That's enough!" I interject. I don't like the way Olivia is looking at Dax, and I'm in no mood to watch those two get into it. Besides, I want to know exactly what Dax's position is on Gage. We have always agreed on everything, but I have a feeling Gage is going to be one of those topics best not discussed by us.

"So, are you going to answer the question?" I ask once the two have stopped staring daggers at each other. "What do you think we should do about Gage if he turns out to be dangerous?"

Dax shrugs. "Simple. Kill him.

THREE

BLYTHE SOL, DAX JANNER, AND OLIVIA MCNABB
RESTORATION RESISTANCE HEADQUARTERS
AUGUST 15, 4010
5:00 PM

THE DINING HALL IS BUZZING WITH CONVERSATION AS ALWAYS, BUT I can't hear a word of it. It's all unintelligible—a jumble of noises and sounds, much like the hum of the hovercraft that brought us home. I stand in line to receive my ration, purposely avoiding Dax's gaze. Olivia is as silent as I am, and I can tell what Dax said out on the steps is burned into her mind as well. I can see it in width of her eyes as she watches him accept a bowl of a soup and a hunk of bread. Neither of us can believe how easily a statement so brutal could have come from his mouth.

Kill him.

I glance over my shoulder to where Gage is sitting alone in the middle of the dining hall, his broad shoulders hunched over his tray. He keeps his eyes lowered and eats methodically, almost mechanically, as if he's doing it because he has to, not because the food tastes good. The little girl—Agata—is at the kids' table with the Hexley Hall matron. She seems happy enough now that she's safe, and I remember that that's all thanks to Gage.

27

Kill him?

Hell no. We should be giving this guy a medal and buying him a drink. He's risked his own life to safe one of us, and that makes him all right in my book.

"Blythe."

I look up to meet Dax's eyes and see the warning there as he shakes his head, twice. My human eye twitches and aggravation causes my jaw to tick.

Nobody tells me what to do and, damn it, Dax knows this. I turn my back on him with a flip of my hair and make my way over to Gage's table. I can practically feel Dax's rage, and I purposely exaggerate the sway of my hips as I go, blatantly letting him know that I don't care what he thinks. He's got little Miss Olivia offering to crack her legs open for him, and I've got a hero to meet and greet.

"Hi," I say as I set my tray on the stainless-steel table across from him and lower myself onto the matching bench. Piercing blue eyes stab me as Gage looks up from his bowl. The pupils widen and he pauses, spoon halfway up to his lips, soup sloshing over the sides.

"Hey," he answers in the same smooth voice I remember from the hovercraft. His tones are cultured, like the people who live in the big cities, and again, I'm left wondering where this guy is from and how he ended up here. His clothes are plain—a white, long-sleeved thermal shirt, brown suede jacket and blue jeans that showcase sinful stretches of masculine muscle—but they're high quality, and it's obvious that he's not hard up for cash.

After a few minutes of slack-jawed staring on my end, and open curiosity on his, Gage goes back to his soup with a shrug, obviously deciding the fish-eyed chick across from him is freaking crazy. I'm just amazed at he isn't staring at my bio arm like it's a serpent.

The dining hall has suddenly gone silent, and I feel about a hundred pairs of eyes boring into me. A few whispers start up, and I know they're wondering why I'm sitting with the outsider in the room. While he's not the only Normal here, he draws the most attention because of his expensive clothes, and the way he talked back to Jenica when no one else would dare. No one knows his relationship to the little girl, and everyone wants to know where they come from. It's obvious they're from money, and people with money have connections... government connections. Knowing no one is going to accept him unless I prove he's harmless, I try to strike up a conversation with him between bites of sausage-and-potato soup.

"That was very brave, what you did today." I start with that whispered compliment and wait to see where it lands me. Gage's eyelids pop up, and he's staring at me again. I shift uncomfortably under his gaze.

"One girl," he says with a shrug. "It won't make much of a difference."

I lean forward, my fist clenched tightly around my spoon. "Are you kidding me? A girl with a bionic brain is just the ammunition that asshole in the White House needs to wage his war against us. If he can convince people that Bios like Agata can read or manipulate minds..." I trail off, shaking my head and sighing angrily. It takes me a moment to get myself together. "You have no idea what you have done for our cause. If nobody else tells you this... well, thank you."

A smile finally splits Gage's face, and I can't help but return the favor. It's as if the corners of his mouth control mine with marionette strings; they can't help but follow the pull of his smile. Across the room, I see Dax's mouth tightening and his nostrils flaring in annoyance. My smiles are usually only for him and Dog.

"I did what I had to do, nothing more. What's your name?" Gage asks, mopping the bottom of his bowl with the crust of his bread.

"Blythe. Blythe Sol."

"Blythe," he repeats slowly as if rolling the moniker around on his tongue and testing its flavor. I guess he decides he likes the taste of it because he nods. "Nice to meet you."

"You too," I say before taking another bite. "Where you from, Gage?"

His eyes harden and his jaw clenches, his knuckles going white around his spoon. "D.C."

My jaw drops. Only the richest and those in the upper echelon of society inhabit the nation's capital. Just as I suspected, Gage comes from a very rich and influential family. My windpipe is suddenly gripped in an iron grasp, and I feel like I'm going to be sick. If Gage is from Washington D.C., then everything Dax suspects could very well be true. It's just too much of a coincidence—the fact that he's so strong and good looking and just happens to be from the city where the Military Police train and the most militant of those against us are located. But then I look at him and the protective way he's watching the girl, and I can't help but chastise myself for jumping to conclusions. If I suspect him without cause, I am no better than the people who would judge me because of my titanium parts.

Gage must suspect the train of my thoughts because a grimace crosses his face before he says, "It's not what you think. I really do want to help. I think it's wrong what the president is trying to do."

"Is that so?"

I make a mental note to rip Dax a new one later as he lowers himself onto the bench beside me, dropping his tray on to the table with a loud 'clang'. His dark eyes are hard and shining like onyx, every muscle in his neck and shoulders coiled with tension. Gage isn't impressed or intimidated, and I admire him for meeting Dax's anger head on.

"Yes," he answers, his biceps flexing in answer to Dax's clenched fists.

"And just who the hell do you think you are, marching in here like some kind of goddamn savior to the poor, deformed outcasts?"

Gage's meaty hands grip the edge of the table as he stands, all six foot, four inches of him solid muscle. Dax is of equal size and just as frightening as he rises as well.

"Better than being some bitter, meat-headed jackass," Gage hisses.

"That's enough!" Olivia interrupts as she joins us at the table. For once, I am happy to see her and her obnoxiously large breasts and perky smile. "Dax, the guy just got here. Lay off him."

Dax's nostrils flair. I can tell that he wants to leap over the table and treat Gage to a roundhouse kick in the chest with one of his prosthetics, but he decides against it. The guys sit back down, and Olivia joins Gage on his side of the bench. I try to ignore the annoyance I feel at watching him turn that wide smile on Gage.

"I'm Olivia," she says. "I thought it was real nice what you did for that little girl."

"It was nothing," Gage answers.

"Damn right, it wasn't," Dax grumbles. Gage tenses but doesn't respond.

"Is this seat taken?"

"No!" I answer quickly to the girl with Kevlar for skin. Her name is Yasmine, I remember, as she sits down on my opposite side. "Please, join us."

The more the merrier at this point. I have a feeling if Dax and Gage ever get a chance to really go at it, it's going to take several of us to stop them, despite the fact that Gage doesn't have any robotic advantages.

"You're Blythe, right?" she asks, ignoring her plate and turning those wide, brown eyes of hers directly on me.

I nod.

"They say you're the one to talk to if I want to meet the Professor."

Gage perks up at this. "I want to meet him, too."

I'm not surprised that they want to meet him. Even before his retreat to the underground and the forming of the Resistance, he became something of a celebrity for heading up the Healing Hands Project after the nuclear blasts to create the bionic technology that saved many of our lives. Everyone knows him as the leader of the Resistance, even the president. They'd like nothing more than to get their hands on the Professor, who is pretty much public enemy number one. This is why we are so protective of him. Very few of us have access to him, and to get to him, you have to go through us.

"Whoa, you guys," Dax says. "The Professor is a busy man. He doesn't have time to entertain."

"I want to join your team," Yasmine answers, irritation edging her voice. I love the way she's eyeballing Dax like she doesn't give a damn. I like this girl already. "I overheard some of the others saying that you go on missions to save others like us from the MPs, and I want in."

"What can you do?" Dax challenges.

Without taking her eyes off Dax, Yasmine reaches for the knife on her tray. She brings it down, full force, on her arm. The blade bends in half on contact, repelled by Yasmine's diamond-hard skin. She arches one dark eyebrow at Dax.

"I can also walk through fire without getting burned and withstand temperatures cold enough to turn you into an icicle," she says. I can hear pride in her voice, and I know that she will be a lot like Jenica, who is proud of her bionic additions. Dax nods approvingly, his eyebrows raised.

"What about you?" she asks Dax, arms folded over her chest. "So far as I can tell, you're just a big lummox with car parts for legs."

Dax laughs and I'm glad to hear the sound. Things have been way too tense since we left the hovercraft this afternoon. He stands and grins at Yasmine.

"Punch me," he says, pointing to his torso. "Right here."

Yasmine stands as if eager to take on the challenge, cocking her fist back. When it connects, the sound of bone connecting with metal reverberates through the dining hall, drawing all eyes to our table. Yasmine cradles her undoubtedly throbbing hand with the other and nods. "Okay, not bad," she acquiesces.

"And you can take that 'car parts' joke up with the Professor," Dax says as he slides back into his place at the bench. "He's the one that made my legs."

"What happened to you?" Yasmine asked, her voice suddenly soft and childlike. I know that she's thinking of the day that changed all of our lives.

"I was living in New York when the bombs were dropped," Dax answers, his eyes lowered to his tray. "I wasn't close enough for burns, but the impact leveled my entire neighborhood. I got trapped under a semi from the chest down. My entire body south of my ribs has been reconstructed with titanium. My legs are enhanced with the Restoration Project's machinery, giving them extra speed, endurance, and flexibility. I'm metal inside and out. My bones from the ribs down are titanium, but I'm skin and muscles over that down to my knees. Calves and feet are all machine."

A few minutes of silence pass before Yasmine looks to Olivia. The petite blonde shrugs and flips her hair over her shoulder like she's talking about a trip to the mall.

"Radiation poisoning," she says as if it were no big deal. "My body was wracked with tumors for years. By the time I finished cancer treatments, my adrenal glands were gone. I got new ones. Oh, and I lost my hand in a totally unrelated incident. Call my new one a bonus."

Gage frowns. "What reason would the president have to be afraid of a girl with enhanced adrenal glands? Look at you; you're hardly more than a hundred and thirty pounds. You're just a girl!"

My bionic eye catches the sneer that crosses Olivia's lips just before she disappears in a blur of blonde hair and black suede. Two seconds later, she's back at our table, holding a chicken leg. Across the room, one of the little ones at the kids' table is bawling his eyes out over his missing dinner. Olivia takes a huge bite out of the chicken and grins as she chews.

"Don't underestimate me, Gage," she says in that throaty voice of hers that always sounds like a cat's purr. "I'm more than just a little girl."

Gage's eyebrows are nearly touching his. "My apologies," he says with a laugh.

After a while, he realizes that everyone is watching him. He glances over at the kids' table and the smiling, laughing Agata. He sighs and plunges ahead.

"Agata sustained a head and spinal cord injury in the blast that hit Stafford, Virginia. She was paralyzed from the waist down, had lost most of her speech ability, and suffered memory loss. We were afraid she'd have to live out her days in an institution, a vegetable. The bionic left brain and modifications to her spinal cord gave her a second chance. It's good to see her walking and running again."

My jaw is nearly on the table, and Olivia is brushing a tear from her cheek. Even Dax has softened a little bit after hearing that. The emotion in his voice is thick, and we can all tell that he truly cares about Agata. Gage shrugs off our stares and admiration, taking a sip of water.

Then he swivels that blue gaze to me. "What about you?"

My mouth tightens involuntarily and my bionic eye fills my vision with readings of my heart rate going up and my core temperature rising as bile clogs my airway. Dax's hand is on my shoulder, but his hard eyes are fixed on Gage in a narrowed glare. Just before I turn and leave the table, I hear my best friend growl, "She doesn't like to talk about it, man."

FOUR

BLYTHE SOL, DAX JANNER, YASMINE ZAMBRANO, AND
GAGE BRONSON
RESTORATION RESISTANCE HEADQUARTERS, THE OFFICE OF
PROFESSOR NEVILLE HINCKLEY
AUGUST 15, 4010
9:00 PM

ENTERING THE FAMILIAR OFFICE OF THE PROFESSOR CALMS ME
immediately, which is good because, for a moment there,
I was totally freaking out. No one around here asks me
about my past, because they know I don't like to talk
about it. I don't talk about the injuries that caused me
to enroll myself into the Restoration Project's Healing
Hands campaign, and I don't talk about my life before
joining the Resistance. Of course, Gage, being new to
the group, didn't know that, and I can't really blame
him for asking. Now I feel like an idiot for running out
on them.

Fortunately, no one calls me out for acting weird.
By the time the rest of the group caught up with me on
the steps of the dining hall, I had gotten myself together.
Gage was silent and so was Dax once he'd asked me if I
was okay. Olivia had said something about a date and
bounced off in the direction of the park we erected a
few years ago.

"I'll take you two to see the Professor now," I said to Yasmine and Gage, ignoring Dax's annoyed glare. I know he doesn't want Gage anywhere near our team, but I have a feeling he would be perfect. Despite my doubts about him being from D.C., I have to say his passion and dedication to helping our kind has me squarely in his corner. Dax can kiss my ass.

As we set off across our small citadel toward the main building housing our Science and Technology center, the guys fall in behind me silently and Yasmine walks at my side. After a few seconds, she looks at me with those soulful, dark eyes of hers and I see my pain mirrored there.

"When the bombs dropped, I was just a normal girl living in San Francisco. I was right at the center of the city when it happened, and I suffered third-degree burns over ninety percent of my body. My parents signed me up for the Healing Hands initiative, hoping to save my life. The pain was so excruciating that all I wanted to do was die. I begged them to kill me, to let me die, but they wouldn't."

"They gave you new skin," I say, hoping that she doesn't mistake the tears in my left eye and my raspy voice for pity. I have nothing but respect for Yasmine and her bravery under the circumstances. She certainly seems to have suffered as much, or maybe even more, than I have.

"Yes," she answers. "They fixed me, and now they hunt me because they hate their own creations. They fear me enough to hurt the people I love to get what they want."

I understand this, and I think she realizes it.

"I just wanted you to know you're not alone," she says as we come to a stop on the front steps. "I wanted you to know that I'm here if you need a friend."

That does it—I'm really a wreck now. No one but Dax has ever even tried to peel back my hard, brittle layers. He's the only one I've ever allowed to get close enough. I force a smile and tell myself that I'm going to try for her, because as brave as she is to offer her friendship to me, I sense that she's truly terrified, that she might need me just as much as I need Dax and Dog.

"I'd like that," I answer truthfully.

That seems to be enough for her, because she falls silent as we enter the building. Dax and I are familiar, but our group draws a lot of curious stares and a few frowns because of Yasmine and Gage. I can tell that the scientists walking past in their white lab coats are trying to figure out whether our two guests are Bionics, or if they should be on their guard. They are all like us, too, many of them having once been prominent figures in the fields of science and technology before nuclear war made us all freaks.

I ignore them and lead our group toward the elevator, which takes us to the top floor that serves as both the Professor's living quarters and work area. When the elevator doors open, we see the Professor in a position we don't often find him—seated in front of the television. The figures of a male and female newscaster are being broadcasted into the room, and the Professor is glued to their 3D images. I know he's heard us come in though, because he waves us forward distractedly.

"Come in, come in," he mumbles around the chewed-up pen hanging from his mouth. Sandy brown curls frame his face in wild disarray and his signature outfit—baggy cargo pants and a turtleneck beneath a white lab coat—is wrinkled and stained with coffee, ink, and God knows what else. His round spectacles frame pale blue eyes that are always darting around nervously. To many, the Professor would appear to be a crazy man, fit for the psych ward. Those of us who know better, see him as the mad genius that he is. A bit distracted when bothered with the tedium of everyday life. Maybe a tad neurotic and jumpy. Quiet and thoughtful, and possibly the kindest person I know.

"Have a seat," he says, motioning to the three sleek, black leather couches surrounding the large television built into the wall. We all trade amused glances before shuffling around books and stacks of paper—they're everywhere. It takes a few minutes but once we've cleared off places to sit, we park it and stare expectantly at the Professor.

"Sir, we have two new additions here who'd like to be added to our team," Dax says, only to be shushed.

"In a moment," the Professor replies without looking away from the television. "The president is about to speak, and I don't want to miss it."

I roll my eyes and mimic a robot for Dax's amusement. He knows how I feel about the president and his speeches. I don't want to hear a thing he has to say, especially not today.

"It's the anniversary of the bombings," Yasmine says quietly, her lips tight at the corners. "This ought to be good."

Seeing as how we're not going to get anything done until the president has had his say, I shut my mouth and lean into the smooth back of the couch. I don't want to sit through this crap—get spoon-fed the horseshit that comes from this man's mouth. He is the reason I am what I am today, and why we are all hunted. Seeing his projection in the room, so close that he looks and sounds like he's really here, fills me with rage so strong that I cannot look away. I don't know what it is about staring into the face of my enemy. I want to look away, but I just can't.

Cool, blue eyes seem to bore into my soul from beneath trimmed, brown eyebrows. His brown hair is pomaded and arranged in its usual style, not one strand out of place. He's got the typical good, clean, All-American good looks of every president before him, with the subtle air of something hard gleaming in his eyes. Maybe it was the two decades he served as General of the Military Police that's put the hard glint there. Whatever the case, I can't stand even the sight of him, despite the vibrant colors of the American flag behind him, or the sparkling white smile stretching across his chiseled face. Even the sky-blue hue of his tie cannot disguise what I've already discovered behind the façade he puts on as easily as a sweater or coat.

President Drummond is a monster.

"People of the United States of America," he begins, his diction beyond perfect, his tones enunciating every T, R, and S, with precision. *"I speak to you on a day of remembrance, a day of celebration for our nation. I am sure*

you are wondering just what I mean when I say that today is a day of celebration, when so many tragic deaths are marked by this date. Even now, many of you are heading out to lay flowers in front of headstones, or gathering around one of several memorials located near many ground zero sites in cities across the country. You wonder how your beloved leader could speak so freely of joy and celebration on this day, and I do not blame you.

"My friends, we have so much to celebrate on this day! As a nation, we are stronger than we've ever been, more united. In the face of adversity and struggle, we have come together to create a better society, not just for the good of our own cities and states, but also for the good of our nation as a whole. Who can forget how we learned to genetically engineer healthy, wholesome foods after our supply of water was reduced by half due to pollution and waste? Because of this development, along with careful rationing of our goods, hunger has been almost completely wiped out. Am I the only one who is grateful for the vigilance of the Military Police? Because of their strictly enforced curfews and gun control policies, our violent crime rate has been reduced by ninety percent."

I clench my teeth as I listen to the president rattle off his inane list of statistics. Every year, it's the same old song and dance. Sure, it sounds good, but we all know that the confiscation of firearms from every citizen other than the peacekeeping MPs was done in an effort at control, not safety, just like every other policy put into place by Drummond.

"No, my friends, I have not forgotten about the devastation that rocked our country four years ago on this date. The North Korean nuclear attacks on Manhattan, Los

election's pretty much a waste of time.

"And now, I want to share with you another cause for celebration."

Drummond's image swivels to the left, and at the center of the projection, a new picture emerges, prompting gasps and shocked reactions from those of us in the room. Over the video feed of about twenty Bionics in a cage surrounded by gun-toting MPs, President Drummond shares his latest development, his voice tinged with barely controlled glee.

"Late last night, our nation's most elite Military Police unit, the Restoration Enforcers, apprehended this rogue band of Bionics living in a secret hideout in Memphis, Tennessee. According to Captain Rodney Jones, leader of the Enforcers, the hideout had been under surveillance for months and the members of this small but dangerous terrorist sect have racked up over eighty criminal charges between them. After the rash of crimes sweeping the nation following the Restoration Project's Healing Hands initiative, I do not think you need to be reminded just how dangerous the Bionics are. My friends, I accept my part of the blame in the creation of these abominations we now know as the Bionics. In our misguided attempts at giving those injured in the nuclear blasts a second chance, we have armed a large part of our population with weapons fit for manipulation, bending, and outright breaking of our carefully rebuilt society's laws. Today, Vice President McCall and I wanted you to see for yourselves the extents of our efforts in finding and eliminating those Bionics who have resisted turning themselves over to us for deprogramming and the exploration of alternatives to suit their needs."

"Fucking liar." Dax's muttered curse is as loud as

a gunshot in the silent room.

Every eye, including mine, is glued to the projection, fixed on the faces of those captured in Tennessee. While we'd been combing an abandoned neighborhood in Dallas, we missed our chance at rescuing several members of our rebellion.

We all know that turning ourselves in to the government is a no go. For someone like me, it would mean a glass eye to replace the bionic one, and a plain old fiberglass arm to replace the robotic one. For a child like Agata, it means being turned back over to her parents as a vegetable once they've done surgery to remove her artificial left brain. And what about Yasmine? Will they pull the skin from her flesh and leave her to die—maybe slap a few skin grafts over it and hope for the best? If at all possible, my hatred of the president, the government, and everything they stand for increases to fever pitch until I feel like I want to hit something.

Sensing this, Dax reaches out and grasps my human hand with his. Our palms touch and in that moment, I am reminded of my humanity and a wave of calm washes over and through me. I squeeze his hand back so tightly I know it would hurt if it were any hand but his. This is Dax, though, and I know his big bear paw can take it. I squeeze with all of my strength until the anger is gone.

I sense Gage's gaze on our clasped hands and ignore his questioning stare. We may have shared a moment in the cafeteria in which I decided he's not a threat to me, and maybe I think his eyes are the most beautiful thing I've ever seen. So what? At the end of the day, Dax is the one I trust with my life. More than that, Dax is the one I trust with my emotions and secrets.

"Because of their rebellion and breaking of the law requiring all Bionics to willingly turn themselves over to the Science and Technology department of the Restoration, these members of the terrorist organization known as 'The Resistance,' will be put to death on the eighteenth of August. Their executions will be televised live as a message to those still holding out hope that this so-called Resistance will accomplish anything. It will serve as a reminder to them that they have no choice but to turn themselves over for the good of their country and for the safety of other citizens. Ladies and gentlemen, I leave you now with this plea—if you have any information that will lead to the capture of one or many rogue Bionics, please do not hesitate to inform the nearest Military Police Officer. Do not try to apprehend them yourselves, as they are often dangerous and violent. Urge any family members that you are harboring to turn themselves in, for they are not only posing a risk to those around them, they are also sacrificing your freedom as well, as any citizen found harboring fugitives faces severe penalties. Any person with bionic apparatuses issued by the government who turn themselves in willingly will not face any penalty.

"And finally, I want to remind the American people that the founders and leaders of the Resistance are still at large. Professor Neville Hinkley and his associate, Jenica Swan, are the voices behind the Resistance. My offer stands, America—five-million dollars each for the Professor and Miss Swan, alive. If we can put an end to their reign of tyranny, we can take a step in the right direction toward ensuring that our citizens are safe. Please, everyone, let us do the right thing for *the good of our continued growth and prosperity as a nation. Thank you and God bless the United States of America."*

The president's image disappears, and the newsroom is now being broadcasted into the Professor's living space. After a few moments, he finds his remote and silences the inane chatter of two newscasters. He knows none of us want to hear the political pundits continually praise Drummond's efforts at creating peace and harmony in our society.

We've heard it all before.

After a few minutes of silence in which everyone works through whatever emotions are the strongest, Dax stands and faces the Professor, who is sitting in his favorite armchair, arms wrapped around his chest as if he's in an immense amount of pain.

"Sir, we should really call a meeting with Jenica and discuss a rescue mission," he says softly, knowing as well as I do that the Professor is probably in emotional hell right now. As one of the foremost scientists leading the Restoration Project's Healing Hands initiative, Professor Neville Hinkley personally created all the bionic and computerized technology used to modify those injured in the blast and, even some like Olivia, who were exposed to radiation and lost vital organs to disease because of poisoning. He never says it out loud, but I know he feels responsible for many of our predicaments. After all, he created us. None of us blame him, at least none that I know of. If anything, we love him for saving us, for going underground with the Resistance, and giving us a safe haven from the tyrannical laws of our president.

"Sir?" Dax says when the Professor doesn't answer.

The Professor's head snaps up and he pulls his pen slowly away from his mouth, blinking several times and looking around the room as if just now realizing that he has visitors. "Hello," he says softly, gazing back and forth between Yasmine and Gage. "I am Professor Neville Hinkley."

"Yasmine Zambrano."

"Gage Bronson."

The Professor cocks his head slightly and studies Gage. "Have we met before? Looking at you, I'm experiencing a rather strong sense of déjà vu."

Gage lowers his gaze from the Professor's and shakes his head. I don't know if it's my imagination or not, but he seems to blush a bit as he answers. "No, sir, I don't think so."

He studies Gage a bit longer and then shrugs, seeming to dismiss the conundrum from his mind. Whatever it is, I'm sure he'll let us know if he remembers. "It's very nice to meet you both." He turns to me, his eyes expectant behind his frames. "How many in Dallas?"

I shake my head. "No more than two dozen. These two were with them. They're interested in joining our team, sir."

The Professor looks at Yasmine and smiles, reaching out to touch her arm. Yasmine flinches, but is otherwise still for the Professor's inspection.

"Lovely," he murmurs as he taps his fingers against Yasmine's skin. "Flawless finish, strong, durable—a girl with impenetrable skin. How much of

48

this did they use on you?"

"It covers ninety percent of my body," Yasmine answers.

The Professor smiles. "A human's skin is his first line of defense against injury and sickness. Tell me, since receiving your skin transplant, have you experienced any illness at all?"

Yasmine opens her mouth to answer, but Gage's voice muffles her response. "I'm sorry, but shouldn't you know these things already? After all, you are the inventor of every bionic organ or body part currently used by the government."

I sense ambivalence in Gage's tone, and I don't think I like it. Dax doesn't either. The Professor fixes Gage with his wide, wise stare, seemingly unruffled by the stranger's outburst.

"My time as leader of the Healing Hands initiative was ended when I spoke out against the treatment of our patients. There wasn't time for me to document the side effects, benefits, or drawbacks of every single case. To date, Miss Zambrano is the first recipient of a skin transplant that I've had a chance to interview."

That shuts Gage up and he allows the conversation to continue uninterrupted.

"I have not been sick," she answers with a smile. "Not once since the transplant."

The Professor beams and claps his hands together in excitement. "Fascinating. Just fascinating."

He swivels his gaze toward Gage and frowns. "You do not possess any modifications, young man."

Gage shakes his head. "No. I came here with a

family member. She has a very unique and—according to the government—dangerous modification."

"A bionic left brain," I add at the Professor's confused expression.

Confusion melts into horror as he removes his glasses and stares at Gage in disbelief. "Young man, you would have me to believe that the Restoration actually approved the use of a bionic cerebrum?"

"You aren't the one who performed the operation?" Gage fired back.

The Professor shakes his head and stands, pacing in front of the now-dead television screen. "I created the bionic cerebrum as an experiment. Theoretically, it could restore full mental function to a person with limited brain damage. It was designed in a way that it could be used as a whole, or in pieces. My main goal was replacement of the frontal lobes, which are responsible for the retaining of long-term memory. It was never approved for use by my superiors. Their reasoning was that it could potentially create a person with the mind of a computer, capable of cracking the codes of a bank safe in under one minute, or even such boggling tasks as mind reading or control. Of course, I never believed in the paranormal potential of such a device, but I could see how a computerized brain could pose a problem. In the hands of a convict or criminal, it could be quite dangerous."

"Well, before President Drummond went on a witch hunt for the Bionics, an experimental surgery was approved," Gage says. "One patient who had been in a near-vegetative state since a head injury caused by the blast was chosen as a candidate. The results were stunning."

"I'd very much like to meet with the child."

Gage shrugged. "I'd be willing to arrange that on one condition."

"Name your price, young man."

"Whatever rescue mission you've got planned for the prisoners from Memphis... I want in."

The Professor rubs his chin and studies Gage as if trying to read him. I know he's trying to decide whether we can trust him. I already know where Dax stands and am sure Jenica would be on his side. As the head of our team, I don't know if it would bode well for Gage if Jenica hates him, but I hope the fact that he brought us Agata will earn him some bonus points.

The Professor does what I knew he would do all along. He throws Gage a bone.

"We've never had an un-modified member of the team before," he says slowly. "I believe it could be to our advantage, especially when trying to infiltrate areas with heavy Military Police Patrol."

"But Professor—" He holds his hand up to stop Dax, who is all ready to protest this decision.

"On a trial basis only," he adds with a pointed look in Gage's direction. "We will see how you perform on this mission and make a decision from there. If Jenica and the others report to me that you are a good addition to the team, I see no reason not to allow it. We need all the help we can get, Mister Bronson, and I'm not choosy about where it comes from, so long as it is genuine."

Gage nods and smiles. "You can count on me, sir."

Angeles, San Francisco, Austin, Houston, Chicago, St. Louis, New Orleans, Atlanta, Phoenix, Miami, Boston, Seattle, and Pittsburg took the lives of thousands of people, and altered the lives of the rest of us forever. From the ashes of the travesty committed against us on that day, we have risen like the mythical phoenix, stronger, better and wiser. We have rebuilt where we could, and relocated those who have lost their homes as well. Those cities that were rebuilt or unaffected by the blasts stand as testament to our strength and endurance. We are now mightier than we've ever been"

"It was my honor as a junior senator from Maine to lead the rebuilding efforts of our country, to throw my hat into the ring and accept your generous nomination for President of the United States. It has been my honor to serve you these four years, and to watch you thrive and fight to overcome the obstacles thrown into your paths. I urge you to join with me now, as we strive for a new order. Believe in me as I believe in you."

He pauses as if allowing all that he has said to sink in, and I feel like I'm going to be sick. President Drummond's approval ratings are through the roof. With the exception of those of us in the Resistance, the people of America see him as some kind of great savior, the charismatic junior senator who came out of nowhere, put the country on his back, and carried it across the desert when it was weak and near dead. There is no doubt in anyone's mind that he will be reelected for another term come November. In fact, no one's really putting up much of a fight, and everyone knows that the Democratic candidate is a joke, a walking punch line. No one's going to unseat Drummond, so the upcoming

FIVE

THE BLINDING FLASH CAUSES ME TO COVER MY EYES AS THE SOUNDS OF screeching brakes and metal slamming against metal fills my ears. The car flips as if someone has pulled the street out from under it, and the seatbelt bites into my shoulder and chest, leaving an imprint that will stay with me for weeks after this day. The windows explode and shards of glass fill the car, spinning through the air in front of my face in a haunting, macabre dance of deadly danger. My hands move to cover my face too late; a split second before I shield my eyes, a layer of blackness blocks out half of my vision. Later, surgeons will pull a three-inch shard of glass from my eye. Without my left eye, my peripheral vision is impaired, and I do not see the foreign object flying through the gaping hole where a car door used to be. Seconds later, I can no longer feel my left arm...

The screams echoing from the walls of my bedroom are deafening. The high-pitched sounds mingle with the howling of some deranged animal, to create a chorus worthy of a full moon. Sweat is dripping down my face, neck, and back as I shoot upright in the bed, realizing through the haze of still-clinging sleep that the noise is coming from me. More precisely, it is coming from both Dog and me. I clamp my mouth shut and fight to catch my breath, bringing my hand up over my closed left eye. As always, the vibration of machinery meets my fingers, and I sigh in both relief and despair. Dog goes quiet, realizing that I am now awake and calm. He licks my hand to console me and I reach down to hug him, assuring him that I'll be okay. A few seconds later, the pounding at my door tells me Dax was awakened by my nightmare-induced screaming.

Again.

"Blythe, it's me, Gage. Are you okay?"

I raise my eyebrows at Dog and frown. Gage? What the hell is he doing in Mosley Hall? I glance at the clock on my nightstand and see that it's three o'clock in the morning. He knocks again, more quietly this time, propelling me into full wakefulness. I jump up and run to the door, realizing that he'll wake up everyone in the hall if I don't answer him soon.

I fling the door open to find him on the other side, still fully dressed with his hair standing on end like he's been raking his fingers through it again. His eyes travel over me, and my face gets hot as I realize I'm not wearing anything but a tank top and a pair of indecently short shorts—both drenched in my sweat. Gage blinks a few times before focusing his gaze back on mine.

He swallows noisily and leans against the doorframe. "I was walking and heard screams coming through your window. By the time I figured out what room you were in and got inside, you'd stopped, but I wanted to make sure you're okay."

"How'd you know which room is mine?"

Gage frowns at me like he can't believe what an unbelievable moron I'm being. "Um... your name's on the door," he said, pointing.

Damn, I'd forgotten about Jenica and her label maker. In perfect, black letters, it says 'Sol' clear as day across the damn door. Still doesn't explain why he's out walking the grounds at three am.

"I couldn't sleep," he says as if he read my thoughts. "Got a lot on my mind."

I nod and open the door a bit wider. "You can come in if you want. I doubt I'll be getting back to sleep either."

He enters without hesitation and I close the door behind him, leaning against the heavy wood and watching him as he moves toward the center of the room. No one else fills up quite so much of my space except for Dax. I doubt they could both fit in here; standing side by side, their shoulders could probably span the width of the cube I call home. My eyes are watching the ripple of muscles that undulate across his torso as he removes his leather jacket to reveal the same white, thermal top he'd been wearing earlier when we met. He turns, looking at me expectantly, and I shake my head to clear it of thoughts of him whipping that shirt off over his head.

"Oh, sorry. Please, sit down."

He lowers himself onto the only available seat in the room. My bed. He's near the foot of it, so I take a spot near the headboard, pressing my back against the rough, chipped wood in an effort at placing some distance between us. I don't know how I feel about the fact that being so close to him makes it seem as if my skin is on fire.

"So..." He trails off and clears his throat, shifting on the bed. "Are you okay?"

I lower my eyes and try to decide what I'm going to say. The only person who knows about the night terrors is Dax... and maybe Jenica since she shares a wall with me on the other side, but I'm not sure. She at least has enough respect for me not to say anything about it if she's heard me screaming until I'm hoarse. Dax says I only do it when I've had a particularly jarring day. I'm thinking that coming back from our trek in Dallas empty-handed and then seeing those poor people from Memphis—many of them elderly and children— branded as terrorists when I know in my heart that they did nothing wrong, has taken its toll on me and brought up memories of my own past. It's always the same— screeching brakes, shattering glass, the spray of blood and gore, that blinding flash of light that started it all and changed my life forever.

"I'm worried about Agata," he continues when I don't respond. "I mean, I know she's safe now. Getting her to Professor Hinkley was my first priority. When I got in touch with his contact in Washington and he told me where to go to find your team, I was happy. I just knew I had to get her here."

"Even if it means death for you?"

His head comes up and his stare is sharp as it connects with mine. "There are some things that are worse than death."

I wonder if he realizes he's preaching to the choir.

"I wish I had died that day," I admit, unable to look away from his gaze no matter how much my mind tells me that I need to. "I wish that all the time."

He inches closer to me on the bed. "Is it really so bad? Professor Hinkley gave you all a second chance at life. It's not fair that the government has decided you and others like you pose a threat."

I think about a news broadcast I saw a couple of weeks ago, showing a surveillance video of a man with an arm identical to mine smashing in the window of someone's car, beating them to a bloody pulp for no reason, before pulling a limp body from the driver's seat and driving off in the stolen vehicle. Of course, the thief was found and immediately executed—no trial, no jury, no questions asked.

"Some of us are dangerous," I answer, and of course, it's the truth.

"Some *people* are dangerous," he insists. "Bionics are still people... just modified."

"Right now, your blood pressure is 124/90, and your heart rate is an elevated seventy beats per minute— not bad, but still high for a healthy male that I assume is athletic. You have a tattoo on your left arm of an eagle and a fractured rib."

"That is amazing."

I shrug. "It's my eye. It is capable of reading a person's body heat signature as well as their vital statistics. It allows me to pull away individual layers, such as clothing, skin, and muscle to expose what's underneath. It's how I knew about the rib." I reach out with my bionic arm and poke his side for emphasis, raising my eyebrows as he winces in pain. "Still think I'm human?"

Gage reaches for my arm—my robotic one—and grabs it by the hand. I can't feel it, or his hand circling the wrist above it. His eyebrows wrinkle as he turns my arm over, inside facing up. He traces the inside of my arm, his fingers sliding over the cool metal and, for the first time since I woke up with that hunk of machinery on the other end of my elbow, I am wishing that I could feel the damn thing.

"Cold," he murmurs as he draws circles on the metal. His fingers stop on the inside of my elbow, on the line where the titanium ends and I begin. I hear his breath catch in his throat and another noisy swallow as the pad of his index finger slides over my skin. I gasp as he trails it up the inside of my arm, flesh now on flesh. The human contact that I've denied myself for years has left me sensitive to every touch, and I feel as if I'm being caressed for the first time.

Of course, Dax has held my hand from time to time; he's even held me against him until I fall asleep some nights when the nightmares get particularly bad. But he's never touched me like this. He's never dared to bum rush past the emotional barriers I throw up so people can't get close to me. A thousand emotions are exploding in me at one time and just as many sensations are following the path his finger traces up to my shoulder, pausing at the strap of my tank top.

"Warm," he says with a smile. "Only about... what... five percent of you is metal? When I got past your elbow, I felt skin, blood flowing through veins, muscle, and... goose bumps?"

He says that last bit with a smile, forcing me to look away in embarrassment. Holding his arm out toward me, he pulls up the sleeve of his shirt and reveals a tanned arm sprinkled with light blond hair, which is standing on end. He leaves the sleeve above his elbow and holds his arm out in front of me.

"See?" he says gently, his head way too close to mine, his breath brushing my cheek. "I have them too."

I reach out with my human hand and touch his arm. His opposite hand comes up to cover mine.

"If anything," he says, his fingers gripping mine tightly, "the additions to your body give you character. They tell a story about where you've been." He pauses, leaning in so close that locks of his hair brush my forehead. "Where *have* you been, Blythe?"

I know he's referring to the screams and my nightmare. I wonder if I can put him off like I do the others, but quickly realize by the glint in his eyes that he's not letting me off that easy. When I clear my throat and open my mouth to speak, no sound comes out. Gage leans forward and presses his lips to mine, taking advantage of my open mouth to nibble on my lower lip.

With a soft sigh, he closes the distance between us and cups my face in his hands, taking my breath away with the simple act of molding his mouth to mine. I haven't been kissed in so long that I'd forgotten what it feels like—to exchange air with another person, to lose yourself in them to the exclusion of everything else in the world. His lips were warm and soft, coaxing gently but still demanding, taking as much as giving.

My hands resting on his thick thighs, I come up on my knees on the bed, leaning into him. Now that he has given me the contact I haven't felt in so long, but didn't know I craved, I want more of it. He shivers as my hands come up to the sides of his face, gripping tightly, my fingers caressing the silky strands of blond hair at his temples. He responds by grabbing my waist, his thumbs caressing my ribs. I'm practically in his lap now, coming dangerously closer and closer to reaching the point of no return.

It doesn't matter that we don't know each other from Adam. Or that I have no reason to trust him. All I know is kissing Gage feels like walking down the street used to before the government labeled Bionics as dangerous. It feels like freedom, and I don't want to stop.

"Hey Blythe, I couldn't sleep and I was thinking..."

Dax's voice trails off as the door to the bathroom we share knocks against the wall, pushed open by my boneheaded best friend who never knocks because he knows I'm never doing anything he can't witness.

Except this time.

This time, guilt propels me away from Gage and back against the headboard, my lowered eyelids shielding me from Dax's dark glare.

"Sorry," he says, sounding anything but. "Didn't realize you'd have a visitor at three o'clock in the goddamn morning."

Part of me wants to rip Dax a new asshole for being such a jerk. What right does he have being mad at me when I know he's screwed Olivia on several occasions, and who knows what other groupies he's got salivating over him in both Mosley and Hexley Halls? Another part of me feels like I just got caught doing something unforgiveable, although I'm not sure if it was that I kissed someone, or if it's the fact that the someone I kissed happens to be Gage.

Gage stands slowly, his hawk's eye gaze swiveling from me to Dax and back again. He nods as if figuring something out and collects his jacket.

"It is pretty late," he says, as if he had no idea what time it was before now. "I'll let you get some sleep now, Blythe. See you at the meeting tomorrow morning?"

With my nightmare and Gage's appearance at my door, I'd forgotten all about the meeting Professor Neville organized for tomorrow morning over breakfast. Jenica will be bringing her intel on the Memphis Resistance group and we'll be formulating a plan from there. Dax hates that Gage was even invited.

"Sure," I say. "Good night."

He leaves with a nod in Dax's direction. The jackass who's supposed to be my best friend just continues staring daggers at Gage until he's out of sight. He then slams the bathroom door and walks to the middle of the room, pauses, runs a hand over his buzz-cut head, and paces to the door and back again, his face a mask of disbelief. When he finally speaks, his voice is a hoarse whisper.

"What the hell did I just witness?"

I rear back as if slapped and, honestly, it's how I feel. "What I think you just witnessed," I hiss, coming to my feet, "was a consensual act between two mature adults that had nothing to do with you."

"Nothing to do with me? How can you say that?" He looks truly hurt, and for the life of me, I can't figure out why. In fact, for some reason, it downright pisses me off.

"You know what?" I challenge, stepping toward him and tilting my head back to look him in the eye. "I can say that, because it seriously has nothing to do with you! Do I come barging in your room when you're rattling the headboard with Olivia?"

His jaw gets so tight I'm afraid it might snap. "That's not fair."

"Why not? Because I'm a girl and I'm supposed to sit around with a chastity belt on while I wait for you to make a move?"

Dax clutches his chest like the wind's been knocked from him. "You've been waiting for me to make a move?"

Shit.

I didn't mean it like that.

Or did I?

I honestly can't say I'm sure about that one. Dax is a sexpot for sure and a great friend, but do I like him in *that way*—want him the way Olivia does? I've never explored the possibility because I've never thought of him that way. He's like Dog—comfortable, loyal, and mine.

"No," I say, a half lie. "What I meant was that I

don't understand why you're so upset when we're just friends. Right?"

Dax studies me for a minute before sighing noisily, bringing his hands up to his hips. He hangs his heads and nods. "Yeah, Blythe. We are friends, and that's why I'm worried about you getting too close to this guy. We don't know him, we don't know where he's from, and we don't know what he wants. I don't trust him."

"You're being ridiculous. You don't know anything about him!"

"And you do?"

I cross my arms over my chest. "I know that he's from D.C. And before you start going on and on about how that makes him even more unsavory, consider this—a guy from D.C. probably has government officials or MPs in his family. That means the axe would fall even harder on his neck if someone were to rat him out for rescuing that little girl. Don't you get it? He's put his life on the line for her and he cares about our cause! You may not be able to see that, but I do."

"So you're going to let blond hair and a set of blue eyes turn your head? Where's your focus, B?"

"From what I've been hearing through this wall between my room and yours, blonde hair and blue eyes have been turning your head at least once a week for months now. And my focus is where it's always been— on finding the others and saving them before it's too late."

Dax turns toward my door, glancing back at me over his shoulder. "I only want to make sure you're okay.

I know that August fifteenth is always hard for you. It's hard for all of us."

I turn my back on him, unwilling to continue to allow guilt to gnaw at me for something I shouldn't feel guilty about. "It's the sixteenth now, Dax, and I'm fine."

SIX

BLYTH SOL, GAGE BRONSON, YASMINE ZAMBRANO, JENICA
SWAN AND PROFESSOR NEVILLE HINKLEY
RESTORATION RESISTANCE HEADQUARTERS, THE OFFICE OF
PROFESSOR NEVILLE HINKLEY
AUGUST 16, 4010
7:00 AM

BREAKFAST IN THE PROFESSOR'S QUARTERS IS TENSE, BUT necessary if we're going to organize some kind of rescue mission for forty-eight hours from now. Jenica has rolled in the flat-screen partitions, filling the conference area with maps and surveillance footage of both Memphis and Stonehead, the maximum-security prison facility where Bionics are held while awaiting their punishment, which is always execution. We are watching a video feed hijacked from the MP station in Memphis of Bionics coming and going from their underground shelter. They did a good job of keeping hidden, only letting those with less-obvious technology leave and only when absolutely necessary. It was the small mistakes that got them caught, and we all watch the footage of the arrest silently. I glance around and see some with anger in their eyes, others with despair. It mirrors my own turbulent emotions at watching members of the Resistance rounded up like cattle and

64

carted off to prison.

Beside me, Yasmine allows a tear to slip down her cheek and, across from me, I can see Olivia is fighting them. Professor Neville has already seen this footage and is busy tackling his biscuits and coffee. Dax and Gage are glaring at each other from across the table and any second now, I'm thinking they're going to pull out the rulers for a dick-measuring contest.

Men.

"That footage was taken by Military Police cameras outside the Memphis hideout for the members of the Resistance arrested by the Enforcers," Jenica says, pausing the video feed and turning to face us with her usual military precision. "Our intel suggests that even though many of them were captured, there are still several down there that need to be rescued. Also an issue, is the fact that the Memphis branch of the Resistance is responsible for procuring fuel for our vehicles. This is not an immediate concern, as we have some in reserve for situations just like this. The important things right now are the prisoners at Stonehead and those still trapped inside of the Memphis Hideout."

"How many still inside?" Dax asks, leaning back in his chair and crossing his arms across his chest.

"At least one hundred," she answers. "Should we undergo a rescue mission, we will need two crafts to bring them back, so we'll need a second pilot. I will, of course, serve as the first."

"It's a trap," Olivia says, popping a genetically engineered grape into her mouth. My whole life I've wondered if the bio-crap the government came up with to replace real produce tastes anything like the stuff that used to grow in the ground. Of course, this technology is at least half a century older than I am and by the time I was born, real crops were no longer an option. Oh, and forget about beef from a real cow. I've never even seen a cow in person, let alone eaten one. Everything is synthetic; the real stuff is reserved for those with really deep pockets. I'm sure the president is eating Grade-A beef with his eggs right now.

The bastard.

"Of course it's a trap," Jenica snaps, her human eye rolling in exasperation. "That doesn't mean we're going to leave them there in the hands of the Enforcers. We need to think of a way to draw the MPs away long enough for us to get them out of there."

"Why not focus on the prisoners already captured by the Enforcers?" Gage asks.

"Because it's exactly what they'll be expecting," I answer. "It's too obvious."

Gage smiles, and I lower my eyes to my half-eaten toast and blush. "Then let's do something way less obvious and way more daring," he says.

Jenica frowns. "I don't think I like the sound of that, but perhaps you should elaborate, Mr. Bronson."

Gage stands, bracing himself against the table with his large fists. He turns his head slowly, looking every one in our group in the eye as he speaks.

"It's simple, really. We go out in two teams: one to Memphis and the other to Stonehead."

"A double mission? Infiltrating Stonehead *and* the Memphis hideout on the same day?"

"Not just on the same day," Gage answers, "but at the exact same time."

"Impossible," Dax snorts. "We don't have that kind of firepower, and we don't have that many people."

Gage glances at Jenica's plans and frowns. "You have hundreds," he counters.

"And it would take all of them to overwhelm the guards at Stonehead," Dax retorts. "Don't you know anything? That place is a fortress, maximum security. Even if we outmanned them, they outgun us. They could pick us off like fish in a barrel."

"The way I see it, you wouldn't need that many people if one of your groups carried a walking EMP," Professor Hinkley interjects, his voice barely above a whisper.

"An EMP?" Gage asks. "What is that?"

"Electromagnetic pulse," Jenica answers, her brow knit with bewilderment as she studies the Professor. "But, that would render us all helpless. Every member of our team would be stuck in the field with malfunctioning apparatuses."

"Can someone please explain—real-people speak—what the hell an electromagnetic pulse is and why it's a problem?" Gage asks, pacing toward the monitors near Jenica and studying the virtual layouts of the two places we need to infiltrate.

"An EMP is a burst of electromagnetic radiation," the Professor says, standing as he goes into what I like to call 'teacher mode'. This is when he's at his best. "Basically, it is a wave of particles, both electric and magnetic that usually results from a high-energy explosion, like a nuclear bomb. It is capable of coupling with electrical systems and producing damaging voltage surges. In short, it can cause a breakdown of an entire network of computerized hardware, rendering it useless. As Jenica and everyone else in this room are fully aware, centuries ago, we discovered that an electromagnetic pulse could be created without the harmful effects of nuclear explosion, enabling a person to harness the same side effects."

"Meaning, if an EMP goes off anywhere near any person with bionic equipment, their gear is going to crap out on them," I say between sips of coffee.

"I don't get it," Gage says to the Professor. "If the EMP is dangerous to pretty much everyone in this room, why would you suggest us bringing in a portable one?"

"Because it would disable MP armor, weapons, and vehicles," Olivia supplies with a shrug.

"The playing field would be even then, but I'd rather have the advantage," Jenica says.

The Professor clears his throat. "I'll clear all that up if you would just follow me to the lab. I want to show you all something."

Through the plate glass window separating us from the pristine, white room on the other side, we see Agata seated in a comfortable chair, surrounded by electronic devices. Televisions blast various programs in a symphony of noise that would drive me nuts if I were her. Robotic children's toys walk across the floor with a chorus of beeps and flashes of flickering light. Music blares from several stereos. I'm grateful that the thick glass blocks out most of the irritating sounds, and I wonder how the little girl can stand it.

"What's she doing in there?" Gage asks. His stance is a protective one, his face full of concern for the little girl. "Haven't you studied her enough?"

The Professor nodded. "Our session last night was eye-opening, to put it mildly. Agata passed every test put to her with perfection and excelled in every area of reason, logic, and mathematics she was quizzed in. Her grasp of the subject matter surpasses that of many of my colleagues and subordinates. It really is quite fascinating the way her mind works. The robotic left brain works side by side with the human right brain in a way that increases her thinking power to ten times that of a normal human being. She thinks faster and better than anyone in this building and is able to compute even the most difficult of equations in less than one minute. And that's not all."

"Her left brain can emit an EMP?" Jenica guessed, her human eye wide with shock. "How is that possible?"

"The technology that was used to build the bionic cerebrum makes it possible," he answers. "Agata is able to emit the energy pulse, but—and this is the best part— she can control it, direct it where she wants it to go with a single thought."

"Watch," he adds, pressing the intercom button that allows him to communicate with Agata from outside of the room. "Agata, how are you this morning? I trust you enjoyed your breakfast?"

The little girl smiles at us from her side of the glass and nods. "It was wonderful, thank you."

"Excellent," the Professor answers with a smile of his own. His eyes crinkle at the corners, and I can tell by the softness in the pale blue depths that he's already in love with the child. Perhaps because she is a walking, talking miracle that he had a hand in. Perhaps it's because she is a symbol to him, proof that all is not lost in this war we fight against the government.

"Agata, would you please demonstrate for everyone what you showed me last night?"

She nods again. "Certainly. Which of the devices would you like me to focus on?"

"The two flat screens to your left, please."

We all look on in awe as Agata turns to the two screens blasting newscasts into the room. In the blink of an eye, they have gone dead with no more than a look from her. Agata smiles at our shocked expressions and decides to give us a show. One by one, she shuts down every piece of technology in the room. Once the stereos fall silent and the robotic toys stop their dancing and chirping, she sits back in her chair, folding her hands primly in her lap.

"Wonderful," the Professor says through the intercom. He turns to the lab aide standing at the back of our group. "Tess, would you please escort Agata back to Hexley Hall?"

"Yes, sir," the aide responds. She enters the room, her gait uneven because of one bionic leg. After a few moments of chatter and smiles, she leads Agata from the room and down the hall—but not before the little girl shoots Gage her megawatt, gap-toothed smile and waves. Gage waves back and puts on a smile for the girl's benefit, but once she's gone, he turns his stony glare on the Professor.

"No," he says from between clenched teeth. "Absolutely not. I will not allow my niece to be used as a weapon."

The Professor removes his specs and wipes them with the bottom of his lap coat. "I expected this reaction from you, although when I thought of the idea, I didn't realize that your family bond with her was so close."

"She's my sister's daughter, and I promised I'd keep her safe."

"She would be safe," Jenica says softly, and it is the first time I've ever heard compassion in her voice. "In order to focus her EMP signal on a target, she only needs to be able to see it. Am I right, Professor? She should be able to do that from the hovercraft."

The Professor nods. "You are correct, Miss Swan, but we will not try to force Mr. Bronson to do something he'd rather not do. If he says no, we have to respect that."

"Like hell we do," Dax hisses, turning toward Gage, his lips curled in a sneer. "Look, you bulldozed your way in here and forced your way onto our team. Everyone here has to make sacrifices for the good of the Resistance, and that means you too. No matter how rich and snooty you may have been before you came here, you're now a fugitive and—because of Blythe and the Professor—a member of this team. Attacking two places at once was your bright idea. The least you can do is contribute."

Gage meets Dax head on, and the two look like jungle cats ready to pounce on each other. I can't say that the sight is all that bad. It's actually kind of stimulating.

"I have sacrificed more than you will ever know to keep Agata safe," Gage says, his jaw clenching in fury. "I will give everything I have to the Resistance, but not her. Agata is off limits."

Dax snorts. "Spoken like a truly spoiled rich kid. Do you have any idea what the people in this room have been through? What those prisoners at Stonehead will be put through if we don't save them?"

"That's enough!"

I can't believe the sharpness of my tone but, really, I've had enough of the bickering. Dax is being an asshole, and the Professor is asking the impossible of a guy who just risked his neck to save a girl we want to use as a piece of equipment. I force myself between the two large men and push them apart, one hand on each broad, muscled chest.

"Dax, Gage is right. We can't ask him to risk his niece for us. You know how valuable a piece of collateral like Agata would be to the government. She's dangerous to them, and they would stop at nothing to use her to get at the rest of us if they had to. If they captured her, she could even be used as a weapon against us. If someone asked you to risk my life, or Olivia's or Jenica's, would you do it?"

Dax looks like he wants to strangle me, but the hardness around his mouth is slowly starting to soften. "Of course not," he answers, his voice clipped.

"Exactly. We are your family. Gage and Agata are

now a part of that family, and we have to treat them as such. If Gage says no, that means no." I look to Gage as I drop my hands from their chests, satisfied that they're calm and not ready to leap over me to get at each other. "Gage, I know that you don't know us very well and you may not trust us. I get it, okay? But, if you would just think about it..."

My voice trails off as Gage brushes past me, stomping angrily for the exit. Without a word, he's gone and I'm left looking like an idiot in front of everybody.

That does it.

Now I'm pissed.

SEVEN

"HEY!"

He keeps walking like he doesn't hear me, and that only fuels my anger. I try not to think too much about the sway of his narrow hips or the ripple of his back muscles beneath his fitted, black t-shirt, or even the cool air that is whipping through those blond strands of hair that make me want to run my fingers through them.

Because those thoughts are completely inappropriate.

"I'm not kidding, Gage, I will smack the shit out of you with my titanium hand and you'll wake up tomorrow with a concussion!"

That stops him right in his tracks and I wonder if it's because he thinks I'll do it, or if he's calling my bluff. Either way, I'll take it. We're alone on The Green, a patch of synthetic grass dotted with trees, flowers, and benches. The kids' playground is a few feet away, but the little ones are probably at the schoolhouse. Just because we're in hiding doesn't mean we don't want our kids to get a good education. One day, when we've righted the wrongs of our country and are able to become productive members of society again, we want the kids to be ready.

"What do you want from me, Blythe?"

The question catches me off guard, even though what I wanted to do at first was convince him to let us use Agata. Now, looking at him and seeing pain wrapped in mystery flashing in his eyes, I am not sure exactly what it is he's asking. Does he need to know what I want from him right this second, or are we talking about something deeper?

"You came to me yesterday and acted like you wanted friendship. You kissed me—"

"I believe it was you who did the kissing," I interject. Despite the breeze, my face goes hot at the thought of his lips on mine.

Gage lifts a blond brow and snorts sarcastically. "Yeah, and it only takes one to tango. Give me break, Blythe. If your boyfriend hadn't come in and ruined it, I could have had you on your back."

Part of me wants to be mad, but the other part of me wants so badly to retort by telling him that I would have preferred it if he were on his back.

Instead, I defend myself with, "Dax is not my boyfriend."

"Are you sure about that? The way I see it, he's awfully possessive of you and not shy about marking his territory. He's a lot like that dog of yours... he might as well have pulled out his pecker and pissed around you!"

"Are you trying to make a point, or are you being

obnoxious on purpose?"

"My *point*, Blythe, is that you're a taker. You are willing to take whatever I give you, look at me with those big, beautiful eyes of yours, and talk to me about trust. With those same eyes, you close yourself off to me and refuse to answer me when I ask you where you've been. How am I supposed to trust you with my niece, with her life, my life, when you won't do the same for me? That family bullshit you were spouting back there doesn't mean shit to me if you're going to take from me without giving back. And don't even get me started on everyone else. They don't trust me further than they can throw me, but no one blinks at asking me to put Agata in danger. And I'm supposed to go along with it? I don't know about you, but where I'm from, people in a family don't treat each other like that."

The howling of the wind picks up and, for a while, it's the only sound that can be heard on The Green. Someone has let Dog out of the dorm—everyone at Mosley Hall helps me look after him—and he's now loping toward us across the grass, his pink tongue hanging sideways out of his mouth. He jumps up and nudges my hand with his head—his way of telling me that he wants to be scratched behind the ears. I oblige him in an effort at distraction, but it only works for so long. Gage has taken my silence to mean that I'm indifferent and he turns on his heels to walk away.

"That's what I thought," he shoots over his shoulder as he disappears back toward Hexley Hall.

As Gage is swallowed up by the doors of the dormitory, I decide against going after him. He was pretty pissed off, so it's probably best to let him cool off. Sinking down onto a bench, still absently scratching Dog behind the ears, I stare off at nothing in particular and let my thoughts wander.

Was Gage right about me, about us? He kind of did have a point about the mistrust being leveled at him, while at the same time so much was being asked. If I were him, I would have said no, too. At the same time, I understand more than he could the reason our little unit acts the way it does toward newcomers. Experience has taught us that we have to look out for our own, even if it's at the expense of others sometimes. Our fierce protectiveness of each other is born of a need to fill the gaps left by the people we've lost. A bond forged by hardship, and months of training together as a unit to become soldiers in a war—a fight for survival...

Two years ago...

"Welcome to your first day of training. My name is Jenica Swan, and while the media has taught you over the years that I am the enemy... I can assure you that I am one of your best chances at surviving from this moment on."

I stand in the formation of about fifty people ranging in age from sixteen to forty, watching the imposing ex-CIA agent pace back and forth in front of us. Her polished black boots click on the tiles lining the hovercraft hangar, and her sleek, black ponytail hangs down between her shoulder blades in a straight line. The titanium of the faceplate covering the upper, top right half of her face reflects the lights overhead.

I am flanked by strangers, people I have never laid eyes on before today. Despite the fact that I've been living at Resistance Headquarters for two months now, I've never left my assigned room. Turning and scanning the row of recruits, my eyes lock on the one person here I do know.

Dax Janner gives me an encouraging smile and a nod. He doesn't have to speak for me to know what he's thinking. I can almost hear him in my head saying, 'You can do this'! Squaring my shoulders and holding my head high, I fix my gaze on Jenica and force myself to focus.

"In the next three months, you will undergo a rigorous training schedule and adhere to a strict personal one. You will wake every morning at 4 am for chow. After chow, there will be a run around the entire dome encasing this hideout. Not through, around... a total of ten miles. After the run, we will engage in hand-to-hand combat training. You will work with partners and other trained members of our team to hone your skills. After that, you will get a one-hour lunch break. From there, you will report back to the main building for time at the range. Our weapons supply is limited, but what we do have, you will all learn to be proficient on. Those of you who signed up for flight lessons will see me each day after your time at the gun range. Every Friday, we will skip our run and meet here for lessons in everything from using your radio COMM devices, to deciphering Military Police code words."

Swallowing past the lump in my throat, I take this all in numbly. In the past, the idea of training to be part of a unit would have lived up to my every dream. Being a recruit, a cadet... it all felt so meaningless now when there was no one here to be proud of me. No father beaming with pride and saying 'That's my girl'. No mother with tears in her eyes. No little sister staring up at me with awe and aspiration.

No one, I reminded myself, except Dax, who saved my life. I can feel him watching me. He does that, as if he thinks I'll break at any moment and he needs to be there to catch me when I do. It's happened often enough since he rescued me and brought me here, so I don't blame him. As much as my insides bristle at his invasion of my defenses, something in me yearns for more of it. Something inside of me misses the bonds I shared with the people who made up my family, and I want those bonds back... more than anything. I want—need—something to live for. Something to fight for.

"Get to know your fellow recruits," Jenica continues, stopping before our formation and turning to face us with her hands clenched behind her back. "You all are going to be spending a lot of time together. Learn to like each other. Live with each other's differences. Get over your petty disagreements, or whatever you walked in here with, because this is it. Look around you, people... the guy to your left and the girl to your right are all you've got. We all remember what life used to be. We all had lives before we came here. Many of you are young and probably thought you had it all figured it out. Your life hasn't turned out the way it planned, but this is it. Some of you will suffer even more than you already have fighting this battle. Some of you will die. So, you may as well make it count. If you don't like each other, tough luck. Forget the past. The people in this room, right now... these people are your new family."

A few hours later, I find Gage in his room with little Agata. The two are lying on the bed together, her head on his chest, and he is telling her a story about a fairy princess. I stand in the doorway and watch them, something familiar tugging on my insides as I remember being in a similar position with my father. A smile is pulling at the corners of my lips as I watch them, silently waiting for Gage to finish.

"And the princess, her prince, and the unicorn robot, all moved into the pink castle together, and..."

"They lived happily ever after," Agata supplied with a grin. "You tell the best stories, Uncle Gage."

Gage looks up from his place on the bed, his eyes flashing in annoyance as they lock with mine. Agata, oblivious to his anger toward me, jumps up and runs over to where I stand in the doorway.

"Hi! I know you; you're Blythe. Your arm is cool."

I hold the bionic limb up and twist it around, flexing the metal fingers. "You think so? Your brain sounds much cooler."

She shrugs and grabs the hand, pulling me into the room. "You know my Uncle Gage, right?"

I glance over at Gage, but he's avoiding looking at me now, so I turn my attention back to Agata. "Yes, I do. He's a great guy, isn't he?"

She pulls me down on the bed, and with Gage's bulky frame stretched across one side of the mattress, it's awful crowded. Agata doesn't seem to mind as she crosses her legs and bounces excitedly, talking a mile a minute.

"Oh, he's the best. He brought me here to get me away from the Military Police. Is that why you're here? Did someone bring you here to get you away from them?"

I nod and smile, finding her innocence and sweetness endearing. "Yeah. My best friend, Dax—the really big guy I was with earlier—he saved me from them, too. They wanted to arrest me for being different."

"Different like me."

"Yes, that's right. He told me about this place and the Professor. He told me I would be safe here and that we could be a family."

Agata frowned, her pale eyebrows scrunching adorably over wide doe eyes. "Don't you have your own family?"

My heart is beating in double time and my eye responds by filling my vision with my stats and vitals. Anxiety claws at me as the details of my past flicker through my mind like a slow-motion film. The little girl inside of me wants to fall to the floor, curl up into the fetal position, and cry. The brittle part of my personality wants to shove this girl across the bed and snarl at her to mind her own business. Another part of me feels Gage's eyes on my face and I know he's waiting for the answer too. And before I can stop myself, the words are coming out and, as I speak them, I am looking into Gage's eyes, not Agata's.

"I had a family," I say, practically choking on the lump in my throat. "They died."

"All of them?" she asks, her rose petal-pink mouth parted in disbelief.

I nod. "Yes. The Military Police killed them trying to get to me. You see, my father didn't want to turn me over to the government. Just like I'm sure your mom didn't want to hand you over."

Agata shakes her head with conviction. "No. That's why Uncle Gage hid me."

"Well, I didn't have an uncle to help me get away. I just had my parents and little sister, who risked their lives to keep me hidden in the basement. Someone found out I was there and told on us. The police wanted to take me away, but my dad tried to stop them. They shot him for it. Then they shot my mom and my sister."

"Why would they hurt your mom and your sister?"

Taking a deep, shaky breath, I decide to be honest with this girl. After all, she's smarter than I am. "Because they can, sweetheart. Because they wanted to hurt me for being who I am."

Agata is crying as she reaches out toward my face, and as her fingers come away wet, I realize that her tears are mirrored on my face.

"You must have been so sad and alone," she says softly.

"Yeah. But I had Dax. He saved me before they could kill me too. He's my family now, and so are the Professor, Olivia, and Jenica."

"That mean one with the robot face?"

I laugh through my tears and ruffle Agata's blonde curls. "Jenica isn't mean. She's just a little too serious sometimes. But, you know what? I can tell she really likes you."

Agata seems to think about this for a minute before answering. "I like her too, I think," she says. "I definitely like you. And that Dax boy is scary and big, but if he saved your life, then I like him too."

"Good."

"Blythe?"

"Yes?"

"Can Gage and me be a part of your family now, too?"

I look up to find that Gage has come to a sitting position on the bed. He stares at me over Agata's head, his face carved in anguish over my story. I wonder if he knows that when it comes to me, this is only the tip of the iceberg. My life, my emotions, my personality... all are epically screwed up, and I'm nowhere near as sweet or as perfect as this little girl asking to become part of my family.

"I don't know, honey. I think that's up to your uncle."

His hand slips into mine on the bed, white fingers intertwining with dark. His lips curve into a half smile, and my heart does a back flip in my chest.

"Uncle Gage wants that," he says softly. "More than anything."

"Good," Agata says as she stands and adjusts the hem of her shirt. "Then we can help the Professor with his mission."

Gage frowns. "How did you know about that, little girl?"

She folds her arms over her chest and gives him a look that screams, 'get real'. "Grown-ups say a lot when they think kids aren't listening. I know what the Professor needs me to do to help those people. I want to do it."

Without giving either of us a chance to reply, she turns on her heels and leaves the room with a swish of her pigtails. I raise my eyebrows at Gage.

"She's got spirit, I'll give her that. Wonder where she gets that from."

Gage laughs. "You haven't met my sister yet."

He's suddenly serious and bringing my hand—still clutched in his—up to his lips. "Thank you," he says. "For telling me that."

I snatch my hand from his and stand with a grin. "I wasn't telling you, I was telling Agata."

He stands from the bed, pulling me up with him. "Well, I'm glad you told her when I was in the room." He faced me, his piercing eyes boring into me. "You are a mystery wrapped in an enigma, Blythe Sol," he says with a smile. "I can't decide if it's going to be fun trying to figure you out, or a pain in the ass."

With a laugh, I turn to leave. Shooting him a glance over my shoulder, I say, "You let me know how that works out for you."

PART TWO: TITANIUM
(Dax Janner)

EIGHT

DAX JANNER AND YASMINE ZAMBRANO
MEMPHIS, TENNESSEE
AUGUST 16, 4010
9:55 PM

SHE DOESN'T SEE ME WATCHING HER. SHE DOESN'T KNOW THAT I am always watching because I can't take my eyes off her. If Blythe knew how beautiful she was, how much I cared about her, or how long I've been waiting for her to return my feelings...

Shit.

We're on a mission now, and I shouldn't be thinking about Blythe. I shouldn't be thinking about walking in on her and that asshole kissing, or his hands where mine should have been. Even now, the thought makes me long for five minutes alone in a small room with the arrogant jackass.

Maybe later.

Right now, on board the Neville I hovercraft, Jenica and Blythe are waiting for Yasmine and me to stage the diversion that's going to clear an opening for them to swoop in and rescue the other Memphis refugees. Jenica's intel showed at least one hundred of them still living underground, unable to come or go because of the steady and vigilant presence of the

Enforcers waiting for us to show up. I'm watching the screen of my COMM device, which keeps me in touch with the other members of my team—team Alpha—and also lets me monitor the movements and progress of team Bravo, who are on board the Neville II and waiting for the changing of the guard shift at Stonehead to strike in five minutes. We don't make a move until they do, as the attacks must be coordinated.

We know our only chance at getting this right will be if everything is as perfectly timed as it should be. At ten pm on the dot, the real fun will begin. As the guards switch out for the night, little Agata will use her EMP signal to cut the power, including the guards' weapons. Despite the fact that I hate Gage with a passion, I can't deny that his niece is useful; I guess we owe him for allowing us to bring her on this mission. As a way to repay my debt, I decide *not* to smash his face in for kissing Blythe.

This time.

I gaze up at the Neville I, taking one last look at Blythe and Jenica where they sit, waiting for us to do our part. The other eight members of our team are waiting in the back of the craft. I feel Yasmine shift beside me and know she's as restless as I am to get going. My gaze lingers on Blythe for a fraction of a second longer than necessary before I return my gaze to the COMM device and note the time.

9:58.

I can hear Jenica's voice through the speaker. "Bravo team is in position. Standby for EMP in two minutes."

I look at Yasmine and find her staring at me, her gaze wide and knowing. She's an attractive girl, a tall and willowy thing, with plump lips and almond-shaped eyes. Her Kevlar skin is cocoa colored and smooth, hinting not a bit at the toughness I know it possesses.

"You love her, don't you?"

It's not so much a question as it is a statement. There's no inflection in her voice to tell me what she's thinking, or why she would say such a thing. Of course I love Blythe; I found her, beaten half to death by MPs and sobbing her heart out over her dead family. I killed the men who hurt her, stole her away, rescuing her from arrest and certain death. I took her family's place—Dog and me—and became her world.

Hell yes, I love her.

I nod, once, the only thing she's going to get out of me on the subject. She nods too, as if satisfied with my answer.

"I can see why you would," she says softly. "She doesn't know what she has, though," she adds.

After that, she goes silent, leaving me to wonder what the hell she meant by that. I'll never understand women and their hints and ever-changing moods. I'm a man with basic needs: food, water, scratch, fuck. You have to tell me things outright and in plain English or I'm liable to miss them completely. Deciding to try to decipher Yasmine's hieroglyphics when I've got more time, I turn my attention back to the COMM device, grateful that she decides not to elaborate right now. Not like we have the time to worry about all of that.

It is now 10:00 pm on the dot and at Stonehead

Prison in Washington D.C., everything has just gone pitch black.

Every muscle in my body is tense as I step out from my hiding place, showing myself to the MPs patrolling the area. Everything that follows this moment depends completely on me and the frightened girl beside me. She doesn't have to tell me that she's afraid, I can feel it. I can see it in the set of her wide, almond-shaped eyes as she joins me in the middle of the road. Looking at her, I can remember my first mission as a part of the Resistance and I know her fear. Today, we are facing the very people who want us dead, who fear us because we are different.

I I'm looking forward to seeing what she's capable of. She stands beside me cool and collected, the sharp angles of her face accentuated by the tight bun at the back of her head. Her eyes narrow as our enemy approaches and I feel her hatred for them. It matches mine.

"Identify yourselves," barks one of the MPs, stepping toward me with his weapon set to stun.

If I weren't focused on my mission, I might have laughed at this guy. *Identify yourselves?* Yeah, I'm so intimidated, Officer Asswipe.

Don't even get me started on the fact that it's 10:00 pm, dark as hell outside, and these jackasses and their expensive armor are lit up like Christmas trees. All they can make out about me is my long, bulky shape, but once they pull out the scanners they're going to know what I really am. Then it'll be time to run.

"Get ready," I whisper to Yasmine as Officer

Asswipe and two of his cronies start walking toward us. They leave behind about ten others, but I'm banking on our discovery drawing them away from the hideout's entrance. Even if one or two stay behind, I know that Blythe and Jenica can handle it.

"You are in a restricted area," the officer warns as he draws near, his weapon still pointed toward the ground, his finger ready on the trigger. His two friends are a few steps behind him, their weapons also drawn and ready. One of them holds a scanner. I brace my legs apart and bend my knees, ready to run.

The officers get closer and the glow from their solar-powered armor—now fueled by a full day's worth of sun—casts enough light for them to see us clearly. I know what they see as they stop in front of me and raise their weapons: six feet, five inches of muscle and brawn stretched beneath dark brown skin, a buzz-cut head, and light brown eyes. What lies beneath will be revealed by the scanners. That's when the fun will begin.

Their equipment starts going off like crazy, clueing them in to my bionic prosthetic legs and titanium ribs. The scanner of the second officer reacts to Yasmine's Kevlar skin as they close in on us, weapons raised.

"Hands up, both of you!" barks Officer Asswipe, his gun trained directly on my middle. Yasmine is unflinching at my side as we silently comply.

The third guy speaks into a COMM device clutched in his free hand. "Sergeant, we've got two Bios here, one male and one female."

A voice crackles from over the speaker. "Aside

from their Bionic additions, are they armed?"

Officer Asswipe and MP number two both step forward to pat us down. My gut clenches in disgust as Yasmine's officer allows his hands to linger a few seconds longer than necessary on her hips. To her credit, she continues staring straight ahead. She doesn't even bat an eyelash.

"No weapons," Officer Three confirms after getting clearance from One and Two.

"Take them out."

The third officer wrinkles his brow and exchanges a glance with Asswipe. He glances as at the COMM device as if confused. "Sir?"

The voice retorts "Those Bios are probably from the hideout. They'd be dead within the next hour anyway. President Drummond has given orders to gas it."

I hear Yasmine's sharp intake of breath and it echoes my own fears. Thank God we got here in time with a plan in place. If we had only run a rescue mission to Stonehead, those left behind would have been killed. I have seen the damage their poisonous gas can do firsthand. I'm talking seizures, drooling and crapping your pants. I wouldn't wish that on my worst enemy.

"Roger," says Officer Three as he stuffs the COMM device back into the clip on his belt.

"On your knees," says Officer Two as he exchanges the laser weapon at his hip for one of the ancient models that relies on bullets. They love to execute our kind with bullets instead of modern laser weapons, because they like to see our blood spilled. The others follow suit.

"No," I respond, lowering my hands back to my

sides. They curl into fists that I can't wait to use on them. Yasmine does the same.

"Who the fuck do you think you are, you *Bio* trash?" Officer Asswipe hisses from behind his helmet. The word 'bio' rolls off his tongue like an epithet. "Get on your knees now, both of you."

"No," we both respond in unison.

This is what I hate about the MPs. They don't just kill us. They strip us of everything, including our dignity. Taking our freedom and our lives just isn't enough for them.

"Doesn't matter," Officer Two says, stepping forward and pressing his gun to Yasmine's head. My gut clenches with irrational fear. If anything, the fact that they've switched to bullets at this point is good. No bullet can pierce her Kevlar skin. "They're dead anyway."

He flips up the visor of his helmet and stares down at Yasmine. "Shame, too. This one's kind of pretty. I wouldn't have minded a go with her if we had time."

"Fuck you, you fascist sack of shit!" She growls defiantly, though her voice trembles slightly.

My eyebrows shoot up and I feel myself reaching a whole new level of respect for the little spitfire hurling insults while staring down the barrel of a gun. In response, he pulls the trigger. The sound is explosive. Yasmine rears back but maintains her footing as the bullet bounces off her head, falling to the forest floor in a steaming lump of dented metal. Shocked gasps ripple through all three of them as she glances up and smiles.

"My turn," she rasps before sticking Officer Two with a right cross. His open face shield ensures that her punch lands right on his nose and as blood gushes in a crimson spray, she twists his arm behind him so quickly he doesn't have time to react. He bends unwillingly at the waist, screaming in pain as she brings her elbow down on his straight arm. The strength of her skin—as hard as diamonds—shatters his armor as well as a few bones.

Realizing that they've underestimated us, the other two officers jump into action. Officer Asswipe doesn't see it coming when I knock the gun from his hand. He takes a swing at me and I let him land it, taking the left hook to the jaw so that he'd get cocky. I see his smirk just seconds before his fist connects with my ribs in a right hook. The sound of his finger bones colliding with my titanium ribs is like music to my ears, which are topped off by his cries of pain as I give him a swift and painful kick to the middle with one of my titanium legs.

Officer Asswipe goes flying away from me and lands at the foot of a tree a few feet away, and I turn just in time to find Yasmine trading blows with Officer Three. I catch him by surprise and knock him out cold before he sees me coming. I can hear the crackle of the dead officer's COMM device as, about a hundred yards away, the others officers check on their fallen comrades. They'll be on us in a matter of seconds, which is exactly what we wanted.

"You good?" I ask as Yasmine bends to retrieve the unconscious MP's weapon.

"Peachy. You think he'll mind if I use this?"

I shrug, kicking at the officer with the toe of my

combat boot. "I think he's okay with it. Didn't know you could fight."

She shrugs as she checks the gun's setting. I follow suit by taking an identical weapon from one of the others. "Dad was a martial arts instructor. It'd be dumb for me to *not* know how to fight."

"I'm impressed."

"Good, but those guys don't look like they share your opinion."

I glance up just in time to see eight MP's rising up off the ground on their sleek hover bikes. They speed toward us, weapons trained and ready. I glance at her and arch one eyebrow.

"Think you can keep up?"

She snorts. "You just better hope one of those mechanical legs of yours doesn't blow a gasket."

"I'll go left, you go right. Try to swivel in and out of the trees and make them crash. The fewer we have to take out ourselves with deadly force, the better."

That's a lesson drummed into me by the Professor. Most days I feel mad enough to kill every MP within a hundred mile radius, but he's the leader of our Resistance and is all about working toward peace. He doesn't want us getting our hands dirty unless we have to. But if it comes down between me and one of those hateful men in gleaming silver armor, the Professor's just going to have to get over it because I'm going for the kill.

As soon as they are close enough to see us, we take off, Yasmine peeling off and going to the right like I'd instructed her. Behind us, the speeding hover bikes give chase, and I hear the hum of the Neville I hovercraft hurtling toward the hideout entrance. I know that the two guards left behind will be nothing for Jenica, Blythe, and the other members of Alpha team to handle. I hope we can divert the others long enough for them to load the trapped refugees into the hovercraft.

I pump my legs as fast as I can, the pistons installed at my joints making me faster than the bikes. I'm hoping to put as much distance between us and the hideout as possible.

I hear Jenica's voice over the COMM device on my hip. "Alpha team moving in. Janner, report!"

"Kinda tied up right now," I mumble as I run, darting in and out of the trees faster than any human ought to be able to. Through the COMM device I hear the sounds of the MPs' weapons firing, followed by a struggle. Behind me there's an explosion, and I glance over my shoulder to see an orange ball of fire and raining debris—all that's left of one of the hover bikes.

"Halt! Stop where you are and put your hands up or I'll shoot!"

The mechanical voice of the MP closest to me, crackling through his helmet, doesn't stop me. I know they'll kill me anyway, and worse, they'll turn right back around and kill Jenica and Blythe, who right now are rescuing those left underground in the hideout. Instead, I veer to the right, hard, forcing the three bikes left to scramble to follow me while avoiding the trees.

I hear the whine of a weapon, the preliminary heating that occurs just before their stun guns fire. Once the core temperature of the weapon reaches near volcanic proportions, the weapon's red-tinted rays can stun or kill, depending on its wielder's intent. I hit the dirt right as a red beam shoots over my head, tucking and rolling just in time to avoid being hit. In my crouched position, I wait for the shooter to get closer.

Just as he zooms over my head, turning his bike at an angle to take another shot, I uncoil my legs and shoot straight up, my legs propelling me several feet above the ground. I grab the foothold and hang on for dear life as the driver swivels and swerves in an attempt to shake me off.

"Shoot him! Shoot him!" he yells to his buddies. Just as I grab onto the side of his bike with both hands and pull, my biceps straining painfully, he turns it so the other two have a clear shot at me. I struggle to climb aboard the bike, and once my foot hits the footrest, I'm good. I am able to swing my other leg over the side of the bike until I'm straddling the seat, right behind my pursuer—who by now is freaking out. He turns and points his gun at me but I capture his wrist, twisting it painfully behind his back. I use his pain and dismay to catch him off balance and throw him from the seat. Scooting forward, I lower my head over the handlebars just as another red beam shoots over my shoulder.

I rev the engine and send the bike hurtling through the trees, feeling a bit more confident now that I've got a bike *and* a weapon on me. We don't have many guns at Resistance headquarters, and most of us have learned how to fight hand to hand. I could turn and pick them both off, but that would leave me blind to the trees surrounding me and I'm in no hurry to relinquish my bike anytime soon. If I can get it back to the hovercraft in one piece, maybe I can talk Jenica into letting me bring it aboard and take it home.

Glancing over my shoulder, I see that the two remaining officers are closing in, one right behind the other. In a risky move, I purposely slow my bike, letting my back bumper kiss the front of his. I stand on the seat of my bike facing him and leap into a front somersault, narrowly avoiding being hit by another red beam and landing on the nose of his bike. He raises his gun to shoot again, but not before I grasp him by the front of his helmet, twisting and throwing him from the seat before shooting him with my gun—which is set to stun. He'll be out for hours.

After I slide into the driver's seat, another shot from my stun gun takes care of my final attacker and sends both him and his bike crashing into a nearby tree. He falls limp on the forest floor as his bike slams into the tree, going up in a ball of orange and red flame just like the first one.

Finally alone and able to take a few breaths, I snatch the COMM device from my belt and call Jenica.

"Alpha team, this is Janner reporting."

A few seconds and Jenica is on the line. "This is Swan. We've infiltrated the hideout and located the refugees. All Military Police personnel guarding the entrance have been subdued. What is your status, Janner?"

"Four MPs on my trail, all stunned and one possibly dead but I'm not sure. Going in search of Zambrano now. She had four on her tail and went in the opposite direction. Once I locate her we will return to the craft within a few minutes. I've got a hover bike."

"Roger that, Janner. There are way more of them here than our intel reported. It will take a while to get them all loaded up, and we sure could use you two to help watch our backs. Get here as fast as you can."

"Roger," I reply, switching channels on the COMM device so that I can find Yasmine. "Zambrano, this is Janner. Are you there?"

Silence.

I frown, lifting the device to my lips and trying again. "Zambrano, please report, this is Janner. Need to know your location."

Even more silence.

"Shit."

By the time the curse has fallen from my mouth I'm back on the bike, turning west in the direction I remember Yasmine taking. I swerve in and out of the trees, keeping my eyes peeled for her. Times like this I wish Blythe was with me. Her bionic eye can pick up heat signatures and save me a lot of time. And right now, time is of the essence because if I can't get to Yasmine before it's too late ... well, it's just not something I want to have to think about.

When I find Yasmine, for a moment I believe that she is dead.

"Oh, God! No!" The words spill out in a rush, my throat constricting with emotion. I stop the bike, park it and jump down, landing amidst a pile of bike debris. I step over two MPs to get to her. She lays sprawled out like a rag doll, covered in dirt and leaves. I kneel down at her side and gently slide a hand under her head, lifting it as I place my free hand around her slender wrist, searching for a pulse with my fingertips. When I feel her blood rushing through her veins beneath my fingers, I breathe a sigh of relief. She's been stunned, but she'll be okay.

I only see two of the MPs, but I have to assume she's taken care of the other two as there are no signs of them anywhere and she's still alive. If the other two had been around when she was down, they'd have killed her for sure.

I hoist her over my shoulder and climb back onto the bike, settling her weight across my lap as I rev the bike again and turn back in the direction of the hideout and waiting hovercraft. I remain on edge, just in case they've sent reinforcements. Luckily, we make it back to the hideout without incident, though Yasmine is still unconscious. As I park the bike and hop off carefully with her slung over my shoulder, Blythe emerges from the hideout's tunnel opening, leading a group of children hurriedly toward the lowered ladder of the hovercraft.

One of our team members, Sayer Strom, is at the foot of the ladder standing guard. He helps the children up the ladder to another waiting team member who will get them all organized and seated in the craft. Blythe, seeing that Sayer has everything under control, trots over to me with concern knitting her brow.

"What happened? Is she okay?"

I glance down at Yasmine, who I've taken from over my shoulder and am now holding against my chest like a child. Blythe reaches out and strokes her hair back from her forehead in a tender gesture and all I can think about is how badly I want to feel those slender, long-fingered hands on *my* face.

"She's just stunned," I answer, once I turn my thoughts away from the possibility of Blythe's hands on my face, stroking the contours of my cheekbones and jaw. These thoughts are dangerous, even more so in this situation with peril pressing in from all sides.

"I hate this happened on her first mission," Blythe says as she watches the last of the children board the craft. "I hope it doesn't change her mind about wanting to be part of the team."

I think back over Yasmine's bold taunts toward our enemies and try to suppress a dry snort of laughter. "Doubtful. How are things going in there?"

She sighs. "There are way more than we expected. Jenica is worried we'll have to make two trips."

My eyebrows shoot up. "And leave the rest of them here without protection? Do they have any supplies?"

"Fuel. Lots of it. Remember, this branch of the Resistance is responsible for smuggling fuel to us and all the others. Jenica wants to come back for it, but the people are our first priority. We have months before we need to worry about a shortage of fuel."

I nod, shifting Yasmine in my arms a bit. She might be thin, but her dead weight is wreaking havoc on my arm muscles. "So, what's the plan? Other than fuel and scared Bios, what else is down there?"

"A little bit of food," she answers as Jenica appears at the mouth of the tunnel with another group. Silently, they make a beeline for the hovercraft and I can't help but feel sorry for them as I watch the procession go by. They are a bedraggled bunch, dressed in tattered clothing with wide eyes full of fear. I remember the feeling of being hunted with no end in sight, so I know what they're going through. That feeling was, thankfully, lifted from me the moment I met Blythe. In her I found someone to take care of and it made me cast off my fear. Then we joined the Resistance and became a family. Fear can kiss my ass.

"Janner, Sol, I need the two of you to stay behind and guard the second group of refugees. We can't take them all in one trip, so we'll have to come back. Is she okay?

I follow her gaze down to Yasmine, who's still out like a light. "Stunned, but fine. She took out the four MPs following her, though. She's a tough girl."

Jenica motions for Sayer to come forward and take her from my arms. My protective nature makes me reluctant to let her go. She's going to freak out when she wakes up from being stunned and I want to be there when she does. But I'm not going against Jencia's orders and I figure it'd be best for her to go in case we are attacked by MPs. I hand her over and watch as Sayer ascends into the hovercraft with her limp form.

"How long will we have to wait?" Blythe asks. I can tell she's annoyed. She doesn't have very much patience, and in this situation I can't blame her. It won't take long for the good folks in D.C. to figure out what's going on here, and once they do, we're in deep shit. Blythe and I can only do so much to protect these people.

"Should be no longer than overnight," Jenica mumbles distractedly as her COMM device crackles to life. I can hear the panicked voice of Gage Bronson on the other end. "This is Swan," Jenica says calmly. "Bronson what is your status?"

"We're taking heavy fire!" he responds through the device. Indeed, rapid gunfire can be heard between every word and I hear Blythe gasp at my side. My arm reflexively goes around her shoulders and I draw her to my side. "We have freed the prisoners but the MPs sent reinforcements faster than we expected. I ... I believe McNabb has been hit!"

My gut twists as Olivia's face flashes through my mind. We weren't exactly involved but we've screwed around a few times. She's the Resistance Headquarters' slut for sure, but she's not a bad person. In fact, she's one of the best people I know besides Blythe. If we lose her, it will be a great blow to the Resistance.

"Get out of there Bronson!" Jenica shouts into the device, her voice rising a bit. The human part of her face is as passive as the robotic half, but her eyes are darting, and I can hear the anxiety in her voice. Jenica pretends not to care but I see through that. Her problem is not that she doesn't care, it's that she cares too much. "Concentrate on getting out and I will put in a call to Headquarters for reinforcements. The lives of Bravo team rest on your shoulders. You wanted to be a part of this thing... this is what we do."

I can practically hear the steely determination in the stubborn bastard's voice as he responds. "Roger, Miss Swan. I won't let you down."

The device goes dead and silence falls over us. The gunfire didn't slow or cease during that short conversation and I know things can't be good at the holding facility in D.C. where Gage and Olivia are supposed to be running a rescue mission.

"Oh my God, Agata!" Blythe cries from beside me, her human eye filling with tears. I know she feels guilt over helping to talk Gage into using the girl as a weapon against the MPs, and she'll be lucky if Gage gets her out alive. "We should never have talked him into taking her. He'll never forgive us if she dies."

"Pull yourself together," Jenica snaps, once again her commanding self. "We can do nothing for them here. You two can get in the hideout and guard those refugees until morning. I can run these people back to Headquarters and call backup for Bravo team. These are things we *can* do. We are the Resistance and we don't have time to fall apart. People are depending on us."

Jenica's pep talk is all we need to get moving. I make sure that Blythe takes a weapon from one of the fallen MPs before we move to the opening of the hideout. We stand in the dark doorway and watch as Jenica leads the last of the passengers up into the hovercraft and steers up and out of sight. I pray silently that she is fast. Something tells me those stunned MPs aren't going to wake up happy. They'll be back with some of their boys.

Once Jenica is gone, I pull the accordion-like

metal gate closed over the opening and secure it with the padlock before pulling the steel sliding doors closed behind them. It won't be enough to keep the enemy completely out, but it will slow them down. After I slide the doors closed, we are cast into complete darkness. Luckily, Blythe's bionic eye has night vision so she wordlessly slips her hand into mine and begins to lead me down the cement tunnel down into the ground where the hideout is located.

The darkness is suffocating, as is the heat that increases with every step that takes us further and further underground. But I trust Blythe to lead me and walk blindly with my hand clenched tightly in hers. I can feel her tension. It's in her grip, but it's also thickening the heavy blanket of hot air around us. I know that despite what Jenica says, Blythe's mind is on what's happening in D.C.

"This isn't your fault," I say as we walk down the tunnel. "You couldn't have known things would go wrong up in D.C. and the girl wasn't supposed to leave the hovercraft."

"Things hardly ever go according to plan," she responds, her voice reaching out to me from the darkness. "Agata should have never been there. Gage either."

My jaw tightens at the thought of the blond Blythe has lost her senses over. She's become way too trusting of him way too fast and there's just something about him that rubs me the wrong way. "He asked to be here, remember? He wanted this. That means he gets to deal with the consequences of his actions. That includes

Agata's and Olivia's deaths."

Blythe gasps and I know I've gone too far. "Don't talk like that! We don't know if they are dead or even if they're hurt. Gage didn't seem sure."

I want to disagree but I keep my mouth shut. Losing everyone I've ever loved has made me pragmatic. I am prepared to face the deaths of those I care about.

"You're probably right," I say to pacify her as light finally appears at the end of the tunnel. "We won't worry until we have to. For now, let's just concentrate on taking care of these folks here. They're probably scared as hell right now."

NINE

DAX JANNER AND BLYTHE SOL
RESISTANCE HIDEOUT IN MEMPHIS, TENNESSEE
AUGUST 17, 4010
11:45 P.M.

THE MEMPHIS HIDEOUT IS CRUDE AND LACKING IN THE COMFORTS we've come to take advantage of at Headquarters. From the large, open main room—which serves as both a living and dining area—to the metal doors of the residents' apartments lining the walls from floor to ceiling, stretching up in five rows with steel-railed walkways and stairs on each level. The people there are as depressing as their surroundings, but that is to be expected. Less than twenty-four hours ago, they'd faced execution at the hands of the MPs.

The people are all gathered around, a mishmash of half-human/half-robot rejects. They are watching us as if they expect us to take charge; which is exactly what we're here to do. We have to hold out until morning, and that means putting several plans of action in place at once and putting them to work so they're not focused on the imminent danger.

I decide to establish myself as the leader, as Blythe is still looking a bit green. It's going to take her a little time to get her shit together and while I understand that, there are bigger issues at stake here.

Finding an empty table, I step up onto its stainless steel surface so that I am a bit elevated, and hold my arms up for attention.

"Good evening, everybody. My name is Dax Janner and this is Blythe Sol. We are a part of the Resistance team that was sent to evacuate this hideout."

"Then why are half of us still here?" shouts a guy from the middle of the gathered crowd. He looks like a body builder and one of his arms is titanium, but the look of fear in his eyes is unmistakable. Others shout and mumble in agreement.

"Our intelligence was off about the number of people being kept prisoner here, and our hovercraft can only hold one hundred, and that's with people crammed into it like sardines. Our pilot had to make two trips. It was important that we evacuate the youngest, oldest, and injured among you first."

I thank God for Jenica's thoughtfulness in evacuating. Among those left are the youngest and strongest, which means that if we're infiltrated before the night is over, we stand a fair chance of fighting them off.

"We have a lot to do before the team returns in the morning for the rest of us. Blythe and I have stayed behind to keep you all safe and organized. It is important that everyone do their part so that we are ready to leave in the morning in an organized fashion."

"What do you suggest we do other than sitting around and waiting for the MPs to return with reinforcements?" asks a woman standing near the front.

She's close enough that I can see the metal plate covering most of her abdomen. Its shiny surface extends up to her shoulders like a breastplate and I wonder how much of her beneath it is machinery. Her Italian New Yorker accent is thick and her dark eyes are narrowed as if she is suspicious of us and our plans. "Obviously, they're not going to just stand back and let us walk out of here alive. They've been watching this place for months; you'd better believe they're already planning an attack on those who are left."

Her words create even more distress, and soon everyone is talking, some yelling to be heard above the others. Some are even suggesting that we make a run for it on our own instead of waiting for Jenica to return with the hovercraft.

"Everyone, please remain calm!" I'm yelling to be heard, but no one seems to be paying attention. They are allowing their fear to tamper reason. "We have protocols in place for this very kind of situation," I continue, trying to remain patient. If I blow my top it's going to upset the situation more. Problem is, I don't have a lot of patience and very little tolerance for bullshit. This is a waste of time and I'm starting to get pissed. I'm just about to scream at those assembled to shut the fuck up, when the shrill sound of a wailing alarm fills the air. It is just loud enough to smother the cacophony of voices that is drowning mine out and render everyone silent.

The sound stops and I notice Blythe has moved over near the wall, her hand poised on the switch of a fire alarm, her expression annoyed. Everyone is looking at her now as she nods her head as if satisfied with their silence.

"That's better," she says, crossing the room and joining me on top of the table. "Panicking and arguing will only get us all killed. She's right," she continues, pointing at Metal-For-Breasts, "the MPs are regrouping right now and they will come back. But if everyone would just listen to Dax, we can get organized, and everything will be fine. We just have to make it until morning and help is on the way. Everybody okay with this?"

Nobody speaks up, so I assume it's okay to continue. "As I was saying," I begin after nodding my thanks to Blythe, "I am going to ask everyone to split up into groups. Those of you with fighting experience, gather over there, near the entrance to this room. There, you will meet with me to discuss securing the perimeter and taking shifts throughout the night to ensure that we are ready in the event of an attack. If you own weapons of any kind, or know of any that may have been left behind by those already gone, gather them. We're going to need all the help we can get. Is there anyone left here who works in the kitchen?"

A few people raised their hands.

"Good. I heard you guys weren't getting much to eat while the MPs were here, so let's get some dinner going. No need for us to starve while we wait. Any items that we can pack up and take with us to Headquarters, get them bagged or boxed up and lined up near the entrance. If there's room for them, they'll be of good use where we're going. Everyone else, gather any clothes or supplies from your rooms you may need once we've moved you. Please remember to only take what's necessary. Your living quarters at Headquarters will be small and you will have to share with others. If your friends or family are already gone and left things behind, bring what you think they'll need. All bags or boxes going with us must be gathered and stacked near the entrance if you don't want them to be left behind."

"What are we supposed to do for the rest of the night?" someone else asks from the back of the crowd.

"If you're not on security or kitchen detail, then once you are packed up and ready to leave, there is nothing else you can do but get some rest. I suggest turning in early in case we are contacted by our rescue party before sunrise. Tomorrow will be a long and trying day. I know it will be hard considering the circumstances, but that really is your best option."

"You heard him," Blythe said once I was done, jumping down from the table. "Let's get gathered into our groups and get to work!"

Most everyone disperses immediately, though there are some who seem to need more time to digest what is happening. I leave these people alone, deciding to give them a bit of time. My impatience would do nothing but upset them more and I know that not everyone is a take-action kind of person like I am.

Blythe and I skirt the room, watching as everyone eventually finds their way to where they need to be. I turn and find her staring down at her COMM device, her mouth a tight, grim line. I know she's waiting for word from Jenica about Gage and the others, but that's unlikely for a while yet.

"Hey," I say, placing my hand on her shoulder. She

glances up at me, the whir of her bionic eye humming as it moves. It starts to beep and I wonder if it's giving her a read on my vitals. If so, I'm embarrassed that she knows how my heart rate spikes when she looks at me. "Thanks for having my back. I was about to lose it for a second there."

She forces a tight smile and shrugs. "Come on, we're the dynamic duo, right? You know I've got you."

I know she means it, but I can't help but wonder if the latest developments won't end our tight partnership. I know she wants Gage and he wants her back, and that realization puts a cold stone of disgust in my gut. I've always been her protector, her best friend. Knowing that some guy has the potential to change all of that leaves me fearful for our partnership. I don't even want to think about what it will mean to have to watch them get romantic. It's enough to turn that stone into a coil of twisting snakes that make my insides quiver with nausea.

Jealousy; it's not the warmest or fuzziest of feelings.

"Why don't you take over with the kitchen crew?" I suggest, hoping that keeping her busy will help her take her mind off what might be happening in the capital. "I'm going to go work out the security detail."

"Sounds like a plan."

She saunters off toward the kitchen and I watch her go, my mouth going dry at the sway of her hips. The timing of my wayward thoughts is completely inappropriate, but then so is my entire obsession with her. I know she sees me as a big brother of sorts, but that doesn't stop me from wanting her with every fiber of my being, or of loving her so strongly that it hurts to be near her—almost as much as it feels good.

I force myself to stop thinking about the lusty images rolling like an X-rated flick through my mind, and turn to join the security team gathered near the entrance. I'm pleased with what I see. The group is small, only about fifteen of them in all, but they are sturdy, strong, and at least half are carrying weapons.

Shiny Boobs is at the front of the group, her muscled arms crossed over her chest. She's wearing a tank top, cargo pants and combat boots, which seems to be the uniform of this group. They look like they're ready for action so I jump right into it.

"I need a rundown of all entrances and exits so that we can post guards at each one. Also, if you guys have some kind of COMM device system, we should break those out. I'd like us all to remain in constant contact."

Shiny Boobs steps forward, dropping her arms to her sides. "Laura Rosenberg, formerly of the U.S. Army," she says.

I smile. "You a New Yorker?"

She smirks as if recognizing the same in me. "You know it. Been heading up security here since I arrived. Got crushed by a pylon in the blasts and took some major damage to my torso. Mostly reconstructed by machinery and covered by this metal plate. Of course they discharged me from the Army, but I put myself to good use here. These guys are all strapped with COMM devices and so am I. I can take you over to the control room and get one for you and your friend."

I immediately snap to attention. "Control room?"

She nods. "It *was* a room with a switchboard that we pretty much used to run this place. It controlled the lights, an intercom system, and even a lockdown mechanism."

"Let me guess, the MPs tore it to pieces when they discovered you guys."

Laura nods again, anger flashing in her dark eyes. "There are switches that control thick, metal doors that slide into place over the regular ones. Too heavy to pry open, too thick to blast through—they are pretty much impenetrable. We were on lockdown when they surrounded us, but convinced our leader to open the doors. They were holding a group of our own hostage, most of them children. We weren't going to just stand there and watch a bunch of kids die while we cowered underground. We had no choice but to let them in. We expected a massacre, but you know Drummond won't miss his chance to make a spectacle out of us. Guess they decided one mass execution would be better than simply reporting that they'd found and killed part of the Resistance."

At the mention of the President's name, some of the guys behind Laura curse or mutter under their breaths. I catch plenty of utterances of 'asshole' and 'coward' and even hear someone spit. Yeah, that pretty much sums up how I feel about him, too.

"Is there no way to physically close the doors?" I ask, thinking about Blythe's mechanical arm. That thing's strong enough to crush a steal beam if she puts enough pressure on it.

Laura shrugs "Never been tried before as far as I know. The doors slide down a hatch and lock in place. If we were to close one, we wouldn't be able to get them back open and we'd be trapped."

"What if we closed all but one? That way, we don't have to break up our group to post guards at every entrance. The MPs will be forced to come through the front and by then we'll see them coming. I'm assuming they left your surveillance system intact."

"Yes, it's how they knew you guys were coming. They called up to Washington for reinforcements. I don't know what's taking so long; I'd think they'd be here right now."

I shake my head. "We're running a double mission. Another Resistance team is working to free the prisoners at Stonehead. Those guys are busy right now. But once they can spare some backup, they'll be here. My friend has a bionic arm. Might be strong enough to yank down those doors. How many other entrances?"

"Four."

I select eight of the guys standing by and send two to each entrance. I make sure that each group of two has one weapon between them. Their bionic additions are the only other mechanism of defense they have. I see another bionic eye in the group, which is good since those things give off heat readings and will catch the MPs coming long distance. I tell everyone to keep in touch and report every half hour via their COMM devices. There are seven more left waiting besides Laura, and I assign them to keeping the peace among those inside the compound. In times like these, people get stir crazy and paranoid and the last thing I need are for these people to start fighting among themselves.

"I need you to show me to the control room and get me those COMM devices. Then, I need a schematic of this place if you have one."

"Of course," she says, snapping to attention like the soldier she is. I am digging the way this chick knows how to follow orders without questions. "Follow me."

We start across the room, ducking and dodging the many people walking through the cafeteria/living area carrying crates, boxes and duffel bags. I notice a group sitting off to the side doing nothing. I pause, my jaw dropping as I take each of them in, because they immediately call for closer inspection. There are about ten of them, and they are nothing like the rest of us.

When it comes to Bionics and their additions, I think I've seen just about everything. For God's sake, half of Jenica's face is made of metal and machinery and Yasmine's skin is made of Kevlar. But this ... what I'm looking at is more extreme than even the most excessive of accessories. They appear to be more metal than they are human, and one could easily mistake them for robots as opposed to humans. Closer inspection reveals that there is something very wrong with these Bionics. Their additions are haphazard and poorly made. Many of them appear rusty and are of poorer quality than the ones designed by Professor Hinkley.

"Who are they?" I ask Laura as a man whose entire scalp is constructed of what can only be described as a metal cap stares back at me menacingly. The skin around where the cap has been bolted to his head is red and enflamed as if the addition was recently added. He's also got a metal arm, but as he lifts it to flip me the bird, a sharp blade slides out of the back of his forearm with a 'whoosh'. Just as quickly, he retracts it and then raises one eyebrow at me, as if daring me to fuck with him. Part of me wants nothing more than to cross the room and kick him in the head to test the strength of his deformed metal head.

"Those guys are bad news," Laura answers with a sneer. She doesn't even try to hide her disgust. "We call them the Rejects because that's literally what they are. Dane, our leader, was going to hold a hearing about having them kicked out of here. They have crazy ideas ... ideas that might just cause people to believe what the President says about us being dangerous."

"You mean, that we're superior to the Normals."

"Exactly. But they take it a step further. Most of them have an original addition or two that they received when they signed up for the Healing Hands initiative. But it's not enough for them. They purposely add on more bits and pieces—they call them 'enhancements'—in order to make themselves more deadly. They think that if they gather up enough Bionics and turn them all into freaks like them, they'll be able to create their own personal little army and storm the capital. They think exterminating the inferior humans is the answer."

Dread floods my veins like ice water at what I'm hearing. This extremist group could pose a real problem. The Professor has worked so hard to show the world that we are just people trying to live normal lives. These assholes and everything they believe flies in the face of that. They are the ones proving President Drummond and the rest of the country right.

"Where do they have the procedures done? I mean, I thought the government held the patent on bionic parts and organs."

Laura scoffs at me like I'm an idiot and I feel my face going hot with embarrassment. "Come on, kid, get real. It's called the Black Market."

"I know what the Black Market is," I hiss from between clenched teeth. I don't appreciate being made fun of. "It's how we supply you all with food and how you exchange it with us for fuel."

"Right, so they've got their own version of that. There is another doctor, one less known than our Professor and much less intuitive. He gets the job done, though. He designed the parts and sends holographic, tutorial messages to the other doctors that are a part of this sick and twisted group. They perform the surgeries, though a lot of those freaks end up with infections afterward because of the conditions these doctors work in. It leaves a lot of them deformed, but they don't care. They only care about creating an unstoppable army."

"Army or not, they're stuck down here like the rest of us. The least they can do is help."

"I wouldn't if I were you."

Laura's warning pretty much goes through one ear and out the other. I don't want to work with these assholes but if they're here, they're going to pull their weight like everyone else, or they're not getting on my hovercraft tomorrow.

The guy I've dubbed 'Blade' stands as I approach, and he doesn't look happy to see me.

"Dax Janner," I say, trying for the friendly approach as I offer him my hand. He looks as if my hand is a snake and decides not to take it. I drop it back down to my side and determine that I was right not to like this jackass from the start.

"You guys look like you could really be of help on our security team," I continue, my eyes searching each and every person seated in the group around him. Not one of them appears to give a damn about what I'm saying. "It'd be nice if everyone here pulled their weight until the next craft arrives."

"I don't take orders, mate," Blade answers. I'm taken aback by his thick, Aussie accent, and wonder how on earth this guy ended up in Tennessee.

"Look, this isn't a pissing contest," I counter. "We were sent here to save your asses, so it might work out for you to cooperate, at least until we get you out of here."

"And who says we need you to get us out of here?" says a chick with metal spikes sticking out of her neck. They are a menacing mix of body art and deadly weapon. As she stands, the spikes elongate and more of them pop out along her skin. Gross.

"I'm sorry, but if I'm not mistaken you all would have been dead by morning if we hadn't showed up," I reminded her. "And for your information, some of our people were hurt and lost during this rescue mission so a little fucking gratitude would be nice."

Spikes smiles as if she realizes she's struck a nerve and shrugs. "My condolences. Still, we aren't exactly interested in joining your little group. See, our idea of a 'resistance' is a bit different than yours."

"So I've heard," I scoff. "If you don't want to leave with us, then what the hell are you still doing here?"

"The food's good," Blade answers sarcastically. I really want to punch this guy in the face.

"We're going to be shutting down the other exits shortly," I warn them. "When I do, there's only one way out and I suggest you take it."

"Who's going to make us?" Spikes taunts just as I turn my back on them.

"Don't screw with me," I answer, turning my head just enough to look back without actually turning around. "I'm not afraid of a bunch of freaks with extra hardware. If I have to disassemble each and every one of you myself with nothing but a screwdriver, I will."

I leave them behind without worrying that any of them will follow or attack me. Laura's following me pretty closely and Spikes looks like she's a bit scared of her.

"That was ballsy," Laura says as she continues leading me to the control room. "Most everyone here just avoids them."

"Yeah, well I'm not much for avoidance."

Except for when it comes to Blythe.

"I like you," Laura says with a nod, as if she is just coming to this conclusion. "You're young but you seem focused. You must have really been something before the blasts."

We enter the control room and memories of flashing nightclub lights, empty liquor bottles and scattered drug needles flashes through my mind. Yeah, I was a real boy scout.

"Not really," I say with a shrug as she hands me two COMM devices. A quick inspection of the control panel reveals that it is, in fact, broken. Even I can see this and I don't know jack about computers. And of course, the one person who could probably put it back together—Jenica—is nowhere near to assist us.

I inspect my watch and sigh with anxiety as I realize it is only half past midnight. So much has happened and no more than an hour has passed. I still need to find Blythe and get those doors closed.

"Let's go," I say before leading Laura from the control room.

TEN

"ARE YOU SERIOUS? WOW, WHAT A BUNCH OF LUNATICS!"

My sentiments exactly. I'd just finished telling Blythe about the Rejects and she'd responded with the appropriate amount of disgust and horror.

"Wait 'til you meet them," I remark as we walk along one of the long tunnels leading to the back entrance of the hideout, Blythe's hand in mine once again as she leads the way. "Real charming."

"Do you think we have anything to be worried about?" she asks as we near the open door leading to the outside. I'm happy to see the two guards here are on the job and not slacking. "The Professor has worked so hard to make this as peaceful a resistance as possible and I don't appreciate those guys screwing it all up."

"One problem at a time," I say with a snort. "If they're a threat, you'd better believe they're on Jenica's radar if no one else's."

It's true. I don't know exactly what Jenica's job was before she joined the Resistance, but we know she has roots in Special Forces, FBI, the CIA, and God knows what else. Whatever the case, she's the best in the business when it comes to covert ops, gathering intel, and keeping a straight face when things go wrong. We talk a lot of shit about her because she's the hard-ass of the group, but we all respect her.

"You're right," Blythe answers as we reach the door. "Let's just hope they don't cause any trouble while we're here. That's the last thing we need."

"I'm kind of hoping they accept my invitation to leave."

"You guys must be talking about the Rejects," says one of the guards, who heard us coming and has turned to greet us. "Those guys are bad news."

"That's what we hear," I say as Blythe drops out of the conversation to inspect the steel frame of the sliding door Laura told me about. "I met some of them personally and it was a real treat."

"I'd have thought they'd be gone by now," the second guard says fiddling with the butt of the gun at his hip. "What's she doing?"

Blythe has taken off her jacket and is stripping off the flesh-colored, polyurethane glove the Professor designed to conceal her bionic arm. Dropping both onto the ground, she stands on her tiptoes and reaches up to grip the bottom of the sliding metal door, tugging gently to test its weight. Even with the slight pressure she's put on it, the door is creaking and groaning in the frame. With another slight tug, it slides down a few inches.

"We're closing off the exits so that we're less vulnerable," I answer as Blythe pauses, her hand poised on the bottom of the door, which is bent a bit from the pressure of her titanium hand.

"You guys coming in or what? I can't hold this door up forever."

Realizing that she's trembling a bit under the force of the door's weight, we all scramble to get back inside. I scoop up her jacket and glove before she slides the tunnel closed. We all link arms and allow Blythe to lead the way. Once we drop the guys back off in the cafeteria—their new assignment being to keep their eyes on the trouble-making Rejects—Blythe and I follow the schematic down two more tunnels and close off the other entrances, sending the guards back to the center of the compound, where everyone is gathering for the hastily prepared meal.

"It's not much," says Laura as she ushers us to a table and our waiting ration of genetically engineered roast beef and a side dish that looks like potatoes and gravy, but tastes nothing like the real thing.

"It's fine, thank you," Blythe says politely. We eat as much as we can manage because who knows when we'll get to eat again.

Throughout dinner, we suffer through the inevitable introductions and explanation of what parts we have and why, though I tune out after being introduced to a dude with a bionic set of ears—not the outer shell, but the inner parts are made of top notch machinery. He can hear a fly buzzing in the next room. It's all very cool, but my mind is on Blythe, who's stirring her potatoes around silently, her jaw clenched. These moments are always hard for her, and I decide to rescue her before she's expected to share.

"Hey, Blythe, can I see you in the control room for a minute?" I ask, leaping abruptly to my feet, my chair scraping back noisily from the table.

"Everything okay?" Laura asks, frowning with concern.

"Of course," I reassure her as Blythe leaves her place at the table. "We just need to make a call in to Headquarters and it's a bit noisy in here. We'll just be a few minutes."

I grasp Blythe's arm and propel her toward the control room and abruptly yank the blinds shut over the large windows overlooking the cafeteria. As soon as we're out of sight, she releases a breath I'm sure she's been holding for about five minutes. She sags against the closed door, her face drawn and pinched with worry, yet also bathed in relief.

"Thanks," she whispers.

She doesn't have to explain why she's thanking me and I don't have to ask. We know each other that way and it's one of the reasons I can't understand why she doesn't see how much I love her. Part of me has always wondered if maybe she just doesn't want to see it. It's not easy for her to be close to anyone and even I get held at arm's length a bit. Loving her is like holding the stem of a rose tightly in your fist. The thorns might prick and tear my skin, but I can't let go because the beauty of the bud has me entranced.

I use the opportunity gifted to me by seclusion and take a few steps closer, stopping once the toes of my boots nearly touch hers. She looks up at me, her eyes filled with worry and pain and I want nothing more than to crush her against my chest and tell her that everything will be okay and I'll protect her from it all. Instead, I settle for resting my hand on her shoulder and kneading the tense muscle gently.

"Come on, B, just make it through a few more hours and we're outta here," I say gently.

"I'm worried that we haven't heard from Jenica yet," she answers. "That can't be good."

"She's got her hands full with all the refugees from this hideout. There were over a hundred of them that needed to be signed in and placed in rooms. I'm sure Bravo team is back by now and both Gage and Jenica are debriefing the Professor on each mission. Don't worry. No news is good news."

"I guess you're right. I can't wait to get out of here, it's too quiet. It makes no sense to me that the MPs haven't showed up yet."

"You're right, but we've got half our security team at the entrance watching for signs of trouble and everyone has a COMM device and knows the plan of action for when they come. Stop worrying." I say this with a smile, which causes her to grin back. Light floods my insides because of that simple gesture and my free hand comes up to her other shoulder of its own will.

"I know I worry too much," she says, her last word trailing off on a groan as I hit a particularly tender spot on her shoulders. "Damn it, Dax, that feels good."

I have to swallow hard to breathe past the lump in my throat as blood surges away from my brain and toward other parts of my anatomy. I can think of about a hundred other things I could do to her that would feel good, and right now there isn't much between us to stop me. Just space and opportunity. And, of course, the mental wall that Blythe erects between herself and everyone she knows. Even I—her closest friend—stand just on the outside of that wall, looking over the top and waiting for her to throw me a bone.

She leans her head forward, resting it on the center of my chest as I work my fingers over her loosening muscles. She breathes heavily against my t-shirt, her warm breath seeping through the fabric and tickling across my skin. I groan and push her away a bit, my arms straining against the impulse to push her against the wall and kiss her senseless.

"What's wrong?" she asks, genuinely oblivious to the pain I'm feeling below the belt.

"Blythe, there's only so much of a warm, soft body against him that a guy can take before nature kicks in."

She raises her eyebrows and laughs. "Dax, you're such a man-whore."

All I can do is stare, my mouth hanging open a bit. No, I'm not a boy scout. I'm a guy, and when I'm itching I scratch; when I'm horny ... well, I handle it. Most of the time with Olivia, but always safely and never with someone who is looking for attachment.

"Is that what you think of me?"

Her amusement melts away and horror replaces it, her eyes going wide as if she suddenly realizes what she just said. "Come on, Dax," she says softly, "I didn't mean it that way."

I can't help feeling hurt, and I'm not as good as

Jenica at hiding my emotions. I place a little distance between us before the anger makes me do something I'd regret.

"It's cool. At least I know how you feel. Maybe you should stay out of my bed when you can't sleep. I wouldn't want you to have to worry about guarding your virtue around the 'man-whore'."

"Dax, wait!"

Her voice causes me to pause in the doorway, just as I'm about to leave. I'm not usually so sensitive, but for some reason knowing that she feels that way about me leaves a sour taste in my mouth.

I turn on her, gripping her shoulders and forcing her to look at me ... and I mean really look at me and not just through me as she tends to do.

"Have I given you any reason to doubt my intentions toward you?" I ask, my voice coming out rougher than I intend it to.

Shocked, she lets out a sound that sounds faintly like a squeak and shakes her head 'no'.

"And have I done anything other than protect you and care for you above anyone else?"

This time, she actually answers me. "No, you haven't."

"But it's just not good enough, is it?" I'm rambling, I know, but I can't help myself. When it comes to Blythe, I've kept quiet for so long. "Maybe what you really want is for me to stop playing the gentleman with you. I mean, it hasn't exactly gotten me anywhere all this time."

I've released her from my hold, but she hasn't moved from her spot against the wall. I don't need a bionic eye to know that her heart rate is climbing and her temperature right along with it. Heat emanates from her, and the sound of her breath sawing in and out of her lungs is the only sound between us until she finds her voice again.

"I don't know what you're talking about," she murmurs.

Those damn walls are back up again, because Blythe can't stand to let someone see her vulnerable. But I know better than anybody how to get to her.

I take the last step separating us, until my hands are braced on either side of her against the wall and our bodies are touching. My blood is at the boiling point, and every fiber of my being has come alive like it always does when I'm close to her. Through her thin tank top and cargo pants, I can feel just about every inch of her underneath; soft, warm, feminine ... mine! Possessiveness grips me and I know—now that she's within my grasp, I can't let her go. I can't stop now.

"Liar," I whisper, my breath teasing the loose tendrils of hair coming undone from her ponytail. "You know. You've always known. But I've let you go on pretending that you don't see what's right in front of your face. Maybe what you really need is for me to stop letting you off the hook. I've never been one to beat around the bush, Blythe. I only do that with you. But I'm done. You want the truth? Here it is."

When I finally touch her lips with mine, the moment is not sweet and my touch is not gentle. It's an outright assault. I've waited too long to even think about going slow with her. I need her to feel what I haven't been able to say with words. She stiffens against me for a fraction of a second, but I'm not having that. By the time my hands come up to her waist in a brutal caress, my fingers digging into her skin as I skim them upwards toward her ribs, she's melting into me in submission.

She might as well have laid out a goddamn welcome mat.

Blythe gasps when I jerk her closer, my hands roaming down to her hips, kneading, caressing, *feeling*— fulfilling every desire I've had since the first time I held Blythe in my arms. A sound like a primal growl comes from between us, and I'm faintly aware of the fact that it is me, but I'm too far gone to care. I want her to hear my sounds of possession as I slide my tongue into her mouth, finding hers and tasting it for the first time, drunk from the feeling of pleasure that the simple act gives me.

Blythe responds in a way I never expected, her hands coming up to the back of my neck and her fingernails making tiny half-moons in my skin as she digs in and holds on for dear life. It hurts, but I welcome the pain as it mingles with the pleasure, racing down my spine in a combination that leaves me weak in the knees.

When I lift her, she wraps her legs around my waist without hesitation. Within seconds, I've got her laid across a gleaming, steel table. COMM devices, batteries and various other odds and ends find a new home on the floor. I lean down to kiss her again, suckling her lower lip between mine before biting down on it gently. She gasps as if surprised and then moans when my hands find their way beneath her shirt. The feel of her bare skin against my fingertips has me so cranked up, I hardly notice the sound of the door opening behind us.

The shocked gasp of the person who catches us registers, though, and Blythe and I leap away from each other as if we've been burned.

"I'm so sorry," Laura says softly. "I need to speak with you when you have a moment," she adds before the sound of her boots and the closing of the door tells me she is gone.

Blythe is still on the edge of the table, though she's scooted as far away from me as she can get. I'm not far from where I was a moment ago, my hands braced on the table's edge as I fight to catch my breath.

Kissing Blythe was like drowning in an ocean of sensations. My senses are in overdrive, and I swear I can practically smell her from across the room. I can't even look at her, because I know her face is flushed and her lips are swelling from my less-than-gentle kiss. The sight of her alone is enough to set me off right now.

Once I'm sure I've gotten my impulses under control, I force myself to look at her. She slides off the edge of the table and turns to face me, though her eyes aren't really reaching mine. She's staring at some point over my shoulder.

She clears her throat. "You should go see what it is they want," she says hoarsely.

I nod. "Yeah, but I—"

"Now's not the time," she interjects.

Damn, I hate when she's right. We're in the

middle of a situation that could turn dangerous at any moment. We don't know where the reinforcements are, but we've dealt with the MPs enough to know that they're coming and that they are pissed. We need to be on our toes and this other stuff—no matter how important it might feel to me—can wait.

"You're right. Talk later?" I ask.

She finally looks up at me and tries to smile, though I can see through it to her uncertainty. She's nervous now, and maybe even a bit frightened of me. Good. I'm sick of being dependable ole Dax, loyal and faithful friend. I have always wanted to be more to her and now she knows. She can't hide from me any longer.

ELEVEN

DAX JANNER AND BLYTHE SOL
RESISTANCE HIDEOUT IN MEMPHIS, TENNESSEE
AUGUST 18, 4010
1:30 A.M.

WHEN BLYTHE AND I REJOIN THE OTHERS IN THE CAFETERIA, A deadly silence has fallen over our group and it immediately sets me on edge.

"Something's wrong," I say to Laura, who's standing there watching me with a grim expression on her face.

She nods. "You two should come with me. You'll want to see this."

What is she talking about? There I go being impatient again. As Blythe and I follow her toward the living area of the large, open space, my mind is reeling with the possibilities. Whatever has gone wrong, it's enough to make people get the hell out of our way as we cut a swath through those gathered in front of a small, flat television panel. It's an older unit, but the picture's clear. Two news anchors are delivering a report, as white letters scroll across a red bar through the center of the screen. The sound is too low but I can see the words as clear as day as two chairs are vacated for our use.

RESTORATION RESISTANCE TERRORIST
CAPTURED IN WASHINGTON D.C.

In the corner, a picture of a blonde-haired, blue-eyed, and very battered Olivia McNabb stares back at us, her eyes wide with fright. Blythe gasps, and my hands clench into fists as Laura steps between our chairs with a remote in her hand. As the volume increases, I force myself to swallow the bile building up in the back of my throat and still the roaring of blood in my ears. I sneak a peek at Blythe and her usually deep, caramel-colored skin is now tinged green. I want to reach out and comfort her, but I don't know if the gesture will be misconstrued as something else after our kiss in the control room.

I return my focus back to the perfectly groomed and starched news anchor reading from a teleprompter.

"This just in ... an attack on the Stonehead facility in the nation's capital, where several Bionics were scheduled for execution in just a few hours, resulting in a standoff that lasted through the night has now ended. According to law enforcement, the terrorist group known as Restoration Resistance, sent in a group of militants to free the prisoners in what has been described as a well-planned and tactical offensive strategy. The terrorists were said to be in possession of a specialized EMP signal, which they used to cut power to the entire facility, without causing harm to their own hovercraft or weapons. Officers say they were eventually able to restore power to their weapons, but not before some of their own were killed in the fray. The scene at Stonehead was eerily dark during the standoff, but night vision cameras captured the footage we are bringing to you now."

The prison video camera feed fills the screen and we watch as Olivia, Gage and the other members of our team fight for their lives. I watch Olivia become a blur as she races from cell to cell, using one of the MPs laser guns to blast the locks before sliding the iron gates open and freeing the prisoners. Gage uses his body to block those running to escape, firing back at the MPs cloistered at the end of the hall in formation, hiding behind their riot shields as they fire back.

Blythe gasps as one of the glowing red beams strikes Olivia, causing her to fall to her face, stunned. Without missing a beat, Gage rushes forward and throws Olivia over his shoulder, careful to keep his weapon trained on the MPs, who are slowly inching forward with their riot shields in place.

"They think he's one of us," I murmur to myself. Otherwise, the MPs wouldn't be tiptoeing around Gage the way they are. They could see that Olivia was fast, but they don't know what, if any, tricks Gage has up his sleeve. He's in deep shit when they find out he's got nothing but a gun and a set of huge balls. The other members of the team close in around him, forming a protective barrier as they fire back at the MPs and I realize that something has gone horribly wrong. Agata's EMP signal should have knocked out the MPs' weapons. That they are still able to fire on Gage and the others has me worried about the little girl. Gage disappears into the circle of bodies and I wonder if this is the moment when he called Jenica for backup.

The video fades as the reporter comes back on screen, the picture of a beaten Olivia taking up the entire right side of the screen.

"Because of the darkness and chaos of the moment, the male accomplices shown in the video have yet to be identified. They are said to have made off with half of the prisoners, but were forced to leave the others behind in favor of making an escape. However, MPs were able to detain ten of the prisoners, along with this young woman pictured here. She has been identified as Olivia McNabb, formerly of Los Angeles, California.

"McNabb was a participant in the Restoration Project, in which she received a bionic prosthetic hand to replace one lost in an accident caused by the nuclear attacks of August 15, 4006. She reportedly re-entered the program one year later to receive a set of bionic adrenal glands to replace those lost to cancer due to radiation poisoning. She was said to have gone missing when the President issued his ban on bionic prostheses and ordered all Bionics to report to the nearest Restoration Project facility for decommissioning. She has not been seen or heard from since, but her recent involvement in last night's attack shows that she has indeed found refuge with the terrorist organization known as the Resistance."

"Goddamn it!" The expletive falls from my lips unchecked as I pound my closed fists against my thighs.

"Forensic experts are now combing the scene in search of DNA evidence that could shed more light on those unidentified accomplices from the video. Captain

Rodney Jones, leader of the elite Military Police corps known as the Enforcers, has vowed to lead the manhunt in search of every member of this terrorist group."

Olivia's picture fades and another video feed shows the Captain at a press conference. The audio switches over and as I look into the cold, dark eyes of the man leading the hunt against the people I call my family, I feel an overwhelming urge to go on a little hunt of my own.

"Good evening citizens of the United States of America," the Captain begins. He's lifted the face-shield on his uniform, but is every bit the soldier from the neck down. He is flanked by two other officers who have decided to keep their faces hidden. The reporters standing by have gone silent, hanging on to his every word. "At approximately ten o'clock this evening, Stonehead was attacked by a group we all know to be against the best interests of our great nation. President Drummond has worked tirelessly to restore peace and order to our lives ever since the devastating attacks on many of our nation's largest cities four years ago. I want you to know that I have spoken with the President personally, and he wants you all to be assured that justice will be served."

"The press didn't want us to release any information about the victims, whose lives were lost tonight in the standoff at Stonehead ... they want to hold the faces of the so-called Resistance up and cause us to forget the real heroes here. Private First Class Marcus Jones, Private April Jennings, Specialist Dirk Hanover, Sergeant Davis Marx, and Lieutenant Lexi Sorenson ...

those are the names of the true heroes tonight. Those are the names I want you to hold in your memory as you shake your heads over this senseless attack. Olivia McNabb is no hero, and neither are Professor Hinkley or his accomplice in the leading of the Resistance, Jenica Swan. They are known terrorists and will be punished within the full letter of the law."

"Now, as for Olivia McNabb and the remaining prisoners here at Stonehead, we fully intend to carry out the execution, but will push it back until tomorrow morning at 9:00 am. Each prisoner is to be killed by firing squad, an event that is slotted to air live. President Drummond is adamant about sending a message to Professor Hinkley and the other members of this rag-tag squad that calls themselves The Resistance. We will not rest until each and every one of you has been decommissioned or executed, as is your punishment according to the law. I will uphold it as my personal mission to ensure that Americans sleep safely at night without fear of half-human, half-machine *monsters* terrorizing our streets."

"That's enough!" Blythe exclaims. Tears are running down one side of her face, unchecked. I know that grief; it is slowly uncoiling itself in my gut and spreading through the rest of me. By 9:00 am tomorrow, Olivia will be dead.

Laura obliges and turns off the television with a click of her remote, casting the room into complete silence.

"I'm sorry," she says softly to the two of us. "I didn't want to upset you, but I thought you'd want to see this. I am sorry about your friend."

I nod my thanks to Laura, but my focus is on Blythe, who looks as if she's going to fall to pieces at any moment.

"Hey," I say, my voice hoarser than I expect it to be. She looks up at me expectantly. "We are going to get her back. Do you hear me? I am going to call Jenica right now and tell her to move her ass so we can get out of this hole in the ground. I don't care who tries to stop me, I'm going to make sure we get her back. You got that?"

Blythe's smile is sad, as if she wants to believe me but can't quite stretch her imagination that far. Hell, at this point I'm having a hard time believing myself. I don't stand a chance going it alone but I'll be hard pressed to find someone willing to help me go in on such an insane mission. Still holding Blythe's gaze, I yank my COMM device from my belt and call Jenica's line.

"Janner, this is Swan, go ahead," she says clearly from the other end.

"Swan, please tell me you've got some good news. We just watched the report about Olivia and we could use some cheering up right now."

"Hang tight, Janner, I'm on my way back to you now. We've just finished unloading and directing the refugees from Memphis to their assigned quarters. Bronson and the rest of Team Bravo have arrived safely from Stonehead, including the little girl. Expect me in the next two to three hours and keep an eye out for the MPs. What is your status?"

"We're packed up and ready to go. No problems so far, although it worries me that the MPs have been so quiet. No sight or sound of any of them, but we're on our guard. Oh, and when we get home and settled, remind me to tell you about these loons they call the Rejects. You aren't going to like it one bit."

"Great," she says sarcastically. "I'm excited to meet them already."

"Well, they're still here and they're a warm bunch. I'll stay in contact with you over the next few hours and let you know if anything suspicious pops up. So far, all clear."

"Roger that. I'm on my way."

I jam my COMM device back in its place on my belt.

"Why don't you two try to get some sleep?" Laura offers, placing her hands on both our shoulders. "I'll take over the security detail until you get the call that they're nearby."

Normally I wouldn't leave my job up to someone else, but Laura has given me every reason to trust her. Also, I'm tired as hell and Blythe looks like she's ready to pass out. A few hours of sleep would be nice.

"That would be good, thanks."

"Here, we'll put you up in one of the empty rooms. Each room has two cots."

Blythe and I follow Laura up to the second level, where she finds an empty room and ushers us inside. Aside from the debris left over from someone's hasty packing job, the room is clean enough and the sheets look freshly washed. Once we're alone again, I turn to Blythe, who is staring blankly at the wall.

"Blythe, look—"

She cuts me off with a palm to the face. All I can think as my cheek starts to sting and my eye tears up, is that I'm grateful she used her human hand.

"What the hell, B?"

"*That* was for earlier!" she says, pointing an accusing finger at me.

"For kissing you or for stopping?" I asked with a smirk.

My question only enrages her further. "For getting mad at me for telling you the truth about yourself. I call it like I see it, Dax, and your behavior earlier only proves my point. I'm not one of your little whores; you can't hit me and quit me like you did Olivia and all those others!"

"No," I murmur, gripping her shoulders—gently this time—and pulling her in toward me. Her scent overwhelms me again—she smells like a green, open field, the likes of which I haven't seen or smelled since the nukes took out Central Park. "You're not like the others. And I have never kissed anyone the way I kissed you today because I've never wanted to kiss anyone that way before you."

That shut her up. She swallows noisily and blinks, her eyes narrowing as if she is trying to figure out the truth from my gaze. It's the first time, other than our moment in the control room, that she's ever held my gaze this long with such honesty and intensity.

"Why?" she finally asks after a while. "Why are you waiting until now to say this to me?"

"Because you are always so guarded, B. And you're my friend ... my best friend. I couldn't risk losing you by freaking you out, even though I've felt this way about you since ... damn, I don't even know when. It just happened."

"You wouldn't risk our friendship before, but you will now. That wouldn't have anything to do with Gage, would it?"

Shit.

She's got me there. Yeah, so maybe the blond hero's coming on the scene put the fear of losing Blythe in me. I never had any competition or risk of losing her before him. Her smirk is mocking.

"That's what I thought," she accuses, turning her back on me. "You don't want me, Dax, you're afraid that Gage will compromise your position in my life and maybe you're a bit jealous. You think you want me because someone else does. You'll get over it."

"There you go again," I say with a snort. "Turning a blind eye to what's right in front of you. Yeah, I might have felt threatened to walk in on you and Gage dry humping—" she scoffs at me, but I call them like I see them too "—but that doesn't make what I feel for you any less real."

"And what exactly do you feel? Lust?"

"If that's what you think, after all we've been through together, then you're blinder than I thought. Ironic for a girl with a robotic eye. You're capable of seeing through just about every layer of the human anatomy, except for the one that really counts. I feel sorry for you."

And as I plop down on my cot and turn my back on her, I realize how true that statement is. I do feel sorry for her. She had everything and lost it in the blink of an eye. Now, she's so messed up, she can't remember how to love anyone. At least not how they deserve. I've always known deep down, that even *if* Blythe ever gave me her heart, I'd only get a piece of it.

"Oh, by the way," I add, turning to glare at her over my shoulder. "In case you need it spelled out all the way, I was trying to tell you that I fucking love you."

Four years ago...

The sounds of the city of New York were the same on that day as they'd always been. Gleaming, silver buildings stretch up toward the sky miles away, and against the horizon, the Statue of Liberty—a structure thousands of years old—still stands as a proud monument, a symbol of freedom. The heat is particularly stifling today, one of the rare occasions when the weather actually matches the season we are in. Tomorrow, there are reports of possible snow. We can all thank the government goons and their experiments with environmental weapons and lack of care for the environment for that.

I wouldn't normally be caught dead outside in this weather, but this deal has to go down today. I need the money, but more than that I need to unload the merchandise. I shudder to think what the MPs would do to me if they caught me with it. Probably turn me over to one of those government agencies that makes you disappear forever. They won't have to work their powers of persuasion on me for long; I'll sing like a canary in a heartbeat. I could care less about the people that employ me, or the fact that their synthetic drugs are more potent than the cocaine and heroin currently approved by the FDA and sold at drugstores all over the nation. What we're doing isn't exactly illegal, but everyone in this business knows that the manufacturers of the now legal drugs don't like outsiders stepping on their turf. The fact that they've got street kids like me selling their stuff for less money and a better high pisses them off.

So, like I said, I need to get rid of the merchandise burning a hole through my pocket.

I'm scanning the street, watching for a man in a black leather jacket with a shaved head, the only description I have to go on. MPs are on every corner, their guns trained to stun, their gleaming fiberglass helmets keeping their identities safe from the rest of us as they scan the crowd for signs of trouble. Hookers work the street freely, and I chuckle as I remember learning in high school US History that their sex peddling was once illegal. I can't imagine today's MPs wasting their time hauling in a bunch of pros. This country's got bigger problems than half-naked girls selling themselves on the street. Though, it does turn my stomach to recognize some of the girls as chicks I knew in school. Not that I'm in a position to judge.

I live in a rat hole, am addicted to the product I'm selling—though I'll never admit it to anybody—and I'll do just about anything for a quick buck. I've done more deals in back alleys than most of the prostitutes passing me by on the street. I am reminded briefly of my mother and how disappointed she would be in me if she were still living. Her presence in my life was the only thing that kept me from losing myself in the streets and now that she's gone, I don't give a fuck about anyone or anything. There is no one else to care about, or anyone left to care about me.

When I spot the guy I'm waiting for, I snap back to

attention, forgetting about everything else except for making the deal and collecting the money—twenty percent of which is my cut for delivering. The flashing sign across the street from me says it's okay to 'Walk' and as I step into the street with about ten other people looking to cross the street, I am not expecting the sidewalk to fall to pieces beneath my feet, or the deafening sounds of honking horns, screeching tires, scraping metal, and collapsing buildings that follows.

I am not expecting the Mack truck that has fishtailed trying to avoid hitting the pedestrians in the street—one of which happens to be me—to pin me to the ground for several days. Even if I wanted to run, there's nowhere to go with cars smashed together and twisted around each other in the street. There's nothing to do but try to brace for the impact...

When I awaken, it is to the gnawing sensation of withdrawal in my gut. I don't know how long I've been out, or where I am. My only clues are bright, white fluorescent lights, the smells of antiseptic solution and blood, and the occasional blurred figures in lab coats. The need for heroin is strong, and as I thrash about on what I assume is a hospital bed, nurses have to strap me down to keep me from hurting myself. The morphine they give me is nowhere near high enough a dose; my body is used to much, much more and it's not happy to be deprived.

I cycle from states of anger and rage, to those so pitiful a newborn baby could probably have kicked my ass. When I do sleep my dreams are a hellish mixture between past and present. I see my mother, who was a waitress at a diner around the corner from the apartment she raised me in. Her mocha skin glistens in the sun and her short, neat afro is the perfect complement to a heart-shaped face. Her plump lips are painted red, because no matter where my mother went, she liked to dress like it was a special occasion, and despite having been on her feet all day, her pumps are three inches high with a metallic sparkle.

In the dreams, she spots me walking toward her and smiles, her perfect, white teeth flashing from between those red lips like a beacon that draws me to her. As I run to her, arms outstretched, I am stopped every time by a speeding Mack truck. It crushes me from the waist down and I am lying beneath it for days, unable to die because somehow, miraculously, the thousands of pounds of crushed steel trapping my body is preventing me from bleeding out completely.

I get flashes, things I think are memories, like the cries and moans of people around me, the wailing of babies and helpless children, as well as the resulting violence that ensued due to looting and riots after the blasts. I have seen all of the news reports about the chaos that engulfed the country after the explosions, and even though I was there for it all, I remember very little. Though, there is the face of a girl in my mind constantly—a brunette with a dirt-streaked face who was trapped beneath the same truck. I can remember holding her hand when I was conscious on that first day, watching as blood poured from her nose and ears.

Even as I watched her bleed to death right in

front of me, I looked her in her hazel eyes and lied to her. "Everything's going to be all right," I said. "Someone will come. They will save us."

By the time they show up with cranes to sift through the wreckage, it is too late for her and by then I know I'm going to die too. More than that, I want to die as I know that nothing can possibly exist from my hips down. I am mangled beyond repair and I'd rather die than live the rest of my life as half a man.

When the withdrawal finally begins to fade, I am able to pick up on the conversations happening around me as doctors and people wearing government badges come and go. I realize that I've undergone several surgeries and that these people are actually attempting to put me back together. Seeing as how I am too weak to lift my head, I have no way of inspecting their handiwork. I honestly have no idea if I'd even want to.

Eventually, a man I've never met before comes to visit. He sits beside my hospital bed wearing a worried expression, despite the many cuts and contusions across his face and the sling holding his arm against his body. As he gazes down at me and cries, I know without having to ask that this man is the father I never knew.

I ask him why he is here now, when he didn't think twice about abandoning my mother twenty years ago. He tells me that the blasts caused him to realize that he'd lost everyone he ever loved in the world. His parents, his siblings ... all dead. In a mad search for anyone he could call his own, he found me bleeding to death in a city hospital. That's when he gives me the news that changes my life forever.

To save me, he signed me up for the Healing Hands Initiative, a branch of the new government project created by then Senator Christopher Drummond called The Restoration. This man would soon become the president that terrorizes people like me.

He tells me about the titanium bones they've created to replace my ribs, part of my spine, pelvis, legs and feet, as well as the never-before-used machinery that will enhance me in ways previously never thought possible. He says that it was the only way to save me from being a cripple for the rest of my life. I ask him how he could dare to make decisions about my life without consulting me, as if he knows anything about me other than the fact that we share DNA.

What the fuck does he want me to do, give him a hug and call him daddy?

He says that he just wanted to know that he hadn't lost everyone. I tell him to get the hell out of my room and not to come back.

I haven't seen him since …

Two years have passed and I am finally accustomed to my new life as a sideshow freak. After months of physical therapy, I now know how to use my prosthetic limbs as if I were born with them. With clothes on, no one even knows that I'm different, yet I know that I can't get too comfortable. Not all of the Bionics are able to hide, and the climate is slowly changing when it comes to people's attitudes about us.

President Drummond won his election in the year 4006 by a landslide, effectively gaining his status as America's savior. His rhetoric against the Bionics begins after a man with a bionic arm was recorded robbing a fueling station outside of Las Vegas. With every day that passes, the hatred and fear spread more and more, and I know it's only a matter of time before the government starts rounding us up and performing mass executions. As we've all legally registered for the program, they now know who each and every one of us, are and where we live and work. We are no longer safe.

I've given up my life as a drug dealer; being sober feels better than anything I've experienced in a long time. The pay I earn hauling furniture for a moving company is barely enough to keep food in my belly and pay to rent my room in a boarding house, but it's an honest life. Almost dying has taught me the value of living.

One day, I am approached by a woman named Jenica Swan. All she can tell me is that she works for the government; her exact profession is privileged information. She's come to warn me, she says, about the firestorm headed our way. Soon, not even she will be safe in her government job and we will all have to go into hiding. She gives me Professor Neville Hinkley's card and tells me that when the government starts cracking down on the Bionics, they will go after those with a criminal past first. That means I'm in deep shit.

I carry the Professor's card around in my pocket for days, torn between calling him and tearing it to shreds and throwing it down a gutter. After a while I shove the card deep into my wallet and forget about it. After all, Professor Hinkley was the ringleader of the Healing Hands initiative; I have no reason to trust him. I never think of him again until the MPs come crashing through my front door, guns set to kill.

As I run for my life, I pray to God that I don't blow some kind of gasket in my machinery. I've never run so fast in my life. Weeks of traveling and hiding in the most obscure places while scrounging and—to my shame, stealing—in order to eat and survive find me on the outskirts of Atlanta. An old friend of mine knew of a monorail operator who would smuggle Bionics in the middle of the night for a fee. After promising to pay him back when I'm able, I board the train on my friend's dime, surrounded by a rag tag bunch of outcasts, many of whom look as scared and uncertain about their futures as I do.

Would we even survive the night? For all I know, the MPs are waiting at the end of the line to cart us all off to Stonehead. The maximum security prison, formerly home to America's most dangerous convicts, has been cleared out to make room for Bionics with criminal pasts. In some areas, there are rumors that the MPs are targeting non-criminal Bionics, and even showing brute force toward those family members harboring them.

Naturally, people are fighting back, but no one ever wants to hear about the desperation of those poor souls backed into a corner by the trigger-happy Military Police. All anyone ever sees were the news reports, which fill the airwaves with images of Bionics acting violently toward MPs. No one seems to care that we act in self-defense. All they see is that people with robotic limbs and organs are capable of things other humans were not. They see us as weapons, and fear that we will inevitably turn on them. The proposals calling for the immediate arrest and disassembly of all Bionics come from all sides of the political spectrum, and President Drummond's rhetoric grows more inflammatory by the day.

By the time I reach Atlanta—after several stops and days spent hiding in the baggage car of the monorail—the manhunt for every man, woman and child who's ever received a Bionic limb from the government is on.

I met Blythe on one of the hottest days of the year 4008. Even though we'd just had snow the day before, the temperature is now a blazing 110 degrees in Atlanta, and Georgia's characteristic humidity is at an all-time high. It is a sign of the times we live in—melted snow streaming down the street in slushy chunks as people in tank tops, shorts, and sandals saunter the sidewalk covered in a glistening sheen of sweat.

I'd give anything to be wearing shorts right now, but I can't let my legs show. The linen pants I'm wearing are thin, but everything feels like a turtleneck and a pair of corduroys in this heat. I'm walking through a well-to-do neighborhood in northern Atlanta, heading toward a safe house for Bios I'm sharing with about fifteen other people. The safe house is run by an old man we call Pops, and he is not one of us. He lost most of his family in the blasts and just wants to help in any way he can. Little do we know that on this day, the hottest day of 4008, we will lose our only friend and protection from the world in a raid.

It is because of this raid that I encounter a girl with a bionic eye, who sits on the lawn in front of a sprawling, three story house with a white picket fence, crying as she stares down the barrel of a gun. Somehow, everything else ceases to exist in that moment. The groceries I'm carrying fall to the ground and the paper sacks rip, spilling the contents across the pavement. I faintly register the smell of fire and smoke coming from deeper in the neighborhood, and in my mind I know they've discovered our safe house and possibly several others.

Families line the street, many of them crying and screaming as MPs cart off their loved ones, shoving them into the back of the hovercrafts lining the street. These crafts are headed for Stonehead and everyone knows once you go in, there is no coming out.

Why this one girl should pull on my heart strings when there are others suffering nearby, I am not sure. Maybe it's because of the three bodies strewn across the lawn behind her; two adults and a child no older than five, all dead. Maybe it's because instead of arresting her for due process, three jackass MPs are taunting her over just having killed her family, and threatening to kill her for fighting back as they dragged her from the house.

As I run to her, she looks up and her eyes connect

with mine. I know I have to save her.

It all happens so fast. Within the span of a minute, I've kicked loose one of the boards of the white picket fence and used it as a weapon against the three MPs. Despite my broken past, this is the first time I will ever kill. I feel no remorse as I shove the pointed fencepost through the face shield of the last officer standing, feel no pity as his blood bathes my neck and shoulders. I feel only primal satisfaction for finally fighting back.

I am tired of running.

The girl is in the fetal position on the ground, clutching dead child against her chest and sobbing in a way I've never heard anyone sob before. The sound will haunt my dreams for the rest of my life.

By now we've caught the attention of others, who have seen what I've done. A riot breaks out on the street, with Bios fighting alongside their families, desperate to save themselves and each other, tired of taking shit from the government.

In the midst of the fray is Blythe, broken, beaten and grieving, lying in the grass like a kicked puppy, waiting to die.

I won't let her.

I scoop her into my arms and lay her over my lap as I straddle the seat of an unattended hover bike. Somehow we make it out of the neighborhood alive and to another safe house I know about across town. Blythe sits and stares off into space for two days without moving or speaking. The woman who runs the safe house, Mae, bathes her and changes her clothes. She tries to coax her to eat or drink, but she won't. She doesn't speak. All she can tell us is that her name is Blythe and that her family was murdered right in front of her.

It is on that third day, when the MP's raids sweep the city in our direction, that I remember the Professor's card in my wallet. There is talk of a revolution, a resistance, an organization started by the very man who created us. I don't know if the rumors are true, but if Jenica Swan can be believed, contacting the Professor will provide me with a safe haven.

On the fourth day, I smuggle her out of the safe house and into the trunk of Mae's car. She's agreed to get us as far West as she can, to get us as close to our rendezvous point with Jenica Swan as she can. We arrive in Oklahoma without incident, where we meet up with another group of Bios headed in the same direction. Weeks later we arrive in Nevada, where we rendezvous with the co-founder of the Resistance. She ushers us on board a hovercraft with twenty others and flies us out over the painted dessert.

As far as the rest of the world is concerned, we are never seen or heard from again.

TWELVE

DAX JANNER AND BLYTHE SOL
MEMPHIS HIDEOUT OF RESTORATION RESISTANCE
AUGUST 28, 4010
5:00 AM

I AM SUDDENLY JOLTED AWAKE BY THE SOUND OF MY COMM device blaring at my hip. The deep, dark haze of my dreams still clings to me, but I am forced to shake it off as I leap from the bed to answer Jenica's call. Now is not the time for confronting old ghosts.

Blythe is on her feet and at my side in a heartbeat.

"This is Janner," I answer.

"Janner, this is Bronson, we've got a problem."

Blythe frowns. "Gage?" She whispers.

"Bronson, where is Swan?"

"She's got her hands full at the controls. We are about five miles out from your location and we're taking on heavy fire here from the MPs. Looks like they set up camp because they were expecting us to come back."

"Goddamn it," I mumble, snatching up my jacket from its place on the floor. Blythe holds my COMM device while I slide it on and we proceed from the room together. "No wonder things were so quiet," I say as I signal Laura from across the room, "they were waiting for the big prize."

155

Jenica Swan is one of America's most wanted criminals, second only to the Professor. If they know she's at the controls of the hovercraft, they don't give a damn about a bunch of Bionics hiding out underground. They know we can't get far without her.

"Jenica's asked me to have you and your security team head our way with as many weapons as you can carry. If you've got hover bikes, that would be nice too. We're holding them off for now, but there's a shitload of them and they just keep coming."

"Roger that. Send me your coordinates and tell Jenica to sit tight. We're on our way."

Laura is at my side immediately as the COMM device's screen fills up with Gage's typed-in coordinates.

"Are they here?" Laura asks, hope in her voice. I notice that there are others—non security team members—standing close by and listening. They look scared and I don't want anyone to panic. I propel Laura closer to the exit leading to the tunnel. Somewhere out there, two guards are standing watch vigilantly.

"They are here," I whisper, eyeing the curious refugees over her shoulder. They are watching us, so I school my face into an expression of calm. "But there's a problem. Five miles out, they encountered the MPs. They didn't attack us here, because they were waiting for reinforcements to come to us."

"What's the plan?" Laura asked.

"We're going out there to help them. I've got coordinates and those who can take hover bikes should, to get there faster. We'll instruct everyone else to stay put, maybe leave a few of the weapons with them just in case. But those on the security team with fighting experience need to come with us. We need as many hands as possible."

"Got it," Laura says with a swift nod. "Meet you outside in five."

Blythe and I ensure that our guns are at our hips before we race off down the long tunnel toward the only open exit. I update the two guards on what's going on and send them back inside to get armed. I'm relieved to find six hover bikes parked nearby and mentally thank our MP friends for leaving them behind. Blythe helps me get each bike started and soon, the gentle hum of energy flowing from each floating vehicle surrounds us like a swarm of bees. I look up at Blythe, who's standing on the other side of the bike I've just started. She's staring wordlessly, her expression equal parts worry, anxiety, and confusion. I know the confusion is there because of me and I feel like shit because of it. This is the worse time for me to start talking about feelings and, in her case, the lack thereof.

"Dax," she says softly, her eyebrows knitting together. I know she's trying to decide what to say. "You told me you love me."

I nod once, a tense, jerky motion. "Yes. I meant it."

"I know," she answers. Of course she knows. She's always known, whether she wants to admit it or not.

"You don't have to say anything," I say, pretending to check the hovercraft's gauges. "Now really isn't the best time but...no matter what happens today I just wanted you to know that."

Warmth fills my palm as she places her hand in mine. She gives it a gentle squeeze and my gaze connects with hers. I'm sure she's about to say something, but I don't know if it's what I want to hear. Laura and the others save us both and by the time the small group reaches us, Blythe has taken her hand back.

"All right everyone," I begin, facing our small group of fighters and ex-soldiers. "I've got coordinates for where the hovercraft has landed. They're taking on heavy fire, so be expected to jump in there and go to work. If you have a gun, make sure it's set to stun. We all know that the Resistance is not about taking lives and we won't do so unless we have to."

"Do you think any of them give a damn whether *you* live or die, mate?" a voice intrudes from the back of the group. I know that voice. The crowd parts to reveal the Rejects, with Blade at their forefront.

"What the hell are you people doing out here?" Blythe asks, stepping between me and them.

Blade steps forward, his metal head gleaming in the light of the slowly rising sun. "You said you needed help. Here we are, at your service."

"We don't need you on our side," Blythe counters, arms folded across her chest. "Everyone here knows about your kind and what you stand for. We are *not* on the same team."

"Well aren't you a fiery one?" Blade chuckles. "I like that. Pardon my rudeness, love. The name's Baron and I think you'll find my cause is the same as yours. I want freedom for people like us. Our methods might be a bit different, but we all want the same thing."

"It's your methods we have a problem with," she answers. "We are not killers."

"Shame, really," Baron retorts with a lazy smile. "You may not have the stomach for it now, girl, but we'll see how long it takes you to change your tune. You've got spirit, I'll give you that. But this war that's brewing won't be won by chivalry and spirit. In the end, I predict that the only accepted method will be punishment by death, for anyone who dares to oppose us."

"That's enough!" I interject. "We don't have time for this. We are going into those woods to help our friends. If you want to help, try to keep up and don't get in the way." I turn to the rest of my gathered men—and woman. "Two to a bike, which means twelve will reach the scene first. The rest of you follow on foot—preferably those with equipment that increases speed."

I read the coordinates out loud to everyone, who program them into their hover bike GPS units and COMM devices respectively. The team quickly divides into groups—those who will be going on foot, and those that will share bikes. I am grateful to see Laura and Blythe sharing a bike. While I know that Blythe has some fighting experience—she knows jujitsu and can handle a gun—I also know that Laura, with her military training and experience, will look after her.

Blythe grabs my shoulder as I take my place at the front of the group, remaining on foot as the machinery in my legs will carry me about as fast as a hover bike could.

"I don't like it, Dax," she whispers, cutting her

eyes over at the Rejects, who have also decided to go on foot. Spikes is flexing her arms, allowing the sharp, jagged pieces of metal embedded there to protract completely. Around her, the others prepare to fight, various appendages sprouting with mechanized weapons. "The Professor wouldn't like it either."

"I know," I answer with a shrug, "but we need the manpower. They've already said they're not interested in coming to Headquarters with us. Once we get rid of the MPs, they'll go on their way and we'll go ours. It's as simple as that."

Blythe sighs and her lips go tight in the way they do when she's got something else to say but chooses not to. She nods her agreement but I know she's not happy about it. I'm not too excited myself, but I'm not in the mood to argue with a bunch of freaks that have deformed their bodies with weaponized bionic parts. Our only way out is with Jenica on that hovercraft and nothing is going to stop me from making it happen.

"Hey," Laura calls out, "take this!"

She tosses me a long, gleaming object that I realize once it's in my hand that it is an automatic weapon.

"The ARX290?" My jaw drops as I turn the large weapon over in my hands, inspecting its flawless, gleaming surface and long barrel. It's one of the most cutting edge laser weapons on the market and I'm wondering how the hell she got her hands on one. The settings are the same as a handgun, so I can chose to stun or kill, but the rapid fire mechanism makes it easier to hit multiple targets quickly.

Laura holds up a matching weapon. "I've got a spare," she says with a wink.

I am so digging this chick.

"Nice, thanks," I say, handing my handgun off to someone else. He gladly accepts it in place of the long, rusty pipe he was previously set to do battle with.

"Okay, let's roll out!" I bellow before taking off at a brisk trot. It takes a few minutes for me to build up speed, but eventually I catch up to the bikes humming several feet above my head. The other group of runners falls behind within minutes, with the exception of one of the Rejects—a guy with matching Bionic arms who is propelling himself from tree to tree like some sort of flying monkey.

I hear the fight several minutes before we see anything, and ready the ARX as I barrel through the last of the trees separating me from my ride home. When we enter the clearing where the hovercraft has landed, I find myself surrounded by MPs on either side. Many of them have taken refuge in the trees, their weapons trained on the hovercraft and the members of our team firing through the small porthole-like windows lining its sides. I readily spot Gage, who has popped open the craft's roof hatch and is sticking out of the top of the craft. Holding a weapon similar to mine, he fires rapidly into the trees, the top half of his body laid across the hovercraft's surface, his legs still dangling inside.

Jenica is at the controls, manning the hovercraft's only weapon, a large gun mounted on a turret a few feet behind Gage. The turret swivels as Jenica fires on one of the three, large tanks parked nearby. Other members of our team fire from their open windows, poking their heads out between the fire coming from the MPs and taking aim on our enemy.

I'm immediately attacked from the left, and I turn just in time to catch an MP in the face with the butt of my ARX. The fiberglass of his helmet shatters and I hear the distinct snapping of a nose being broken before a gush of blood follows. That guy is out cold, so I'm on to the guy coming at my right, who tries to grab me and punch me in my titanium ribs. The force puts a dent in his body armor and he cries out in pain as the sound of metal against metal fills us both with the vibrations of impact. I use his moment of weakness to deliver a roundhouse kick to the head, putting another dent in his armor and knocking him out next to his friend. It's taken years of practice to be able to get my leg that high, but it's paid off.

As I duck down behind a large rock and take aim at a group of three MPs trotting toward the hovercraft, those on their bikes swoop in and out of the trees, their weapons firing as they duck and dodge and return fire. I spot Blythe, who is pointing toward something in the trees and yelling in Laura's ear, and I realize her Bionic eye has picked up on a heat signal in the woods.

After stunning the three guys in my sights one by one, I jump up and take off in the direction Blythe and Laura are taking, anxious to get a look at where they're headed. I come up short as I spot it—a weapon known as the Annihilator. Manned by a group of four MPs, the large cannon being wheeled slowly toward the clearing is capable of reaching temperatures so high it could melt flesh from bone. Only very specific types of body armor can withstand the heat and the only person I know that could survive without said armor is Yasmine.

Seeing as how the rest of us don't have impenetrable skin, I whip out my COMM device and quickly put in a call to Jenica.

"Swan, this is Janner. We have a problem."

Jenica's voice crackles over the line and I turn the volume down so that the MPs can't overhear. They're nowhere near close enough, but one can never be too safe.

"I'm kind of busy here, Janner!" Jenica snaps, her voice tinged with annoyance and strain. The sound of the Hovercraft's weapon and the hum of hover bikes zooming through the air fills our frequency with background noise.

"Just thought you'd want to know these bastards have an Annihilator out here," I say casually. "No big deal."

"Shit!" Jenica yells as she fires again. "We've got to find a way to take it out! What is your position?"

"A few hundred yards from where you are, in a southeastern direction. I've got eyes on the big boy; they're wheeling it toward you now. Sol has eyes on it from the sky so I think I'll see what she's got in mind. Just wanted to give you a heads up."

"Roger that, Janner, do whatever you have to. Take it out. Now!"

The line closes off and I immediately pull up Blythe's frequency. "What do you think, B?" I ask, watching as the Annihilator creeps through the underbrush, slowly making its way to the clearing. I'm separated from it by several feet of brush and trees, so I continue watching its progress from relative safety.

"Rosenberg here," Laura says from the other side of the COMM device. "We've got a plan, but we'll need your help."

"Go ahead, I'm open to any ideas that don't involve us getting fried by that thing."

"I need you to catch Blythe. I'm going to fly as low as I can and she's going to jump to you. Then I'm going to crash this thing into the Annihilator."

My eyes widen at her crazy-but-genius idea. "Are you nuts? You're going to get yourself killed!"

A feminine laugh filters through before Laura says, "Kid, when the blasts hit in '06, I took a six inch shard of glass to the chest, and so much shrapnel they had to replace my tits with a metal plate and my heart with one that has a V-6 engine. I've already cheated death once—I think I can do it again. This isn't a kamikaze, okay? I'll jump at the last second, once I'm sure the bike is aimed at the Annihilator."

I don't like it; the risk of losing Laura is too high. In the short time I've known her, I've become attached and I want her on our team permanently.

"Use your head, kid," she says when I am silent for too long. "Even if you lose one man, it's worth it to save the rest of you from getting your faces melted off. Trust me."

She hasn't steered me wrong yet, so I'd be an ass to ignore her plea for trust. "All right, Rosenberg, you're up. I'm about a hundred yards from the target now and they're approaching the clearing. If we're going to do it, we need to do it now."

"I see you," Laura says just as the hum of a hover bike's engine grows louder. "Heads up."

I have about two seconds to react before Blythe's body comes hurtling at me out of the sky. I catch her and we both go tumbling into the underbrush. I turn to my back so that I take most of the impact, bringing her down on top of me as we skid across the dirt and brambles below. I barely have time to register the sting of branches scoring my back through my t-shirt before Laura's bike comes whizzing out of the sky at full speed, aimed right at the Annihilator.

The MPs scatter like cockroaches, all but two of them getting out of dodge in time. An orange ball of flame billows upward, followed by thick black smoke, as Laura's aim proves true. I swiftly switch mine and Blythe's positions, placing her under me and covering my head as shards of metal and fiberglass rain down in a cloud of smoke, dirt and debris.

I flinch as a shard of falling shrapnel embeds itself in the back of my shoulder, but remain in my position until I'm sure most of the falling wreckage has cleared. When I lift my head, a flaming hunk of metal rests where the annihilator used to be. What's left of the bike lies in pieces around the now useless weapon, and the bodies of two MPs are in just as many bits on the ground.

"Did she make it?" Blythe asks, reminding me that I've got her pinned to the ground. I stand and give her a hand up, brushing my clothes off and ignoring the shooting pain running up and down my arm from the shrapnel. Whatever is in my shoulder is in deep and hurts like hell.

"I don't know," I rasp between deep breaths of smoky air. The ash and smoke are so thick, I can barely see. I am unprepared for the attack, but Blythe is not. By the time I realize the two MPs that survived the blast are on us, Blythe has stunned one with her gun, and smashed in the face of the other with her bionic arm.

"Nice," I mumble with a nod of thanks.

"It's the least I can do after you let me use you as a human shield," she jokes, nudging me with her elbow.

"Ah," I groan, flinching on contact.

"What's wrong?" she asks, grabbing me by the arm and turning me to inspect my shoulder. Her gasp confirms what I already suspected. "It's in deep," she says, gently poking at the skin around the chunk of metal sticking out of my back. "I don't think I can pull it out by hand."

"Let's not try it then," I say, instinctively inching away from her searching hands. "I'll be okay for now."

"Are you kidding me? That's barely a scratch," jokes Laura's voice from behind me. I turn to find her striding toward us through the trees, her once shiny chest plate now charred and blackened. A nasty burn covers the left side of her neck and her face is stained with ash, but a huge grin is spread across her face.

"You'll live, and so will I," she says, inspecting her ARX for damage.

I laugh as we turn and tramp through the woods, back toward the clearing. "Rosenberg, two, Death, zero."

THIRTEEN

DAX JANNER, BLYTHE SOL, AND LAURA ROSENBERG
MEMPHIS HIDEOUT OF RESTORATION RESISTANCE
AUGUST 18, 4010
6:30 AM

BY THE TIME WE REACH THE CLEARING, THERE HAVE BEEN LOSSES on both sides, with the majority of those being on the side of the MPs. While the ones hiding in the tree are of concern, it's the three massive tanks firing at the hovercraft that pose the biggest threat. If we can take them out, we're home free.

The Rejects have arrived, along with the others that came in on foot, and I see them mixed in with our own, fighting ruthlessly. I spot the guy with the bionic arms, swinging down from his perch in a tree and landing on the back of a tank before grasping the head of the MP manning the turret and snapping his neck like a twig.

"No!" I bellow, racing toward the tank and leaping up onto the top of it with him. Monkey Arms frowns at me as I push one of the MPs out of his grasp and stun him with my ARX before taking down three others in the same way.

"What's your problem, man?" Monkey Arms asks, his face a mask of rage and bloodlust.

"My problem is, we don't kill unless we have to. I thought I made that perfectly clear to you and your band of freaks. Taking lives is an action we save for desperate situations. You purposely broke that man's neck when you could have just as easily knocked him out!"

"Take it easy, mate," says Baron from the ground as he head-butts one of the MPs into unconsciousness, cracking through the fiberglass front of the guy's helmet with his metal-domed head. "Joe here's just having a bit of fun."

Ignoring them both, I jump down into the tank's turret. "Rosenberg, you know how to drive one of these things?" I ask as she runs by, her ARX firing into the trees.

Her eyes widen and she grins. "You bet your ass I do."

Laura jumps into the driver's seat below me and steers me toward one of the other tanks, which is parked a few hundred yards away, still firing on the hovercraft. Jenica returns fire from her place at the controls. The tank bounces over uneven ground, but is swift as we approach the second tank. I fire a warning shot, hoping to scatter some of the MPs before I blow the thing to smithereens. One is all I give them, though; I uphold the Professor's peaceful Resistance mumbo jumbo, but only to a certain point. I'm ready to go home and these sons of bitches are in my way.

I let loose with everything in the tank's arsenal and within seconds, the tank is blown sky high, flipped upside down with smoke billowing from its engine. A few bodies lay in the wreckage, but those that remain are merely stunned by the members of our team who have been lying in wait for this moment.

Laura turns toward the third tank, but Jenica's already on it, the hovercraft's weapon blowing holes into the tank's tough exterior. I add my weaponry to hers and take out the second tank, rendering it as useless as the first.

Now left without their tanks and their precious Annihilator, the MPs are turning tail to run, disappearing into the woods in the opposite direction of the hideout. Laura and I leap from the tank and give chase, stunning as many of them with our ARXs as we can. Blythe, Baron, Spikes, Monkey Arms, and all the others join us, and pretty soon, every last one of them is gone.

A cheer goes up from the crowd, our victory sweet after hours of wondering if we'd ever make it out alive. I scan the crowd, counting those that remain, sad to see that we have lost many members of our security team, but knowing that it is necessary. In the end, those who remain at the hideout are safe because of our sacrifices. I notice that we've lost two of the Rejects and while I can't say I care too much for any of them, I can see the sadness in the eyes of those that remain. Their brotherhood is as strong as ours, so I know that Baron, Spikes, and even Monkey Arms are in mourning as well.

Jenica exits the craft and Gage jumps down from his perch on top, and the two head in our direction. I try not to let it show, but my gut is knots as I watch Gage rush forward and crush Blythe in his arms.

"Thank God you're okay," he says as he holds her away long enough to look her over before hugging her again.

"Me?" Blythe laughs. "You're the one we were all worried about. I'm glad you made it out."

"You did good, Janner," Jenica says as she steps between me and Blythe and Gage. Thank goodness too, because I'm about three seconds away from giving into the impulse I've felt since meeting Gage, and kicking him square in the face. I focus on Jenica and try not to stare at them over her shoulder as they talk in hushed tones.

"Hey, this is the person you should be thanking," I say, grabbing Laura as she walks by. "Jenica Swan, this is former army sergeant Laura Rosenberg. She was an integral part in helping keep the hideout safe, as well as getting rid of the Annihilator. We were lucky to have her on our side today."

The two women shake hands and Laura smiles warmly. Jenica, of course, keeps her stoic expression, a stony mask she hardly ever takes off.

"Nice to meet you," Jenica says as her hand drops back down to her side, "and thank you for all you've done. We should get moving before they come back with reinforcements. I wouldn't be surprised if they had a hovercraft or two nearby. We still have over a hundred people to load up before we can lift off."

"I'll ride ahead and get everyone ready," Laura volunteers, already throwing one leg over the seat of a hover bike. "We'll be at the entrance and ready to board quickly. Dax had us gather food and supplies too, so if we have time, it might be good to load that up."

Without giving us time to answer, she's off and whizzing over the trees, leaving the rest of us to board the hovercraft. I turn to find the Rejects standing on the outskirts of our group and am glad to see that they don't appear interested in coming with us, which takes the task of telling them they aren't welcome on board our craft squarely off of my shoulders.

"You're a good leader and a strong fighter, mate," says Baron as he steps forward and extends his hand toward me.

I keep my arms crossed over my chest. "Thanks for your help, but now is when we part ways," I say. "That stunt your boy pulled over by the tank wasn't cool. It reminded me of exactly why we don't need people like you among us."

Baron smiles, curling his hand into a fist as his blade retracts back into his arm. "Ready or not, mate, we are here. There are more of us than you realize and we plan to take our lives back. And we don't plan on doing it nicely."

"Why do you want to go against Professor Neville?" asks Blythe as she and Gage join our little powwow. "He is working for peace between us and the people of the United States. It's not their fault the president has them afraid of us. His lies and dangerous rhetoric are the reason we have to hide. Violence won't go too far in convincing them that we aren't dangerous."

"See, that's where you messed up," Spikes chimes in, stepping up next to Baron who puts his arm around her waist, careful to avoid her jagged barbs. "We aren't interested in convincing anyone that we aren't dangerous. In fact, I'm more interested in showing them just how dangerous I can be."

As if to emphasize the point, her spikes elongate, sticking out of her neck like one of those clichéd biker chick dog collars.

"You can't win a fight against the government," Gage challenges. "Any action you take against them will be used to show the people that they are justified in their treatment of the very people they created. Your logic is flawed. You aren't helping the Bionics … you're dooming them."

"We're enlightening them," Baron says, his voice edged in cold steel. "I wouldn't expect you to understand, *Normal*. Aren't you fighting for the wrong side?"

"I'm fighting for what's right," Gage answers, a deep growl creeping into his tone.

"That's enough," Jenica chimes in as she steps into the middle of our group. "Everyone going to Restoration Headquarters, get on the freaking hovercraft. The rest of you had better get out of my sight as quickly as you can. I won't let you go so easily next time."

Baron bows regally at the waist in a mocking gesture. "As the lady wishes," he says before motioning for his crew to follow him. They disappear into the woods as we board the Neville I.

"We have to warn the Professor about the Rejects," Blythe says as she takes her place at the controls beside Jenica.

When we are all together, Blythe or Olivia navigates and mans the guns and Jenica pilots. Gage and I take seats on opposite sides of the aisle as the others slide into the rows behind us.

"Professor Hinkley and I are well of aware of the activities of these so-called Rejects," Jenica says, her face twisted in a snarl of disdain as she expertly steers the Hovercraft back toward the hideout. "We have been for months now. We've been waiting to see if their little uprising would grow beyond the pitiful numbers they began with."

"Do you think there's cause for concern?" I ask, watching the trees speed by below us through my window. "They seem pretty damn serious."

"I think that our main concern is Stonehead, and the fact that they still have several of our people, including Olivia. The Rejects are a problem that will have to wait until another day."

"What will we do?" Blyth asks, her voice low. "About Olivia, I mean."

Gage reaches over the back of Blythe's seat and places a hand on her shoulder. "Don't worry, we'll think of something," he says, his voice soothing. "I promise."

My teeth are grinding together so hard it's no wonder they don't shatter.

Blythe seems to take comfort from his words. She turns and gives him a small smile. He smiles back and I see in his eyes the same emotion I know is in mine when I look at Blythe. I feel as if I've swallowed a molten rock. Blythe looks up and finds me watching them. She swiftly turns and shrugs Gage's hand off of her shoulder, her eyes lowered to the control panel. Twin spots of red appear on her cheeks.

This is exactly the kind of shit I don't need right now. I remind myself that our mission is not over and concentrate on counting the minutes that pass as we near the hideout.

I am almost grateful when the hum of another hovercraft fills the air and Jenica spews a string of curses. Almost.

Through the back window of the craft, I can see that there are not one, but two military-grade Hovercrafts speeding through the air behind us.

"Sol, the gun!" Jenica cries as she banks right, hard. I grip the seat behind me before I can go hurtling across the aisle toward Gage.

Strap yourself in next time, idiot.

"Everyone, windows open, guns up!" I command, throwing my window open.

Those with guns follow suit and as I stick my upper body through the window, I barely miss having my head taken off by a zooming hover bike. There are about six of them closing in on us, poised to shoot us through the windows. I have no doubt that after the beating they took, their guns are now trained on 'kill' instead of 'stun'. As I take aim on the bike that nearly hit me, I am surprised to find Baron on its seat. He pulls up beside my window and salutes mockingly.

"You didn't think I'd let you have all the fun, did you, mate?" he bellows over the wind, his face split in a wide grin.

"Hold your fire!" I command as I recognize the rest of the Rejects as the occupants of the other bikes. "The bikes are friendlies."

"They don't look like any friends of mine," Gage snorts from his position across the aisle.

"Yeah, well they're not the ones firing on us!" Blythe yells as she takes aim on the craft directly behind us using the radar screen.

The hover bikes fall back, surrounding the craft that Blythe has blown a few holes into behind us. It's going to take a lot more than that to take down the military craft, and we all know it. Jenica is working some impressive piloting skills, swooping low and veering through trees, but only so much evasive maneuvering is going to save us.

"Hey, Bronson," I call across the aisle, catching Gage's attention. "Feel like getting some fresh air?" I ask as I point to the roof hatch above out heads.

To my surprise he smiles and stands, his gun at the ready. His CBX1000 is nowhere near as badass at my ARX, but it'll get the job done.

"Now that you mention it, it is getting kind of stuffy in here."

"What are you doing?" screams Jenica as she banks left again, throwing Gage into me before righting the craft again. "Do you want to get yourselves killed?"

"No, but we'd rather not let you go down with us if we do," I answer as Gage pops the hatch open. He gives me a leg up first and once I'm out, I lean down through the hole and help pull him up. The current of air on either side of us is strong and each of us has to grab on to one of the steel handles on either side of the hatch to keep from falling off.

"We need to get on those bikes," I say, watching as the Rejects swarm around the hovercraft, smashing in its windows and laughing with glee as they snatch MPs through the circular holes and throw them to the ground. "Pick one and jump on. Throw the other guy off and try not to get killed."

"Got it," Gage says, taking off before I can tell him to go.

"Impatient bastard," I mutter as I stand and take off after him, picking up as much speed as I can before reaching the edge. There are three bikes within our reach, and I opt for the one furthest away to give Gage the best chance to reach one of the closer ones. With one good leap, I am able to propel myself close enough to grab on to the footrest of a bike piloted by Monkey Arms.

"What the hell?" he screams when I swing my legs up and settle behind him on the seat.

He swings back at me and I block the blow with my arm, my shoulder screaming in protest. Pain radiates up my arm and into my chest as bone connects with titanium and I realize I've picked the wrong bike. This dude could knock me senseless with one punch. He takes another swing at me, but I dodge it before bashing the butt of my ARX against his jaw. Blood gushes from his mouth, but he's relentless, going for a choke hold, but missing my neck as I lean back in the seat, nearly losing my place on the bike.

"You Resistance idiots just don't get it, do you?"

Monkey Arms snarls, spitting blood. "We have a chance to change history, to take our place as the most powerful people in the world. Why do you want to ruin that?"

I grip Monkey Arms by his shirt collar and pull him close, having had enough of him and his stupid friends by now. The bike stalls, but remains in the air, hovering among the other whizzing bikes, one of which I can see is piloted by Gage.

"I won't waste my breath explaining it," I growl as I lift him clear off the seat, snatching his legs over the sides. "Just know that if you survive today, I won't hesitate to rip one of your arms off and beat you senseless with it if we meet again. I've had it up to here with you, your friends, and your shit!"

I let go, sending his body flying through the air. I slide forward on the bike's seat, gripping the handlebars just as his hand wraps around my ankle with crushing force. If my ankles were still made of bone, this one would be broken.

I glance over the side to find him hanging on, trying with all his might to crush what he thinks is a normal ankle.

"Eat metal, bitch," I say with a smirk as I cock my foot back and bring it slamming down on his face. That knocks him loose and he hurtles downward. I watch as he latches on to the branch of a tree, swinging himself deeper into the woods and out of sight.

Gage swoops past me on his bike, his gun aimed at the second hovercraft pursuing the Neville I. The first one is overtaken by Rejects, most of whom have dismounted their bikes and are climbing in through the vehicle's windows.

"Take out the thrusters!" Gage yells to be heard over the wind.

Fucking brilliant idea; I can't believe that jackass thought of it. Grudgingly, I follow Gage as he swoops under the second craft, aiming my ARX at one of the two thrusters located beneath it. Taking out the thrusters won't ground the craft, but it will make them about as slow as a person on foot, giving us a chance to get away. Our red lasers tear through the thrusters, leaving two smoking, gaping holes in the bottom of the metal tube. The craft shudders, then stalls.

"Yes!" Gage shouts, whooping excitedly as we make our escape from under the craft.

"Nice work guys," Jenica's voice crackles from over my COMM device. "Forget about the other craft; looks like the Rejects have hijacked it. Now do you think you can follow us back to the hideout without getting yourselves into any more trouble?"

Gage shoots me a grin as we fall in behind the Neville I. "Race you there," he says with a laugh.

Despite the fact that this dude wants my woman, I can't resist. My hand tightens on the throttle, and Gage and I are off like twin bolts of lightning.

FOURTEEN

WE'VE BEEN HOME FOR LESS THAN AN HOUR AND MY BODY IS crying out for food, a hot shower, and a change of clothes. Despite the fact that I'm operating on very little sleep, adrenaline is pumping through my veins and it's not likely to stop until I know we've got some kind of plan to rescue Olivia in place.

Yet, I know I can't think about any of that until I've gone to check on my partner from the last mission. After loading the passengers into the hovercraft, Jenica flew us home, all while telling us about how things had been going back at Headquarters. She was sure to include that Yasmine had begged to be allowed to come back to Memphis with her and Gage, but the Professor and Jenica wouldn't hear of it. I am glad they made her stay behind; even a girl with Kevlar for skin needs her rest after being stunned.

She looks no worse for wear now, sitting up against the metal headboard of one of the many cots in the infirmary, her willowy body encased in a hospital gown. An IV is stuck into a portal built into her inner left arm—a clever device created by the Professor so that those with the Kevlar skin can still receive fluids and medicine in an emergency situation.

Her thick, wavy hair is loose around her shoulders and I'm amazed by how much of it there is. I've only seen it pulled back and wound into a bun. Now it frames her slender face like the perfect picture frame, causing her eyes to appear larger and the angles of her face softer. As I sit in a chair beside her bed, I'm surprised at how attractive I find her. The strength of my reaction is something I haven't experienced for any girl since meeting Blythe.

It frightens me.

"Hey you," I say, my voice gruffer than I intend it to be.

"Hey yourself," she answers, a smile lighting up her face. "Glad to see you made it back in one piece. Well," she adds, eyeing the bandage on my shoulder, visible through my undershirt, "Almost."

Stripping my t-shirt off and submitting to the Professor's poking and prodding to dislodge the shrapnel from my back was not fun. The pain was so intense, I nearly blacked out from it, but now that it's been cleaned and stitched up, I am enjoying the numbing effects of something he injected into my shoulder for pain.

"Yeah," I answer, touching my shoulder lightly. "It's nothing. I'll be fine."

"Sorry I got shot," she says, her expression one of embarrassment. "Rookie mistake, it won't happen again."

"Are you kidding? You took out three MPs by yourself! For your first mission, you did a hell of a lot better than I did."

"Really?" she asks, her voice telling me she's not convinced.

"Yeah, but you get no details. That's a terribly embarrassing story for another time. I just wanted to come by to make sure you were okay."

"I'm fine," she answers. "Professor Hinkley says my skin saved me from burns."

I nod. "It's true. Getting stunned from one of those things doesn't just knock you out; the heat from the lasers is known to leave second degree burns. I guess the neural effects got to you, but not the heat."

I gaze down to see her trailing her fingertips over the back of her arm. In a flash of memory, I see myself waking up in a cot that looks a lot like Yasmine's, my body altered permanently for the rest of my life—my life saved, when I should be dead. I look up from her arm to see her staring at me, her eyes wide and earnest as if she is willing me to see into her. I find her stare disarming.

"What does it feel like?" I ask, gesturing toward her skin.

"You can touch it, if you want," she offers, holding her hand out to me. "I don't mind."

I smile. "Thank you, but that's not what I meant."

She frowns as I reach out to touch the back of her hand. "What did you mean?"

My brow wrinkles as my fingertips skim over her hand. "Wow," I whisper. "It feels so ..."

I trail off, not sure how to say it without being insulting.

"Real? Soft?" Yasmine offers with a laugh. "A lot of people are surprised by how real it feels. It is made of Kevlar, but the Professor created it using real live, donor skin grafts. It has all the properties of armor but it feels like skin should feel."

I jerk my hand away when I realize I've trailed my arm all the way up to her shoulder in my exploration. I clear my throat noisily, embarrassed.

"What were you meaning to ask me?" she asks, not missing a beat, pretending she can't see how embarrassed I am to have felt her up like that. "Before, when you asked what it felt like. What did you mean?"

"I meant the blast. You were much closer to the explosion in your city than I was in mine. I was far enough that I only suffered from the impact, not the heat and light."

Yasmine sighs, folding her hands together in her lap. Her eyes grow distant and watery and her voice is haunted as she speaks. "It feels like dying," she whispers. "It's the only way I can think of to describe it. It's like dying a thousand deaths and wishing that each one were the last one. The white light is so intense, you think you'll never see again. And just when you've gotten over it—the pain of realizing that you may never lay eyes on green grass, blue sky, or gleaming city buildings again—the burning starts and it's so intense, it feels like tiny needles invading every pore of your skin and stabbing deep, lighting you on fire from the inside. It feels like Hell."

A lone tear slips down her cheek and my insides jerk, hard. I swallow past the lump in my throat and blink rapidly to get rid of the extra moisture pooling in my eyes.

Yasmine swipes at the tear on her milk-chocolaty cheek and forces a smile. "So," she says, recovering nicely, "is there a plan for rescuing Olivia?"

"I'm not sure yet," I answer. "As soon as I got home I came here. I wanted to make sure you were okay first. Now I guess I should go shower, change, and meet up with the others. Getting into Stonehead a second time won't be easy."

"Go," she says, reaching out to squeeze my hand. "Don't worry about me. As you can see, I'm fine now. Just do me a favor, will you?"

"Sure," I offer. "What do you need?"

"Try to sneak some desert in from the cafeteria. They won't give me any real food until tomorrow morning and the nurses keep making me drink these God-awful protein shakes."

I pull a face and grunt in remembrance of the chalky taste of the protein shakes she's referring to. "Ugh, you poor girl. I've got your back. Chocolate mousse or vanilla cake?"

"How about both?"

I laugh. "You got it."

When I enter my room, I immediately peel my shirt off and begin rifling through my drawers for clean clothes to wear. I passed Jenica in the hallway and she informed me that we were meeting in the Professor's quarters in twenty minutes—just enough time for me to shower, shave, dress and scarf down a few strips of beef jerky and drink some water before joining the meeting.

Without thinking, I throw open the bathroom door, forgetting to knock like I always do. The connecting door to Blythe's room is hanging open and I can see her and Gage inside, seated on opposite sides of her narrow bed, talking.

"I'm sorry I failed you," Gage is saying as I drop my clothes onto the bathroom counter. My jaw tightens as he reaches across the bed to take her hand. "I failed all of you."

"What happened to Olivia wasn't your fault," Blythe says, curling her fingers around his. "I don't blame you."

Gage shakes his head and lowers his eyes. "You should."

"Hey," Blythe says, reaching up to his jaw with her free hand. "No more guilt, okay? Remember, we're a family here. There is no condemnation here. The operation was dangerous and we should never have attempted two rescue missions simultaneously. It put all of us at risk, including you. I would never have forgiven myself for being part of making that decision if something had happened to you."

"Hey guys," I call loudly from the bathroom, as if I've just walked in on them. "Meeting in the Professor's quarters in twenty."

Blythe drops Gage's hand as if burned and stands quickly. "Oh, hey Dax. I guess we better get ready then."

"Right," says Gage, shooting me a glare as he stands as well. "I need to change, too. I'll meet you guys there."

He turns to Blythe and bends down to kiss her cheek. Murderous thoughts fill my mind and I find I'm starting to enjoy them.

"Thanks," he says before leaving the room, pausing to shoot me another glare.

I raise my eyebrows and shrug as if I have no idea what he's so pissed about. Asshole.

Once he's gone, Blythe turns to me, arms crossed over her chest, a hint of a smile curling her lips. "Stop it, Dax!"

I hold my hands up and shrug. "What? What did I do?"

"You know exactly what you did. Stop acting like my guard dog."

"Hey, speaking of dogs, where is Dog?" I haven't seen our wiry, furry little friend since we got home.

"He's in Mosley Hall with the kids, and stop trying to change the subject."

"Okay, fine! I'm sorry, okay?" I say, stepping forward to pull her into my arms. I'm done playing the nice guy. "It's just ..."

She pulls back, but not completely out of my embrace, which leaves me feeling a bit smug. "It's just that you told me you loved me, and I haven't told you how I feel."

I nod, giving her a little squeeze and reveling

in the feel of her pressed up against me. She places her hands against my chest and pushes slightly, forcing me to let her go.

"Look," she says, taking a step away. "You want the truth? I don't know how I feel."

I shrug and rub my chin nonchalantly. "Fair enough."

"I need time to figure it out, but the problem with that is there's is no time. The government is breathing down our necks, Olivia is imprisoned at Stonehead, we just had to shut down one of our most valuable hideouts and fuel-smuggling operations, and don't even get me started on those Reject freaks."

"I get it, B. I understand."

She sighs as if releasing a ton of doubt and worry. "So, we're agreed. I'm allowed to be undecided for now."

"For now."

"And you don't get to make me feel guilty about it."

"Duly noted."

"And you'll stop treating Gage like shit."

I wince as if her statement has physically hurt me. "Now, see, that's going to be tough."

Blythe folds her arms over her chest and pretends to frown. "Try harder."

Coming in close again, I grasp her shoulders and pull her up against me. Her arms drop to her sides and her body melts into mine.

"That's the thing," I say, my mouth inches from hers. "When a guy wants the same thing I want, I tend to get sore about it."

"Just remember that I belong to no one," Blythe says, the quavering in her voice betraying the straight face she's wearing. "This isn't a pissing contest and I am not a prize to be won."

"No," I say, my lips brushing hers lightly. "You are not a prize, you are *the* prize. And I don't intend to lose you."

She sways into me and it's all the permission I need to cover her mouth with mine, groaning deep in my chest as she opens her mouth to me, the warmth of the inside of her mouth mingling with mine. When our tongues touch, she pulls away her eyes wide.

I smile and chuck her on the chin lightly with my knuckles. "I said I'd let you go on undecided, I never said I'd stop showing you just exactly where I stand."

She continues to stand there, silent and motionless until I finally grab her by the shoulders and steer her back towards her room.

"Less than twenty minutes, B. Unless you want to see me take my pants off, you should go. Or stay, it's really up to you."

My laughter follows her as she runs from the bathroom and slams the door.

Everyone is gathered and waiting in the meeting room in the Professor's quarters when Blythe and I arrive. The Professor is at the head of the table, his characteristically messy brown hair like a bird's nest around his head, his clothing rumpled and unkempt.

Jenica sits at his right side in a fresh, black flight suit, her hands folded on the table. Gage is at the foot of the table, slouching with one foot resting on the opposite thigh. As Blythe and I take our seats, I am acutely aware of the fact that Olivia's chair, across from Jenica, is empty. A cold fist knots in my stomach as I notice the video panels pulled up on either side of the professor, each depicting scenes from Stonehead. I blink and look away from the one showing Olivia's battered and bruised face.

Once we're all seated, Jenica stands and begins the meeting. "I trust that you all have seen this footage. It's been all over the news since Olivia was captured at Stonehead." Everyone nods silently and she continues. "Olivia—and the others imprisoned at Stonehead—are scheduled for execution at 9:00 o'clock a.m. eastern time. That only gives us a few hours and a very narrow window of opportunity. Our last attack was well-planned, but we did not anticipate that our EMP would be targeted."

My gaze swivels to Gage as I realize that no one has explained yet how things went wrong at Stonehead. Agata's EMP was supposed to knock out the MPs weapons, but it's obvious from the footage that this is not what happened.

"They knew about Agata," Gage says in answer to my unspoken question. "I don't know how, but they did. They had some kind of device, something that emitted a high-pitched frequency that only Agata could hear. It rendered her unable to do what we brought her to do."

"Is she okay?" Blythe asks.

He nods. "She's got a little headache, but it's nothing a good night's sleep won't cure."

"I am working on trying to figure out how they knew about Agata," Jenica says, "but we all know that the most pressing matter is getting back into Stonehead and getting Olivia and the other prisoners out alive."

"I hate to sound negative, but how the hell do you propose we do that?" asks Blythe.

"With these." Jenica reaches behind the panel and comes out with two MP helmets. She drops them onto the table with a 'clunk', their white, gleaming faces turned toward us. I can see myself in the reflection of one of them.

"Sayer Strom from Alpha team was thoughtful enough to strip two of the stunned MPs of their armor and identification last night. We're going in covertly this time. Two of you will pose as Military Police escorting in a group of prisoners. With these ID tags, you will have access to even the most secure levels of Stonehead. Olivia will be in maximum security lockup, the hardest to get to. Luckily, one of these guys is an officer and his credentials will get you in."

"Wait a minute?" I ask, my mind racing as I try to wrap my mind around Jenica's plan. "Those officers were stunned, not killed. Surely by now they've reported back and had their old IDs voided."

A hint of a smile pulls at Jenica's lips. "Strom took care of that for us by chaining the officers together and dropping them down into a ditch. If we're lucky they won't be found for days and by then it won't matter. If the credentials are rejected, the prisoners that you're bringing in will trump all else. Or I should say, the main prisoner. They won't be able to resist letting you in with this guy as bait."

"Who's the bait?" Gage asks. I can tell he's as intrigued by this plan as I am.

The Professor stands and speaks for the first time since the meeting began. He removes his glasses and I can see that tears have pooled in his eyes. He is afraid, not for us but for Olivia. I know he sees her like a daughter. We are all like his children.

"I am."

Part Three: Secrets
(Gage Bronson)

FIFTEEN

GAGE BRONSON AND DAX JANNER
RESTORATION RESISTANCE HEADQUARTERS SCIENCE AND
MEDICAL BUILDING
AUGUST 18, 4010
9:00 PM

I AM AFRAID.

It is not something I would admit to a lot of people and if anyone asks, I'd rather die than let them know the truth. I've been afraid since the day I arrived at Restoration Resistance Headquarters. I am afraid that the secrets I've kept will get me in hot water with the people I think are beginning to trust and accept me. I am afraid for Agata, and I worry that she will someday come to resent me for the decisions I've had to make for her. Will she ever understand that I'm only acting in my sister's stead; doing the things for her that Trista could never do?

More than anything, I am afraid of being exposed for hiding the truth about my past to the only person whose trust I care about keeping. She's watching me as I pull the MPs armor on over a black flight suit provided by Jenica. The armor is a perfect fit and all that is left to put on is the helmet. Blythe approaches from where she's been leaning against the wall, the helmet clutched between her slender fingers. Her eyes are filled with fear, the same fear that I feel. I am grateful for her presence. It calms me, but also reminds me that it's okay to be afraid. We have every reason to be.

"I don't like this," she says as I take the helmet from her and drop it on the cot beside me. The pristine, white exam room where I was escorted for changing is right up the hall from my final stop before boarding a craft headed for Washington D.C. "You could be killed—you and Dax—if they find out who you really are."

"If the Professor is willing to risk his life to save those people at Stonehead, then I'm willing to risk mine too," I answer, realizing that it's the truth. I have never felt right about the way our government treats the people that were saved from the results of the nuclear fallout by their own inventions. "I kind of wish you would listen to me and just stay behind on this one," I add as I step forward to cup her face in my hands. Her skin is so incredibly smooth at my fingertips, and all I want to do is trail my hands lower to explore more of the same. "I don't want what's happened to Olivia to happen to you."

"I'm going," she says firmly, and I know there's no arguing with her.

Fortunately, Jenica put Blythe's assertion that she pose as one of the MPs to rest. Even with the DNA altering serum that will be injected into my and Dax's blood in a few moments, Blythe cannot be transformed into a male and we need two men to pose as officers. We were able to talk her into posing as a prisoner along with Jenica, Professor Hinkley, Laura Rosenberg, and Sayer

Strom. While the Professor and Jenica are the big prizes, Blythe and Sayer are an added treat for the enemy.

"Then we'll just have to promise to look out for each other, won't we?" I tease, tweaking her nose playfully. "I won't let anything happen to you, as long as I live. Do you understand?"

Through the glass behind her I see Dax walking by, suited up in the same armor I am wearing. I can feel his dark eyes boring through me with intense dislike, but I ignore him. This moment is about me and Blythe, and I won't allow it to be cut short because of some prick's jealous tendencies. She submits to my kiss, and for a few seconds I experience heaven. Her lips are soft and she tastes like vanilla and cinnamon...or perhaps it's her scent invading my senses and influencing my sense of taste. Surely, no woman could taste this sweet. Somehow, Blythe does, and her pliant lips urge me to take more. She doesn't resist when I wrap my arms around her and hold her close, savoring the moment for as long as she'll let me. When it's over, I find confusion in her eyes—the same confusion I know she feels over Dax.

"I'm sorry," I lie. I am not the least bit sorry for stealing a kiss with the girl who's slowly stealing my heart.

"It's okay, I think," she says, her eyes lowered. "I'm sorry, Gage, I just—"

"Hey," I interject, raising her chin so that she'll look at me. "I understand. There's so much going on right now and you and I barely know each other. Then there's Dax ..."

I trail off and she rolls her eyes. "He can be such a jerk sometimes."

I laugh. "Yeah, but he's your jerk. If I were him, I would be protective of you too. I wouldn't be too fond of the new guy making eyes at you from across the cafeteria, or kissing you in the middle of the night in your bedroom. He has every reason not to like me. Can't say I'm all that fond of him either."

Blythe laughs too, a sound she hardly makes but when she does, it's musical. "Thank you for understanding."

How could I not understand? She's just as mixed up as I am, as everyone else is here. These are pivotal times, for both our lives and the history of our country, and tensions are high. Nothing is simple and nothing is cut and dry. How can I, in good conscience, ask Blythe to give me her heart, when I can't even tell her the truth about me? The last thing I want is to see those dark, velvety eyes of hers filled with disgust and disappointment. Both are probably inevitable and that hurts me more than the thought of possibly dying tonight.

At some point, I vow to tell her the truth, but now is not that time.

The room is silent, except for the beeping of the heart monitors attached to both me and Dax. We are lying on cold slabs of steel, strapped down and slightly elevated, as nurses in white scrubs and lab coats move about the room, preparing things for our departure.

Our disguises will go much deeper than what we're wearing on the outside. The DNA altering serum that Professor Neville invented just a few months ago, has never been used, making us the test dummies.

"Explain to me how this works again?" Dax asks the nurse as she removes the armor on his left arm and peels back the sleeve of his flight suit. He sounds as nervous as I am.

The nurse smiles at him and patiently explains. "Professor Hinkley found hair and skin fibers in the suits you are wearing, and was able to extract the DNA of the officers wearing them. These syringes contain the DNA of Captain Jack Knightly and Sergeant Grayson Barnes, along with the serum that will connect their DNA to yours temporarily. The bond lasts twenty-four hours. Once you are injected, their DNA will latch onto yours, temporarily changing your appearance to match theirs. Should the guards at Stonehead decide to do a DNA swab, your blood or saliva will pass for theirs. No one will have any way of knowing your true identities."

"Sounds simple enough," Dax says with a shrug. "Does it hurt?"

The nurse's smile gets a bit tight, but she keeps it plastered to her face in that way nurses do when they want to reassure a patient. "We are not sure, but the Professor's research indicates that the transformation could be a bit ... jarring."

Dax nods grimly. "Great. Sounds like fun, let's do it."

The nurse visibly relaxes. "Wonderful. I will just

step out of the room for a moment, and return shortly with another nurse to assist me."

Her steps are noiseless as she leaves the room, the sliding door swishing shut behind her. A few moments of tense silence pass before I finally turn to Dax. "Look," I say, deciding to get right down to business. "I know you don't really like me, and I'm okay with that. To tell you the truth, I'm not crazy about you either for reasons that have nothing to do with Blythe, and some that do. But you and I made a pretty good team out there today, and in the end, we both want the same outcome for the Resistance. Can we just agree to put that aside and work together without it getting weird?"

He seems to consider this for a moment, watching me through narrowed eyes as if trying to figure me out. "You're right," he says slowly. "I don't like you."

Silence follows and I roll my eyes, scoffing out loud at the idea that I could try to make nice with this jerk. It was a dumbass thing to do.

Dax's laughter is unexpected and my head whips around at the sound. I find him looking at me, his shoulders and chest shaking with humor. The tension melts from my limbs and I laugh as well.

"Now that we got that out of the way," he says, once the laughter has passed, "I don't trust you, and I'm not shy about admitting that. I think there are things you aren't telling us, things that could affect us all in the long run. You have to understand that the Professor is like the father I never had, and these people here, the Bionics, are like his children. I won't let anyone, not even you, fuck with that. You don't like me, I can tell. But like each other or not, we do make a pretty good team. You're a quick thinker and you've got big balls of steel. That, I do like about you. So I agree, let's do what we have to do without letting the other stuff get in the way. This is about the Resistance. It's bigger than us, you know?"

"Yeah," I say with a slow nod, deciding that I might not dislike Dax as much as I thought.

The nurse comes back in with her assistant and each of them takes a place beside us. The other nurse quickly removes the armor from my left arm and rolls up my sleeve like the other nurse did Dax. Moving as one, they clean us with alcohol swabs and tie off our arms with tourniquets, each searching for a good vein. Again, as one, they lift their syringes from the silver tray between them, careful to ensure that they each have the right one. My nurse pauses, needle poised inches above my skin.

"Ready?" she asks as the other nurse asks Dax the same.

"Just get it over with," Dax says, his voice a bit edgy. "I hate needles,"

"Oh, come on, you can do this," I encourage him. "We're doing this for the Resistance."

"For the Resistance," Dax agrees as he turns back to his nurse. "Do it."

The prick of the needle is nothing compared to what follows. Tiny pinpoints of light flood my vision before melting into swirls of color as pain explodes like fire in my veins. My entire body goes tense and spasms uncontrollably as if I'm having a seizure. I writhe and grit my teeth to keep from screaming. Even if I did scream, I doubt anyone would hear me over Dax's enraged bellows as the transformation grips him. I am soon to follow and the pop and snap of bones realigning in my face is unlike anything I've ever felt. What feels like hours, is really only a few minutes by the time the pain ceases. The burning in my veins slowly subsides into a slow tingle, a side effect we were warned would occur but would only last for a little while.

The tingle feels good, like a flood of extra adrenaline, rushing from my head to my toes. As the nurse releases me from the table by unbuckling the straps holding me down, I leap to the floor, energized and ready to go. Dax does the same. When I look at him, I'm stunned by what I am seeing. He has been transformed into a Caucasian man in his mid-thirties. Green eyes stare at me from beneath brown eyebrows, and much thinner lips curl into a smile.

"Sergeant Grayson Barnes, at your service, Captain," he says with a laugh. Even his voice sounds different, its pitch higher. The Dax I know is gone. "Dude, you look like you're going to be sick."

"It's just so weird," I say, tilting my head and staring into the unfamiliar eyes. "I know it's you, but my mind is telling me you're someone else. This is crazy."

"Me?" He laughs and points at the mirror behind me on the wall. "Take a look at yourself, bro."

I turn slowly, my shoulders stiff with tension. I know that I will not see my own reflection but I am unprepared for what meets me in the mirror. The face staring back at me is not my own.

SIXTEEN

GAGE BRONSON, DAX JANNER, BLYTHE SOL, JENICA SWAN,
SAYER STROM, LAURA ROSENBERG AND PROFESSOR NEVILLE
HINKLEY
STONEHEAD PRISON FACILITY
WASHINGTON D.C.
AUGUST 18, 4010
1:00 A.M.

As the Neville I hovercraft drifts over the darkened
Nevada desert, I turn my head to gaze out the window.
Because of the darkness outside, my reflection is what
greets me and I stare into unfamiliar eyes. The man
whose face and name tag I'm wearing as a disguise is
Captain Jack Knightly, a high-ranking officer of the
Military Police. He is middle-aged with nondescript
features and dull, gray eyes that seem stripped of any
uniqueness or emotion. I guess that's what it takes to
be an MP—murder people in cold blood, and follow the
dictates of a broken government like a stupid, soulless
sheep.

My mind should be on the mission ahead of
us. Infiltrating the maximum-security levels of the
Stonehead prison facility will not be easy, despite the
advantages that our disguises have given us. Everything
has been carefully orchestrated and there can be no

deviation from the plan like there was on the last mission. I have gone over the details dozens of times in my mind since the meeting but it still doesn't seem like enough. I rehearse it, over and over, playing out all scenarios and contingencies as the hovercraft zips through the sky at a steady and rapid pace.

Across the aisle from me is Sayer Strom, a member of the resistance that I have not gotten to know just yet. He has one bionic leg and a pair of bionic lungs, as his own were severely damaged by radiation poisoning after the nukes took out Austin, Texas. Like everyone else here, he became a part of the Restoration Project looking for a second chance. I'm sure the insurance salesman's son did not expect to one day become part of a secret organization targeting the very government that had promised him redemption. He's young, no older than eighteen, but I can see that years of running, hiding, and fighting have changed him. The harsh lines of his face are further enhanced by a scar running across his face in a jagged, diagonal line, the only flaw in his perfect, all-American looks.

Next to Sayer is Laura Rosenberg, the newest member of our team. Unlike me, she is trusted by everyone with no question, and I can't help but wonder if it's because she's 'one of them'. Without a bionic prosthetic—the only one in the group besides the Professor without one—I'm the odd man out. Laura's gleaming chest plate and bionic heart aren't the only things that make her, though. The former army sergeant is tough as nails and raw as a slab of bleeding beef How she can sit there, with fresh, angry burns marring the side of her neck and one shoulder, as if she doesn't have a care in the world, is beyond me. She insisted that she was fine, allowed someone at the infirmary to slather burn ointment on it, and demanded to be let back into the fray. I have to say that I admire her dedication.

In the row in front of her Blythe sits alone, one row behind the cockpit where Jenica and the Professor are seated at the controls. I can only see her profile from where I sit, and can't help tracing the sloping lines of her face with my eyes. Her hair is pulled into a ponytail at the top of her head, the long strands brushing the back of her caramel neck teasingly, making me want to come up behind her and press my lips to that very spot, that stretch of skin just above where her neck meets her shoulders. This girl is a mystery to me, as much as I think I am to her. I think it's what has drawn us to each other. In the end, I also believe it is what will tear us apart, and the thought leaves me sick to my stomach. If there is anyone I want to be completely honest with, it's her. The deepest shadows of my heart are hers and she doesn't even know it. Or maybe she does. It could be what has her keeping me at a distance.

Or, it could be Dax. I scowl unwillingly as I shoot him a glance out of the corner of my eye and find him watching her too. Even in disguise, the naked hunger he feels for her is obvious. Anyone paying the slightest bit of attention could see it. The only mystery is where Blythe's heart is in this tug of war. I don't think even she knows; which only makes the chase that much more desperate for me. I don't know how or when it happened. I've always been the kind of guy to keep things casual when it comes to girls. I don't do commitment and I've never been in love. At least, not that heart-pounding, tragically beautiful, painful love portrayed in books and movies. Yet, one look in those buttery brown eyes and I was lost. The broken, hardened woman peering at me from the dark depths pulled on my insides, gripping my soul like marionette strings and leading me along effortlessly.

And yet, Dax has just as much, if not more, stake in this battle for Blythe. Their friendship is a deep one and it makes me feel like an intruder. They understand each other on a level beyond anything I've ever seen. This intimidates me about as much as Blythe's brittle outer shell does. I'm not stupid. I know my chances are slim and I'm the odd man out. A smarter man would leave it alone, let Dax have her, and bow out graciously. But I've never been one to take the easy way out, and am known to pursue the things I want with intense ferocity.

Maybe if she hadn't given me the smallest glimmer of hope, if she hadn't opened herself up and told me her story, if she hadn't kissed me as if stealing my last breath... maybe then it would be easier. Blythe doesn't even know what she's done by giving me even that much. Just a taste of the corner of her mouth would have been enough, but now I've tasted the heady tang of her tongue and felt the slide of her thick hair between my fingers. I've felt her breath on my cheek and taken her intoxicating scent in on far too many occasions.

She's looked at me with those soulful eyes and showed me a glimmer of promise, a lingering of doubt and intrigue when she looks at me, one too many times.

Blythe has given me just enough that I know the fight won't be in vain, just enough hope to spark a flame that grows by the day, and now I'm on fire for the girl with the saddest eyes I've ever looked into. I want to be the one to soothe that hurt, the one to use the tips of my fingers to wipe away tears, and smooth lines of agony away with the touch of my lips.

She has given me hope and she doesn't even know what she's done, God help her. If she did, she would have never let me kiss her. I guess no one ever told her what hope can do to the hearts of men. I've seen it happen, and continue to watch the same effect unfold within the Resistance. With the smallest bit of hope, men have risen against their oppressors with fists raised, even when they knew they stared into the face of death. Women have held infants against their breasts and covered their eyes and ears against the horrible sights and sounds of war, because they believe that even in this terrible world there is innocence to be preserved. Nations rise up against their government, screaming that they've had enough, that injustice will not be tolerated any longer... no matter how many of them have to sacrifice their lives for the cause.

That is what Blythe has done to me. She doesn't even know it, but I would gladly follow her into Hell.

When the sparkling city of Washington D.C. comes into view many hours later, several thoughts and memories assault me at once. The emotional impact is almost as strong as a physical one, not unlike taking a sledgehammer to the gut. For most of my life, this was is all I knew—this sparkling city that is a façade for all the corruption and greed that drives the people running our government.

To the untrained eye, the gleaming white buildings and towers surrounding millennia-old national monuments are beautiful, sparkling white tributes to America's greatness. When I look at them, all I see are cracks, deep, dark, and oozing putrid sludge out into the streets. Our monuments are bathed in blood and that sludge surrounds the dazed citizens on the sidewalks without their knowledge. The mire pulls at their feet, sucking, draining the very souls from once good men. Yet they continue on blindly, believing in a man who elevated himself to the position of most powerful man in the world during our country's most devastating event in history. What a joke.

The streets are well lit and heavy with traffic as the sun rises, more so than usual on a weekend. But this is no ordinary day, and the people out on the street aren't just going about their daily lives. They are hungry for blood, Olivia's blood, and they lust for the stench of death. The public execution is set for four hours from now, and already the twisted and convoluted streets are filled with people making their way to the lawn of the nation's capital building, where Olivia and several others will be executed by firing squad. The event will be televised live, and all over the nation, people will cheer and celebrate her death.

As Jenica lands the craft on the outskirts of the

city, I am reminded of my adolescence and my time spent living the same lie as so many of the people here. I was just as blind to the injustices, just as oblivious to the lies and propaganda being fed to a frightened nation. At least, I was until the nuclear bombs destroyed our country—and the perfectly laid out path of my life— forever.

Four years earlier...

Tamryn Bell is a sweet pixie of a girl, no taller than five feet, with a waif's frame and a short haircut, boyishly cute and blonde. Blue eyes portray an air of innocence and a cherry-red mouth brims with unwitting seduction and promise. She is from a prestigious family, which makes my mother happy, and everyone assumes that we will get married someday. I am in no hurry to take that step, but I am not exactly intimidated at the thought either. At this time in my life, a future with Tamryn seems like a no-brainer. It is just one of many steps in my life plan, just after getting a degree in law and securing a job at a prominent firm. With my father's influence, I am sure to land that dream job with enough money to place a golf ball-sized diamond on Tamryn's finger. When I picture a life with her, it is filled with sweetness and comfort, possibly made all the better by the pitter-patter of little feet and a white picket fence.

Of course, all of this changes on the day of the attacks. I am fortunate enough to be thousands of feet in the air on a flight back from a trip with my parents to Hawaii—which is now no more than a series of charred lumps surrounded by an ocean long depleted of its wildlife and stripped of its sapphire hue, the results of another, unrelated and completely heinous

THE BIONICS

attack that followed a few years later.

My sister and Agata are crush victims, their home in Seattle collapsing on top of them. My brother-in-law is killed, and Agata nearly goes with him. It is the Restoration Project that will give her a second chance when her injuries turn her into a vegetable. Her bionic cerebrum also makes her smarter than the average four-year-old child.

Tamryn is given a second chance as well. Although, I will always remember the day of the blasts as the day our relationship died. Coincidence—or fate if you believe in that sort of thing—has her square in the center of Los Angeles on that day. She is found beneath a pylon and, a few weeks later, declared a paraplegic by the doctors. There is no hope that she'll ever walk again. But even then, I stand by her. I sit beside her hospital bed and hold her hand, praying especially hard in those first days that she will live and then, in the days that follow, that she will regain the use of her legs. I can't imagine her confined to a wheelchair. Tamryn loves to dance. She loves to run, jump, and twirl girlishly down the sidewalk everywhere we go. Like some kind of fairy, she is constantly in motion, her hands and face full of animation and vivacity. Life without her legs will be worse than death for Tamryn.

She begs me to go, says she is no good to me with a broken body, but I won't abandon her. Guilt over having avoided the tragic day mixes in my gut to do battle with my relief that I've been spared.

The road to recovery for her is full of hardships, and mirrors what is happening across the rest of the country as we struggle to move past what has happened. Even then, I believe it all, believe my parents when they tell me about the Restoration Project and the Healing Hands initiative and how

208

it will change so many lives. Believe them when they tell me it is our government's way of trying to piece our broken country back together.

She wants nothing to do with the project, nervous about being labeled as a freak. She is scared but I urge her on, telling her everything will be all right. 'Don't you want to walk again?' I ask her, knowing the answer will be yes and that she'll trust me just because I'm telling her it will all be okay. Tamryn, despite what she's been through, is still as naïve and innocent as ever. It is one of the things I liked most about her.

The procedure is a success and, after a few weeks' recovery, Tamryn walks out of the hospital with a bionic spinal cord and a new set of legs. Around the same time, my sister, Trista, makes the heart-wrenching decision to put Agata's life in the Restoration doctors' hands. Before her bionic cerebrum, she is well on her way to becoming a vegetable for life, a possibility that leaves us all paralyzed with grief. A few months after Tamryn, Agata is released as well, better than she had been when she was brought in.

It does not take long for the hate speech against Bionics to begin. On the airwaves, the media fills television screens with images of the Bios looting, rioting, stealing, and committing violent crimes. To be fair, there are just as many non-bionic perpetrators—our history has shown these crimes to be a natural side effect of disaster—but fair and balanced reporting has never been a strong suit of the American media. The Bionics are painted as villains with mutations—as if they'd been born that way, not created by doctors and scientists working for the government.

This is all it takes for the politicians to start weighing in. Soon, every campaign from mayor to senator to president becomes about the Bionics and their place in society. They are vilified and persecuted in the media. It is right around this time that I feel a deep rift develop between Tamryn and me. She will never say it out loud, but I know she resents me for pushing her to enroll in the Healing Hands project. She hates her bionic additions and fears the day when the Bionics will be rounded up and... well, at this point, we have no way of knowing what the government will do. But Tamryn just knows it would be awful.

It's funny that I have always thought of her as the naïve one. But just now, our roles are reversed. I keep my faith in our government and the project. After all, it is doing so much good for our society. Each division is responsible for rebuilding and reshaping our world in different ways. Our citizens are getting their lives and their health back. Our cities are being rebuilt and are now bigger, brighter, and more beautiful than before. What evil is there to be found?

Even when the MPs start storming the city, rounding up all Bionics with an unsavory past, I believe that Tamryn is safe. After all, she comes from a good family, a well-known family. She can be protected by her father's name, just as Agata is protected by mine, her grandfather's. It isn't until the day she goes missing that I realize how stupid I've been. Her mother shows up at my parents' house, tears in her eyes, begging to see my father, wanting his help in getting her little girl back. I watch from a darkened hallway as she is turned away, the hard set of my father's jaw revealing the nature of his resolve. He can help her... but he won't.

Nothing that I say will change his mind, not when he has invested so much into his image. He can't be seen as siding with the enemy. 'Not even your niece', he says in that cold tone of his. In that moment, I realize just how sheltered I have been and how it has crippled me. I am completely incapable of understanding this new world, where the rich and entitled aren't protected by their bank accounts or prominent names. I realize how spoiled I've been, how blind I am to the plight of the Bionics, as well as anyone less fortunate than I am.

I'm not a bad person, I know that deep down. But having the blinders ripped off, and the true nature of society shoved in my face, has left me angry and filled with purpose.

Within a few weeks, it becomes increasingly clear that my father will force my sister to turn Agata over to the authorities. Even though I'm the younger brother, I immediately take charge of the situation. I won't lose her like I did Tamryn. My guilt over not doing more to save her is a deep and raw ache, but there is nothing I can do for her now. In Agata, I can find my redemption.

Rumors of a secret Resistance led by Professor Neville Hinkley himself seem too good to be true. Yet, I know firsthand how the government turned on him when he opposed the mutilation of those he'd fought to save. When the government declared that all Bionics would be stripped of their prostheses, the Professor objected strongly. It cost him his job, his life, and got him branded as a terrorist.

It took a lot of digging around, but I eventually found an underground railroad of sorts, a chain of people who would send you on the right path to the Resistance for little or nothing. Some would take food, some money, and others wanted nothing at all. It seemed enough for them to be able to stick it to the MPs, even if it could cost them their lives. In their faces, I see all the horror and hardship that I've been saved from by the coincidence of my last name.

By taking Agata and running away with her, I have made us both fugitives. But the alternative is simply unthinkable. I am now one of these people—an outcast, running from the enemy and fighting for a cause. I can never truly be one of them—my organs are all original parts of my body and I'd never known a day's hardship before running away with my niece—but losing Tamryn taught me a very valuable lesson.

Injustice is as blind as justice, and no one is safe. And if injustice can pick and choose who it targets, then I am free to choose which side I stand on.

SEVENTEEN

GAGE BRONSON, DAX JANNER, BLYTHE SOL, JENICA SWAN,
SAYER STROM, LAURA ROSENBERG AND PROFESSOR NEVILLE
HINKLEY
STONEHEAD PRISON FACILITY
WASHINGTON D.C.
AUGUST 18, 4010
4:00 A.M.

JERKING MYSELF FROM MY WANDERING THOUGHTS AND SHAKING
off the dark mood my memories have brought on, I
stand and mutter to no one in particular that I'm going
to the bathroom. The tiny, tube-shaped room at the back
of the craft is small and cramped, with hardly any room
for a guy with shoulders as broad as mine to turn one
way or the other, but it'll do. I handle my business and
leave, ready to take my seat again, when the rumble of
voices speaking in hushed tones stops me in my tracks. I
pause in the doorway, cracking it just enough to find the
Professor and Jenica standing to the left of the aisle, in a
darkened corner. I realize that we've stopped, the craft
hovering several thousand feet above our destination.
Toward the front of the craft, I can see Dax, Blythe, and
the rest of our crew standing to stretch and prepare for
the next phase of our plan.

It makes sense that these two would want a

quiet moment to go over any last minute details of our mission, yet something about this feels wrong. I feel like a voyeur watching them, and I don't really know why until the Professor reaches out to clasp Jenica's hand. The touch is not one of friendship, or even camaraderie and reassurance. There is more there, and as I watch the human side of Jenica Swan's face soften— an expression I would have never thought her capable of—I understand what I am seeing. Between these two, who fight at the forefront of the Resistance, there is more than friendship and respect.

There is love.

"Stop it, Neville."

My eyebrows shoot up at Jenica's gentle tone, as well as the fact that I've never heard anyone refer to the Professor by his first name before. With all her formality and hardness, she's the last person I would have expected to hear it from.

"I'm sorry," he says softly, his voice quavering in the darkness between them. "I just thought it might be worth trying to convince you one last time."

"I won't stay behind. You can't ask that of me."

He smiles, his eyes crinkling at the corners behind wire-rimmed frames. "I know. You are loyal to your crew and to the cause and I love that about you. But this isn't about you or me, it's about—"

"Don't!" she interjects, a bit of her usual harshness pulling at the corner of her mouth. "Don't you dare try to use that to make me feel guilty!"

The Professor sighs, his shoulders sagging. "It's not just you and me anymore, Jen. We have to think about it, even if you don't want to. At some point, you're going to *have* to face it."

"I will," she insists, her voice dropping even lower as her gaze darts about the craft as if afraid the walls will overhear them. "Just not right now. This mission—Olivia—it's all too important."

The Professor nods but I can tell, even in the darkness, that he's not happy about letting her off the hook. "Just be careful," he says, grasping her slim waist and pulling her in toward him. "If something were to happen to you..."

He doesn't finish, his words screeching to a trembling halt as if he's afraid of what he'll say.

Jenica exhales noisily and lays her head on his chest. "I will, I promise."

After a few quiet moments, the two leave the back of the aircraft and return to where the others have gathered. I count to thirty slowly before emerging from the bathroom and making my way up the aisle to where everyone is receiving last-minute instructions. When I come up on the back of the group, I feel Jenica's narrowed gaze on me. I meet her eyes and try to smile, but my lips are frozen. Her cold, dark eye—the human one—appears to be boring into me. The other one, a piece of machinery built into the metal covering half her face like an opera mask, whizzes and whirs as she watches me. She knows that I spied on her. She knows that I heard them.

As I tear my gaze away and try to refocus on the task at hand, I can't help but wonder how a love affair between the Professor and Jenica Swan came to be. They seem like a very unlikely pair, but then, so are Blythe and I. In fact, I know if we ever crossed paths in our previous lives, we would probably have never noticed each other. The same has to be true for them, but I can see how desperate times have caused them to cling to each other. I can also see that I'm not the only one around here with secrets.

We have three and a half hours to infiltrate Stonehead, locate Olivia, and break her out of there as safely as possible. It seems like an infinite amount of time, but when you factor in all that could go wrong, it feels more like three and a half minutes. Each of us has our roles to play, but the pressure is on for Dax and me. Our disguises aren't enough to get us through. It's going to take a lot of bluffing and confidence to take on the roles of officers Knightly and Barnes.

One thing that will help is the bait we've brought. The Professor and Jenica have been at the top of the most wanted list for years. Throw in a few of the Resistance's key players and it makes for one very tasty treat the officers at Stonehead will be salivating for. They are our ticket in. Balls and firepower will have to be enough to get us out.

Our first move is getting our prisoners looking like actual captives. They already appear exhausted, which they are, and with Blythe's fresh bruises and Laura's burn from the fight in Memphis, they look as if they've been in a struggle. We ruffle the Professor's hair and then bend his glasses a bit before lining them up one behind the other and chaining them together using an intricate system of cuffs used by the MPs for transporting multiple prisoners. Each pair of cuffs is attached to the other by ionized chains. The negative ions of the chain are attracted to the positive ions of the cuffs, causing them to fuse together in a bond that can only be broken by a special device, a remote of sorts, which Dax now has control of. Once each of them is cuffed, he links them together in a straight line, hands behind their backs, with the Professor in front followed by Jenica, Blythe, Sayer, and Laura.

In the massive storage hold beneath our feet is a Military Police vehicle that is small but fast. It is what we will use to gain entrance to Stonehead, leaving our own hovercraft right where it is, masked by the clouds until we can return. We form a procession and take the stairs down to the storage hatch in silence, each of us sinking into our roles before we are even seen. I try to mimic the stiff cadence of an MP's steps and notice that Dax has done the same. In my hands, I clutch the same CBX laser weapon I carried for the rescue mission in Memphis. I shoot Dax a frown lined in jealousy. His automatic ARX is far superior, but a gun is a gun. At the end of the day, I'm grateful not to be empty-handed.

Dax has some rudimentary piloting skills, which is enough to get us to the landing strip at Stonehead quickly and safely. As we land, a ground crew dressed in white flight suits comes racing toward us. They are probably surprised to see the craft, as Sergeant Barnes and Captain Knightly were no doubt presumed dead when they didn't return from Memphis. Dax brings us in for a shaky landing and, within moments, we and our 'prisoners' are standing on the paved landing strip, surrounded by the curious employees of the facility.

"Is that who I think it is?" one of them asks, his wide brown eyes fixed on the Professor. "And you got his partner too?"

The Professor lowers his eyes, playing the perfect role of the frightened prisoner. Or, maybe he *is* scared. Jenica simply raises her chin, staring down the gathered men with an air of arrogant superiority. It's no act; Jenica is above these men and she knows it.

"Well, what are you waiting for?" I bellow, jumping straight into my role as the commanding officer. "Someone find Warden Daniels and tell him to get down here. Tell him I have an early Christmas gift for him."

Three men jump to do my bidding and we our prisoners across the tarmac toward an entrance. Before our mission, Dax and I were drilled over and over on our knowledge of Stonehead's layout. We didn't have a lot of time to steady Jenica's schematic and get down the basics of where everything is in the country's most secure, maximum-security prison. First, there's a set of doors that won't budge without the proper identification. Of course, a facility like this one hasn't bothered with paper credentials in decades. It's fortunate, then, that we have been injected with the DNA of the men whose identities we've stolen. It insures that the retinal and thumbprint scans go smoothly.

The doors slide open for us welcomingly, and

we usher the Professor and the others down a long, narrow corridor shaped like a tube. The glass walkway is identical to the others around us, that tunnel their way to and from various levels of Stonehead. Of course, Olivia and the others are situated near the very heart of the prison, down a winding path of twisting tubes. During our initial rescue attempt, we had the benefit of my niece Agata's special abilities. Her bionic cerebrum's electromagnetic pulse knocked down Stonehead's power just long enough for us to break through the many checkpoints requiring fingerprints, retinal scans, and voice recognition. Even though they were able to stop her with some kind of weapon—we still aren't sure what kind—by the time we reached the center it didn't matter.

Now we have the liberty to walk through these doors without attracting suspicion, though we do gain the attention of every officer we pass in the tubes. They stare, openmouthed and envious, clearly unable to believe that two officers were able to bring down the most wanted criminals in America and a few of their accomplices to boot.

When we reach the main doors leading to the wing of the prison reserved for criminals marked for execution, we are met by Captain Rodney Jones, the dedicated soldier tasked with heading up The Enforcers, whose sole mission is the capture or termination of all Bionics. Dressed in a simple uniform of slacks and a button-up shirt decorated with medals befitting his high rank, he is still as menacing as he appears when decked out in his armor. He is as tall as Dax, which is insane, and twice as broad. No way is he that big naturally. If I had to guess, I'd say he takes full advantage of the steroid injections offered to the Military Police. To level the playing field, the government says. His dark eyes are narrowed and gleaming dangerously as he approaches. He is flanked by several other officers as well as Callius Daniels, the infamous warden of Stonehead.

Just behind them are a series of doors leading to small rooms where prisoners are processed in and questioned. I shudder as I remember passing these rooms on our first mission. The door to one is hanging wide open and the white tiles are bathed in blood... Olivia's blood. It takes everything I have not to open fire on the MPs right then and there. Instead, I grip the butt of my weapon tightly with one hand and execute a perfect salute with the other.

"Captain Jack Knightly reporting," I say in a soldier's rough bark.

Dax salutes as well and the other officers return the gesture—all except Jones. He is circling us and eyeing the prisoners with a predatory smile. "Well, well," he says, his booming voice reverberating from the walls and ceiling, "I must say I am surprised to see you Knightly, Barnes. When you didn't return from Memphis, we feared the worst."

Dax launches into the story we fabricated to explain our—or rather, their—absences. "We took a chance on following a Resistance aircraft, sir," he says in perfect imitation of a subordinate soldier. "They were trying to escape as the other Bios attacked us. Captain Knightly and I pursued the craft and shot it down.

220

Imagine our surprise when we found *them* inside."

Jones's eyebrows shoot up. "You deliberately defied orders, but I am willing to let that slide, Barnes," he says with a shrug. "Sometimes following your instincts is worth it. And in this case..." He trails off, sauntering toward Jenica with a smirk. He leers at her, leaning much too close, so close I'm sure she can tell what he had for lunch. But she doesn't move an inch. "I'd say it was more than worth it."

Jenica is defiant, staring the captain down as he glares at her. After a few seconds, his eyes shift toward the rest of our prisoners. "Excellent work," he says, clapping his hands together loudly and spreading them wide as if welcoming the prisoners to Stonehead. "Have them processed in and caged, Warden," he says to Daniels. The warden is a rail-thin snake of a man with shifty, beady eyes and pointy teeth. I don't like the way he's eyeing Jenica's headgear, as if she's a shiny new toy he wants to play with. No one talks about it, but everyone knows that the torture of the Bionics is a regular occurrence on his watch. The government has assured the people that the 'decommissioning' of a bionic enhancement is humane. But behind closed doors, parts are removed without anesthesia, and of course, many who lose their parts cannot live without them. Those that can are now mutilated beyond repair and most likely wish they were dead.

"Make sure they're comfortable," Jones adds with a chuckle. "Meanwhile, I'll put a call in to the higher-ups. I'm sure they will want to interrogate America's most wanted terrorists."

Dax and I step away as the warden and his officers step forward to take the Professor and the others. My jaw clenches and my fingers curl around the butt of my gun as their shackles are deionized and they are separated. Blythe's scent curls up through my nostrils as she's taken past me, shoved roughly by a guard. Her eyes meet mine for a brief moment, and I can see her fear. I want to tell her everything is all right, but have to settle for letting my facial expression do the talking. Though, I don't know if the desired effect is achieved since this face is not mine.

"Did you hear? Intelligence has found three Reject hideouts, including a weapons cache. Jones is going to make a move on it soon."

I meet Dax's glance from across the round, gleaming steel table as the chatter of other MPs goes on around us. In a men's locker/break room of sorts, we are surrounded by men changing, grabbing a quick bite, and gossiping like a bunch of women. We decided to slip in long enough to find out if there are any new developments. There is nothing else we can do until it is time for the prisoners to be taken for execution. As of now, we have another hour. We both pretend to be too hungry to talk and fall silent as we listen to the conversation a group of officers is having at the next table.

"It's a suicide mission," one of them says, his voice filled with disdain. "Those Reject nuts are nothing like the Resistance. They're a bunch of freaks."

"They're all freaks," scoffs another. "There's no difference between them."

The first guy shrugs. "I don't know, those Resistance people... they at least seem human. The Rejects..." he shudders. "They're insane."

"Either way, Jones is ready to take them down," Guy Number One responds with a shrug. "And I intend to get on that mission. Might even bring one of their limbs back as a trophy."

His companion laughs before draining his coffee cup and the two stand up to leave. Many others are clearing out and I can tell that it's time for the morning shift to start and the night crew to leave.

"Maybe you can get one of those arms they've outfitted with guns," Guy Number Two says as they make for the exit. "Get it mounted on your armor."

The two share a laugh and are joined by several others on the way out the door. Dax and I find ourselves conveniently alone. Our eyes lock from across the table.

"We've got to get our hands on that intelligence," he whispers, his eyes darting back and forth as if the eyes have ears. They most likely do.

I glance down at my watch. "We have a little less than an hour until execution," I murmur back, careful to keep my voice as low as his.

His smiles at me and his eyes are gleaming. My answering smile is wide. "Jenica will kill us for going rogue," he answers. "She hates deviation from missions."

I shrug and stand. "Well, Jenica's in a holding cell and isn't expecting to see us again until 8:30. What do you say we poke around Jones' office? In a place like this, there's no need for him to hide anything. With both of us looking, we could find it and be out of there in no time."

Dax doesn't even bat an eyelash. "Let's do it."

As I follow him from the locker room, I am once again surprised to find myself feeling a bit of admiration for him. All bullshit aside, I'm actually coming to like the guy. We fight well together and I admire his instinct for acting on his own conscience when he feels it's necessary, instead of always blindly following orders. For me, rule breaking is new. It wasn't until very recently that I learned to start thinking for myself.

Six months ago...

Tamryn is gone, but her eyes haunt me every day. The pages of my sketchbook are filled with her image, scratches of charcoal in black and white with the eyes colored in a perfect shade of sky blue. Thinking of her haunts me, and when I close my eyes at night, those eyes are in my dreams, filled with tears and accusations as she asks me without words why I didn't save her. Even as I try to convince myself there was nothing I could have done, my own uselessness angers me.

Her loss has triggered a change in me, and as I watch news broadcasts of people—yes, they are part machine now, but they have always been people first—being abused by the government, I know that change has become apparent to my family. They watch me with eyes filled with confusion. Well, at least my parents do.

My sister sees me through a lens of hope. I am starting to believe that she was never as naïve about the Bionics and the state of our government as I was. She always knew that things would happen this way and, after Tamryn is gone, she is starting to realize that Agata is not safe. Though she has not said it out loud, I know she is counting on me to help her should things go wrong. After all, she is a widow now and the only male figure in Agata's life is me. My father is too busy with his own affairs to bother to be a grandfather to a child he now sees as a freak.

It is not easy to hide—the change in me. Really, I'm not sure I want to. Our country, our world, is broken. Seems to me a little change is needed, even if it only starts with the individual. Because I am my father's son, I am well educated in America's history, and over the centuries, we have seen time and time again how the spark of the individual can trigger something enormous. We've seen less and less of it as time has marched on and our world—and courage and honesty—have become buried under depravity and corruption. But I like to believe the potential for that spark still lies deep within our collective subconscious. I am proven right when I discover the Resistance. The spark had already begun, and I didn't even know it yet.

To cope with the turmoil swirling in my gut, I fall back on my passion, which is art. Drawing by hand, specifically. It's an antiquated pastime, as nowadays most artists prefer a digital canvas and create by touchscreens. I favor the feel of pencil and paper, the honesty of it, over dots and pixels. It's a waste of time, according to my father, since he's been priming me for a law career since Kindergarten. I was all fine with it when I was one of the blind sheep. Law is the career of choice for young people in Washington, as it is the center of the judicial system and politics. Most who reside in D.C. live their lives knowing they will grow up to work for the government. All of a sudden, I am not okay with this, and my father can't stand it.

"Have you finished your application?" This question is from my father when he walks in on me drawing one day, a picture of Agata with an intense expression on her face in profile. I've drawn the side of her head as if it's being seen under an X-ray; beneath her skin and skull, machinery churns away. In my imagination, an invisible pulse of energy radiates from the bionic cerebrum.

I shrug, and continue shading, barely sparing him a glance. My tablet sits nearby, the unfinished application an unopened file just as it was when it was sent to me. Tension rolls off him in waves as he stands in my doorway, an imposing figure in an Armani suit and tie. His nondescript brown hair and soft blue eyes fool people into thinking he's warm and friendly, even a bit bland. He is none of those things.

"I'll get to it."

He steps into the room slowly, each movement calculated to intimidate. He has no idea how much he and others like him have diminished in my estimation. I am not intimidated or impressed.

"Gage, we've discussed this. You've been out of high school for three years now. My connections can only hold your spot open for so long."

"I wasn't aware that your power came with an expiration date," I scoff sarcastically, my eyes still on the drawing taking form under my fingertips.

The book is snatched abruptly from my hands and I finally spare my father a glance as he flips through it swiftly before hurling it against the wall, his chest heaving with barely controlled rage. This is the side of him no one outside of our house ever sees; I wonder if people would think so highly of him if they did.

"Everything's a goddamn joke to you, isn't it?"

"Absolutely not," I say nonchalantly, standing to face him with my arms folded over my chest. "It is my future we're talking about here, and I've given it a lot of thought. I've decided that I won't be going to law school."

There's a vein in his forehead that's going to blow any second. "And just where is it you think you will be going?"

"The Art Institute, of course. You know, the one I've been telling you I want to go to for years."

His smile is derisive and his eyes are glinting with malice as he closes in on me, leaning forward into my face. His every word is sharp and succinct. "This is about your little girlfriend, isn't it? She's gone and now you've made yourself out to be some kind of pitiful, tragic, love-story hero. Well, allow me to put some things in perspective for you. She's gone—get over it. She made a decision to become one of those freaks and is now paying the price."

Disbelief rips through me and mixes with anger to make me feel like I'm going to be sick all over his shoes. "Choice? What choice did she have? What choice did any of us have in this? And while we're on the subject, where's the accountability on behalf of the government? They're the ones that created the Bionics."

"A grave mistake that our nation is now paying for," he says solemnly, as if he truly believes it. "We must all make sacrifices during this time in our nation's history, son. It is not an easy thing to have to live with, but it must be done and the rest of us must move on."

"And what about people like Tamryn, Dad? What are they supposed to do? What about Agata?"

At the mention of my niece's name, his mouth goes tight at the corners and his shoulders go stiff. Horrified, I realize the path of his thoughts. He doesn't have to say anything out loud—I just know. Agata is not safe. He will not protect her. It won't be long before my sister is called on to give her up and he won't do a damn thing to stop it.

I let the subject go and make false promises to fill out the application. I let him think that my sudden outburst is because of my grief over losing Tamryn. That is only half-true.

A few weeks later, I am gone, never to be heard from again. Agata mysteriously disappears with me. Even though my father is a prominent figure in D.C., no one comes looking for us. No missing person's reports are filed and no media campaign is launched to locate us. We are simply gone—Agata clinging to me as I run through alleys and subway tunnels in the dead of night, toting a single bag filled with the meager possessions we will bring with us. Nestled at the bottom is that sketchpad. Even from inside that bag, buried under a few changes of clothes, bottles of water, and packages of protein bars, Tamryn haunts me, reminding me that I have succeeded for Agata where I once failed her.

EIGHTEEN

GAGE BRONSON AND DAX JANNER
STONEHEAD PRISON FACILITY
WASHINGTON D.C.
AUGUST 18, 4010
8:30 A.M.

"GOT IT!"

I hold the small, palm-sized cartridge up in my hand, catching Dax's attention from across Jones' office. In a file cabinet in the corner, which is filled with classified files, I have found all the information the government has on the Rejects. "Good," Dax says, pulling his COMM device from his back pocket. It has a handy slot for file reading on the back. "We've got to report to escort the prisoners to execution. We barely have enough time to copy the information and get back to the cell block."

I come around the desk and place the slim, rectangular cartridge in his hand. He quickly plugs it in and presses a few buttons on the touch screen to begin copying the file. The transfer happens almost instantly, and Dax hands it back to me. I carefully place it back where it came from.

"Let's move," Dax says, leading the way toward the exit swiftly. A solemn silence falls between us and

I know his mind is on what will happen next, just as mine is. The information about the Rejects, we can't do anything with now. It's of no use at the moment. Now is the time to focus on getting Olivia and the others safely out of Stonehead.

When we arrive at the cell block, a team of twelve officers is assembled, led by Captain Jones. Behind the glass doors on one side, I can see Jenica chained to a steel table in one room, the Professor in one next to her. The raised voices of interrogators are muffled as they pace back and forth in front of the tables, fists flying and blood splattering the walls as they work to get the information they need. It takes everything in me not to cringe as an officer's palm makes contact with Jenica's cheek. To her credit, she barely winces, her human eye narrowed murderously at the man abusing her as he takes out his frustration on her. The Professor is in worse shape, one eye nearly swollen closed, his wild curls now beyond repair and hanging in a battered face.

Hang on.

The thought echoes in my head as if I'm trying to project it at them, and I wish that some higher power would carry the message on from me to them. Soon, this will all be over. I trade glances with Dax as we fall into the formation of officers and I can see by the tight set of his jaw that he is not happy with what we've seen. But there is nothing we could have done to avoid it. By volunteering themselves as bait for this mission, Jenica and the Professor had to have known it wouldn't be easy. As America's most-wanted criminals, they had to be aware of the possibilities. That doesn't make it any easier to watch them beat senseless.

On the other side of the circular space, cells are being opened and shackled Bionics are emerging in chains and linked together. Blythe is first and her hair and clothes are rumpled as if she's been in a struggle. Laura is next, and the angry burn on her neck, which had started to scab over, is bleeding and raw. There is a bruise on her left cheekbone that wasn't there before and she's bearing all her weight on her left leg; I believe she has injured the right one. Sayer is next, followed by four others who were taken with Olivia. Sayer is a bit battered too, like Blythe and Laura, but it's the condition of the four other prisoners that turns my stomach.

Their faces are nearly unrecognizable masses of purple and black bruising, swelling and blood. One of them sports a bandaged and bleeding stump and I can only assume a bionic arm used to be there. I choke back bile as a red haze of rage slides over my vision at the sight of the armless young man. Execution just isn't enough; they had to mangle him too, subject him to the pain and humiliation of losing his limb before death. The girl chained behind him is wearing an eye patch and I shudder to think of the now-empty socket behind it.

And then, they bring out Olivia.

They make a big production of it, walking her slowly past the other prisoners as if on parade, before shackling her in front of Blythe to lead the procession. She has to be held up by two officers, as she is clearly unable to stand on her own two feet. She is wearing only a paper hospital gown, her petite frame swallowed up by the thin garment. Across her collarbone and shoulders, ugly bruising is turning green beneath her skin. Her shallow breathing hints at broken ribs and the bridge of her nose is at an angle—clearly broken. Her eyes are ringed in black, the normally vibrant blue of her irises muted and lackluster. Her lip is split right down the middle and dried blood is gathered and caked at the corners of her mouth. Her head has been shaved, leaving only a fuzzy patch of blonde down. Just like the young man with the missing arm, I can see that Olivia has been under the surgeon's knife as well. Her bionic hand is gone, the wound dripping and bleeding beneath a white bandage.

One of the other female prisoners begins sobbing at the sight of her, a loud wail that echoes from the walls around us. "You monsters!" she rails at the guards, yanking against her chains and causing those attached to her to shift a bit with her movements. "You sick sons of bitches! What have you done to her?"

She's answered by the butt of a gun. It slams into her face, filling her mouth with blood as she crumples to the floor. The guy beside her kneels to help her, propping her up in his arms and glaring at the officers through swollen eyes.

"Was that necessary?" he growls defiantly. "Haven't you taken enough from us?"

He is treated to the butt of an MP's gun as well, with a foot to the gut for good measure. The officer is cocking his foot back for another go when another voice intrudes.

"That's enough!"

My body tenses from head to toe at the sound of Blythe's voice as she jerks against her chains, staring rebelliously at the officers closing in on her, prepared to punish her for daring to speak up for the others.

"Yeah, big tough group of guys you are," she sneers, her lips curling as if she's smelled something putrid. "You gotta beat up on a group of injured people chained together."

One swing from the officer closest to her and her mouth is filled with blood and dripping down the front of her shirt. My gut clenches and I feel Dax jerk violently beside me as if it physically hurts him to watch.

"Shut your fucking mouth, you Bio whore, and get back in line. All of you! Next one to open their goddamned mouth gets a laser in the ass. It doesn't make a bit of damn difference to me if we have to drag you before the firing squad stunned and drooling."

Blythe spits a mouthful of blood in the MP's face and the motion sets off a chain reaction. The officer raises his weapon at the same moment I lunge for him, taking him down to the floor. By the time I bash his head against the ground and knock him out cold, all hell has broken loose.

The officers converge on the prisoners with weapons drawn. I hear the crunch of bones connecting and groans of pain as Sayer takes one of the officer's down with a well-timed head butt. Laura and Blyth grab the heavy chain linking them together and swing it out like a whip, catching a third officer across the face. An alarm is triggered as Dax sprints toward the holding cell where Jenica's captor is emerging from the doorway in response to the commotion. A roundhouse kick to the face knocks him out cold and I find myself jealous of his long, titanium legs. Goddamn showoff.

As Dax unchains Jenica, I work my way toward the Professor's holding cell, taking out two more guards by stunning them with my weapon before kicking the door in. The MP that guards him lunges at me and pins me to the wall. We struggle for a moment before I manage to take him to the floor and crack his temple open with the butt of my gun.

No killing. It's the Professor's policy, one the members of the Resistance try to follow whenever possible. At this point, though, I'm seeing red and don't give a rat's ass if the man at my feet bleeding from his head ever wakes up again. After what they did to the Olivia and the others, they don't deserve to live.

I quickly unchain the Professor, noticing that he is limping as well. Obviously, the beating he took while being questioned has taken its toll on the scientist. I tuck him under my arm and bear half of his weight, guiding him as fast as I can back into the vestibule. Dax and Jenica have managed to unchain everyone and gunfire is being exchanged across the space—the MPs hunkered down behind the large, circular desk where prisoners are processed, our guys scattered and crouching in cell doorways and behind interrogation room doors. Only Dax and I had weapons, but I can see that Blythe and Jenica have picked up the discarded guns of the men we took down.

Jenica and I exchange a glance as the gunfire continues and I know she's realized the same thing I have—we are going to have to make a run for it. The alarm is blaring and reinforcements will be here at any minute. She gestures toward the door leading down the tunnel that will bring us back out to the tarmac with her gun before firing across the room and stunning another officer. I take the silent order and crouch low, my sights trained on the doorway.

"Cover me!" I shout at Dax before motioning for one of the captives to follow me. The girl with the eye patch crawls across the floor toward me, careful to keep her head low. I place her between the wall and me, careful to shield her with my body as we make a run for the tunnel. Sayer is standing watch there, a handgun clutched between his fingers as he guards our way out. Eye-Patch Girl makes it to him safely and hunkers down in the doorway as I reach for the girl who got smashed in the face for speaking up against the MPs. She makes it easily as well, clutching Eye-Patch Girl tightly as they cower beside Sayer, trembling with fear.

"Go!" I command Sayer once the fourth one has made it safely. "Don't wait for us; we're right behind you. Go!"

Sayer hesitates for a split second as he shoots a glance at Jenica. She ordered no such thing, but I know it's better this way. If Sayer makes it to the hovercraft first, he can get it fired up and ready. Besides, it'll be slow going with Olivia, Laura, and the Professor injured so badly. He nods once, his jaw clenched grimly as he ushers his rescued hostages down the tunnel and out of sight.

Jenica appears at my side. "Time to blow it," she

says. "Do it now and let's get the hell out of here."

I nod, reaching for the hand grenade on my belt. "Dax, roll out!" I shout, just as I pull the pin. Dax swiftly crouches to lift Olivia, who has been cowering and trembling on the ground through the whole fight, before barreling toward the tunnel at a sprint. Blythe has the Professor under her arm and is practically dragging him toward the exit, while Laura brings up the rear, limping but still moving and providing cover fire.

"Shit!" I curse as I realize my grenade toss is coming up short. Blythe's eyes jerk up toward mine just as the grenade sails over her head. Before I can blink, she's shoved the Professor to the floor and is leaping to snatch up the grenade—which would have landed near Laura's feet—out of the air before chucking it further across the large space. It's barely left her hand and began traveling in the right direction when it explodes, throwing her back into me before rocking the room. Bits of ceiling tile fall and crumble on the MPs' heads and the large, circular intake desk is blown to bits. Pieces of the steel frame are bent and warped, while the fiberglass has broken apart into shrapnel and injured several of the officers.

I hear the sound of popping and crackling and glance up to see blue lines of electricity dancing down Blythe's bionic arm, which is now missing two fingers, before a whirring sound and then silence. The arm goes limp at her side and she slumps a bit, thrown off balance by the heavy piece of machinery that has just gone dead. Blythe simply shrugs and bends to pick up the two metal fingers before shoving them in her pocket. I must be wearing a look of horror because she laughs as she runs past me toward the exit. Bloody and battered MPs are struggling to their feet, disoriented—we don't have much time left to get out of there.

"Get a grip, dude, it's fixable," she teases, grabbing my hand with her human one and propelling me through the exit.

Get a grip. I fumble for one as we run, trying not to dwell too long on the fact that I nearly killed her with that grenade. As she runs, she holds the bionic arm close to her body with the opposite hand, cradling it as if injured, but she's keeping up just fine. Bursts of gunfire are going off behind us, interspersed with the sound of pounding footsteps. I sneak a glance back over my shoulder and see that Jones has managed to scrape a few guys off the ground. They are joined by reinforcements, who arrive just in time to join him in pursuit down the tunnel.

"We've got company!" I shout to the rest of our group.

Jenica spins on her heels, barking orders over her shoulder as she runs back to where Blythe and I are bringing up the rear. "Janner, get Olivia to the hovercraft and make sure Strom is ready for takeoff the minute we reach the tarmac."

Dax stops and turns, shooting Jenica an annoyed glare. I can tell he can't stand being left out when it's time to fight. "Are you shitting me?"

Jenica points her gun at a door leading to another series of tunnels and fires. She blasts the hinges off and the door falls out of the frame. I reach out to catch the heavy door just before it hits the floor.

"Shield," Jenica explains curtly before turning back to Dax, who's holding a trembling and silent Olivia. I lay the door on its side and it spans the width of the tunnel. I pull Blythe down beside me just as Jones opens fire, and crouch down beside her. Dax—clutching Olivia tight—the Professor, and Jenica follow suit, crouching to take shelter behind our makeshift riot shield.

As we aim our weapons over the door and return fire, Jenica proceeds to rip Dax a new asshole. "Janner, you are never again to question a direct order from me, do you understand?"

"But—"

Jenica growls in frustration. "But nothing!" she says, her voice still surprisingly calm, while edged in cold steel. "Saving Olivia and the others is our priority and I am trusting you to see to their well-being until I can get there. Now, you can stand here and argue with me while we're being shot at, or you can suck it up and follow orders. Do you think you can handle that?"

Dax doesn't hesitate because, really, we all know Jenica is right and he is nothing if not a dedicated member of the team. "Yes," he throws over his shoulder before disappearing down the hallway at a sprint. Olivia's haunted eyes peer at us from over his shoulder as she clings to him, her white paper gown flapping against her body like a sail in a storm.

Once they're out of sight, I turn my attention back to Jones and his cronies. Blythe and Jenica are returning their fire from either side of me, and the

Professor is crouched on Jenica's other side. From between shots, I hear her berating him for not leaving with Dax.

"You shouldn't be here," she grumbles as she takes aim over the side edge of the door and stuns an MP. They've broken out the riot shields, but they have to poke their heads from around them to see us and there are too many of them to take cover behind the shields, so it's like shooting fish in a barrel. The problem is the sheer number of fish and it seems we'll never be done with it.

"I'm not leaving your side for a second," the Professor answers.

The murmured exchange is heard only by me and I can't help but think of the private moment I witnessed between them on the hovercraft. The statement is loaded and I find myself, once again, feeling like the worst sort of intruder.

After a few more minutes of exchanging fire with no leeway on either side, I've had enough. "Fuck this," I mutter before turning to Jenica. "I'm making a move. When I jump over this door, make a run for it."

Jenica shoots me a scowl that's hot enough to burn the eyebrows off my face. "Do I need to remind you who's giving the orders here?"

I roll my eyes. "Yes, Jenica, you're the man. You have big brass balls of steel. Now that that's out of the way, would you just freaking run for it? We're not getting anywhere fast and we're outnumbered. It'll be better if you guys just go and let me catch up to you."

Blythe's hand clutches my arm tightly and when

I turn to look at her, she doesn't speak. She merely shakes her head, her eyes wide. She doesn't have to say anything. We all know I won't be catching up.

"Do it, Jenica," the Professor says firmly, his fingers biting into her skin as he grabs her forearm. His eyes are dancing wildly behind his glasses. I've never heard him speak so authoritatively before. The meek scholar is gone and in his place is a man in love protecting his woman... even if she is a stubborn bitch with ice in her veins. Another silent moment passes between them, in which all the emotion in the world arcs and flashes in their eyes. I've decided not to give them any more time to reason with me. Once I'm gone, they would be foolish not to run.

Their shouts fade beneath the pounding of my own heart in my ears as I vault over the door, immediately drawing the MPs' fire. I shed my helmet, finding my vision is better without it, and open fire. My legs are pumping faster than they ever have in my life as I zig-zag down the tunnel, dodging the red glow of lasers now set to kill. Adrenaline surges as I switch my weapon's settings from stun to kill without hesitation. Screw this peaceful, kumbaya, holding hands in harmony shit. I promised Blythe last night that I wouldn't let anything happen to her as long as I live. I intend to keep my promise, even if it means taking out as many of these shithead MPs as I can before I die.

A red laser beam grazes my temple, burning on contact as I take down an officer just to the left of Jones. He's removed his helmet too and has murder in his eyes as he lifts a second pistol from his belt and proceeds to double his efforts at killing me. Somehow, I manage to last a full minute before someone kills the lights. The shots continue and I wait for death, knowing that in the few seconds it takes for the MPs' night vision to kick in, I'll be a goner.

What happens next defies all reason. I hear the scrape of a metal door in the frame behind me seconds before a pair of hands grasps me and propels me across the threshold. When the door slams again, I find myself in a darkened room, with the sound of heavy breathing indicating another presence in the room. A beam of light cuts through the darkness, barely illuminating the face of a woman.

I feel as if I've been punched in the gut as I stare into blue eyes identical to my own... at least they would be identical if I weren't borrowing Jack Knightly's gray ones. My mouth goes dry as my sister, Trista, stands in front of me in a prison employee's uniform, her eyes wide with fear but her mouth set in determination beneath the glow of a flashlight.

"What are you trying to do, get yourself killed?"

I am unable to speak for several moments. I'm too busy drinking her in, running my eyes over her to make sure she's okay while simultaneously wondering how she ended up working at Stonehead. "Trista." I don't realize that I've said her name out loud until she wrinkles her eyebrows and frowns.

"How do you know my name? Have we met?"

My heart sinks as I realize she can't possibly know she's standing right in front of her own brother. The time we've spent apart has not been good to her.

She looks exhausted and grieved. I swallow past the lump in my throat and shake my head.

"No, we haven't met but I know your brother."

Life pours into her expression and she grips my arms tightly. "Gage? He's alive?"

Pain lances through me as I realize she's thought me dead all this time and probably Agata too. So much has happened since we left home that I hadn't thought to try to send word that we are all right. I hate myself for making her worry.

"Yes," I answer, dropping my voice to a whisper as the pounding of boots sounds just outside the door. In the meager glow of her flashlight, I see that Trista has propped something up against it, but it's only a matter of time before they get the lights back on and start checking doors. I talk quickly. "He is safe with the leaders of the Resistance."

Her smile lights up the dark room. "Oh, thank God. And Agata?"

I smile reassuringly. "She is well. She misses you, but is well taken care of. There are lots of other kids at Resistance Headquarters and they even have a school and several pets. She's happy."

Tears roll down Trista's cheeks and she trembles, her fingers tightening as she clings to me, presumably a stranger. "He did it," she whispers. "He actually did it."

"What are you doing, Trista?" I ask, hoping to get some answers before I have to run again. I could never forgive myself if she's found with me and punished for committing what amounts to an act of treason. "You could get yourself killed if you're seen as being in league with a bunch of terrorists."

She raises and eyebrow at me and crosses her arms over her chest. "So could you."

That's my sister. The girl I know gives as good as she gets. "Point taken," I answer. "I have my reasons."

Trista nods decisively, grabbing my arm again and propelling me through the room—which turns out to be a large storage bay. "We don't have much time. Your friends got away, but you'll have to hurry if you don't want to hold them up. I assume you need to get to the tarmac?"

"Yes," I confirm as she leads me through a maze of shelves storing uniforms, armor, and weapons. "If they have any sense, they'll leave without me."

"I'll try to get you there as fast as I can and maybe you can catch up with them. If you stay here, they'll kill you... after they've tortured you for information on your friends. First, you gotta ditch the armor."

I quickly oblige, peeling off the heavy pieces and laying them gently in a dark corner so they don't clatter. I stand there in my black flight suit as she rifles through containers on a shelf beside me before tossing a bundle in my hands.

"Put these on," she said. "It's a pilot's uniform. Put the hat on and yank it down low. Hopefully, no one will look too closely at your face. It should work just long enough to get you to the airstrip."

I pull the slacks, button-down shirt, belt and hat on before slipping into the boots she tosses at me, cringing as I realize they're a size too small. But I'm not complaining. "Why are you doing this?" I ask, not because I don't know, but because it's a question Jack Knightly would ask, and right now, that is who I am.

She turns to me, the light of her flashlight casting shadows against her haggard face. "Because I refuse to live in a world where an innocent child—my daughter—is considered an enemy of the country. I refuse to stand by and watch this government persecute the innocent. If you are for the Resistance, then I will help you in any way I can."

I don't like it, her involvement. I took Agata away so that she wouldn't have to fight this battle. By taking my niece out of the equation, I've put myself in the position to fight for her. Yet, I realize now that none of us can be exempt from this. Revolution is here and the time will come when we all have to choose sides.

Trista gives me a once over, sweeping me from head to toe with the flashlight and nods her approval. "Good enough. Once you're out this door, take a left and follow the tunnel out to the side of the building. Stay close to the wall; you're less likely to get picked up by the cameras. Keep walking along the building—to the left—and you'll see the tarmac when you round the corner. Once you're there, run like hell and don't look back."

I nod and tuck my weapon into the belt around my hips and turn to face Trista. "I have a message from Gage."

Her confusion is evident but I don't have time to explain. There is no way for me to tell her how Jack Knightly would know she'd be there when seconds before he'd been surprised to see her. None of that mattered when I was facing the possibility of never seeing her again.

"He says he loves you," I say, my voice hitching a bit on the last word. I clear my throat and take a deep breath. "And he says to stay strong. He'll come for you."

Trista smiles but her eyes say it all. She knows she can't go on double-crossing the government forever. She has signed her own death sentence by siding with terrorists. I steal one last glance at her before I open the door and slip out into the empty tunnel. As I walk—as quickly as I dare without drawing attention to myself—I fight the urge to look back. Yet, I am resolved to return for her, to rescue her from certain death when she is found out. I now add Trista to the list of people counting on me. One more reason why I cannot fail.

NINETEEN

GAGE BRONSON
STONEHEAD PRISON FACILITY
WASHINGTON D.C.
AUGUST 18, 4010
9:30 A.M.

WHEN THE AIRSTRIP COMES INTO VIEW, I KNOW THAT WE'RE IN deep shit. Jenica, Blythe, and the Professor haven't even made it to the craft yet and are ducked down behind a row of hover bikes, taking cover. I can see our hijacked government craft several hundred yards away, its guns raised and swiveling on their turrets as Dax and Sayer try to help us pick off the MPs one by one. It is an impossible task—there are too many of them. The smart thing to do is run, but I know Dax won't leave without the others. As I weigh my options as quickly as possible, I realize that there is no way we're getting out of this together. I start across the tarmac, gun in one hand, raising my COMM device with the other.

"Janner!" I bark as Dax as I make a beeline for a craft parked on the other end of the airstrip. With so much manpower concentrated on the others, this craft is unguarded. I've never piloted a hovercraft in my life and what little I do know has come from watching Jenica at the controls, but I can't think about that now.

The MPs are closing in on Blythe and the others and there is nowhere for them to run. "Do you know how to fly one of these things?"

Dax's voice—or rather, Sergeant Barnes' voice—crackles over the speaker. "Not that particular model, but Strom does. What are you thinking, Bronson?"

"I'm thinking you need to get out of here and get our rescued prisoners home," I say as I reach the hovercraft and proceed to climb up toward the closed hatch, all the while praying that it is unlocked.

"That's a negative, Bronson," Dax answers, yelling to be heard over the sound of gunfire. "We're not leaving without our team intact."

"That's not exactly an option," I answer, trying the hatch and find it open. I quickly scramble inside. "We're going to have to split up. Put Strom on the line and tell him I need a five-minute piloting lesson. I'm going for Jenica, the Professor, and Blythe."

Dax hesitates for a split second before I hear his heavy sigh over the speaker. "You'd better not get them killed," he grumbles, and I can picture him grudgingly handling the COMM device to Sayer. "Or I will seriously kick your ass."

"If I don't do something, we're screwed either way," I retort before Sayer comes on the line.

"Strom here."

"Strom, give me the basics," I say as I run up the hovercraft's center aisle and find the pilot's chair. Rows of foreign buttons, gauges and screens line the panel in front of me. I watch through the window while the space between Jenica, Blythe and the Professor and the

MPs grows smaller. I don't have much time.

"See that clear plastic box to your right near the throttle?" Sayer asks over the COMM device.

I nod. "Yeah."

"Pop it open and flip that red switch."

I do as he says and immediately the hum of the hovercraft tells me it's turned on. "Done."

"There's a series of silver switches to your left."

I locate them. "Yeah, there are six of them."

"Those control your elevation. Each one will lift you higher into the air. Flip the first two and that'll get you high enough that you're flying but still low enough to swoop down and grab Jenica, Blythe, and Professor Hinkley."

I quickly follow his instructions and the hovercraft jolts as I flip the two switches, then it ascends, hovering several feet over the ground.

"Now what?" I ask, dropping into the pilot's chair and fastening the harness. My hands shake as I grip the throttle.

"Fly," Sayer answers before the connection is cut. I drop the COMM device into my life and swallow past the lump in my throat. *Fly.* That's it? It sounds simple, but I know there's more to it than simply steering. Yet, it's all I have to go on, so I grip the throttle and accelerate forward the way I've seen Jenica do so effortlessly. The craft jerks and shoots off way too fast, propelling me halfway across the tarmac in one very clumsy motion. I'm thrown off balance as my hand jerks on the throttle, causing the craft to bank right, hard. My teeth gritted, I fight to get control of the massive thing, nearly going upside down as I overcompensate by jerking left and nearly plowing into another, parked aircraft.

I gain enough control to point it in the right direction and come in for a very rough landing, the nose of the craft pointed down and scraping the pavement just inches away from where Jenica is crouched behind the row of hoverbikes. After mashing the button to open the craft's door and lowering the ladder, I leap from the pilot's chair and climb up to the hatch on top of the craft, sticking the upper half of my body through the hole and providing cover fire as Jenica, Blythe, and the Professor scramble up the ladder one by one.

"What are you doing, Bronson—trying to kill us?" Jenica screams as she throws herself into the pilot's chair, strapping herself in and going to work on the control panel. Blythe takes a seat at the controls beside her—taking control of the guns—and the Professor pulls up the ladder and slams the doors closed. I am barely in my seat and buckled in before Jenica has us in the air and hurtling across the airstrip, steadily rising higher and higher.

I sneak a peek out of the window just in time to watch a swarm of hover bikes take to the sky, one large hovercraft at their center like the queen bee.

"We've got company!" I bellow as I pop my window open and stick my gun out to take aim.

"Shit," Blythe murmurs as she works to swivel the guns to the rear of the craft, her eyes clued to the radar screen. "There have to be at least two dozen of them, Jenica."

"You just shoot," Jenica answers, her jaw clenched

in concentration as she increases our speed and pulls up higher. "I'm going to try to find a thick patch of forest to lose them in."

That's easier said than done. Maybe in some other areas of the country, where cities have been decimated by nuclear war, poverty, and famine, there are miles of woods that have overtaken civilization to hide in. But here in D.C., every square mile of trees has been mowed down to make room for gleaming skyscrapers, condos, and national monuments. The outskirts of the city are usually the best bet for the coverage of trees and foliage, but we are at least half an hour from being out D.C.

We're pretty much screwed.

Sweat breaks out over my brow as I try my best to take aim. It's hard in the moving craft. Plus, my weapon isn't made for distance shooting. I'm pretty much just wasting my weapon's charge and soon it will die and become completely useless, or overheat. Deciding to conserve power for when I might really need it, I toss the gun aside and join Blythe near the radar screen, watching as she takes out bike after bike. Yet, she doesn't seem to be making a dent in their numbers. Then there's the other hovercraft to deal with. It's becoming very clear that we are going to be shot down in a matter of minutes and they are gaining on us.

Jenica must realize this, because after a while, she sets it to autopilot at top speed and unbuckles herself from the pilot's chair.

"We're going to have to use the escape pod and make a run for it."

"Are you *insane?*" Blythe screeches, her knuckles

nearly white where she's gripping the guns' controls. Her hair is plastered to her neck and face from sweat, her eyes wide with fear, the human eye's pupil dilated by adrenaline. "Landing in D.C. is a death sentence!"

"We don't have a choice," the Professor interjects, his voice surprisingly calm. How the hell does the man do it? "We can try to lose ourselves in the crowd and find a hotel to hole up in until we can form a plan. We have to try to disguise ourselves, even you, Gage, as Jack Knightly's face is now undoubtedly all over the news along with ours."

Jenica reaches into one of the many pockets of her flight suit and comes out with a syringe. "Let's do it," she says as she pulls the cap off the syringe before jamming it into her carotid artery.

Blythe shrieks in reaction to the sight and I cringe. Jenica doesn't even flinch ... and then she is on her knees, groaning through clenched teeth as the familiar sound of popping bone and stretching cartilage tells me what she's just done. She's used the same DNA altering serum that gave me my disguise. Only her transformation isn't nearly as dramatic and when she stands, I find myself staring into a familiar, yet unfamiliar face. The titanium plate that covers half her face like an opera mask is gone and I am now able to see what Jenica looked like before the blasts tore off a huge chunk of her face. Two dark, slanted eyes and a cute, button nose are cover by flawless, porcelain skin. My jaw drops.

"Since I have a prosthetic that is harder to hide than the others, I always carry one," she says with a shrug. "Most people don't remember what I looked like before the blasts anyway and it's easier to use my own DNA than someone else's. My genetic material holds the code for the missing parts of my face."

I snatch off my baseball cap and hand it to the Professor, who tucks his wild curls under it and pulls the brim down low. Of the four of us, his face is the most recognizable. He takes off his glasses and hands them to Jenica, who slips them on, taking focus off her very distinctive eyes and sloping cheekbones. Blythe slides open the door to the escape pod and finds two MP uniform inside. She quickly dons one and though it is oversized, it more importantly comes with a helmet that will cover her face. I shed my pilot's uniform and throw the other set of armor on over my flight suit, putting on the other helmet. We step into the escape pod, which barely fits the four of us. We are pressed together like sardines, with the Professor and me standing shoulder to shoulder. Blythe is in front of me, with her back pressed against my front. For a split second, I reach for her hand and clasp it tightly. She is trembling, but that stops the moment our hands touch, as if she's drawing strength from me. I let her have as much of it as she needs, placing my other hand at her waist and pulling her close in an embrace.

"It's going to be okay," I whisper as Jenica presses the button to release the pod. "I won't let anything happen to you."

My earlier promise to her bears repeating after all that's happened today. Things have gone horribly wrong once again and I need her to know that no matter what the cost to myself, I will stay true to my word.

"I know," she says, even though her shaky voice says otherwise. I give her another squeeze as the pod shoots away from the hovercraft. It hurtles downward toward the city so swiftly my heart drops down into my stomach.

"Hey Jenica," I ask conversationally, trying to detract from the dread growing in my middle. Once we hit the ground, it's time to start running. "If you can change your face back with a simple injection of DNA and hide your titanium plate, why wouldn't you?"

Jenica's eyes are sharp and her voice cuts me like a knife as she shoots me a glare over her shoulder. "Because," she says, her voice shaking with years' worth of suppressed rage, "I shouldn't have to."

The hovercraft lands smack in the middle of the city's industrial district. Rows of factories and warehouses line the streets and workers wearing jumpsuits in bland shades of white, black, and beige walk in neat little rows to work like ants. MPs linger on the corners with their weapons lowered. But I can tell their eyes are scanning the streets, keeping on alert for trouble. Most likely, a broadcast has gone out with our descriptions. They are watching out for us.

"We should split up," I say as quietly as I can once we've stepped from the pod. "By now they realize the others have escaped and are looking for four people."

"You're right," Jenica says, her eyes darting back

and forth behind the Professor's glasses as she scans our environment. "Let's split up and wait it out for a bit, let things cool off. Keep your COMM device on and close by. I'll call you in a few hours and we'll go from there. Hopefully, Janner and Strom will get the others back safely."

The last I saw of Dax and Sayer, they were hightailing it away from Stonehead. For their sake, and the sake of their rescued prisoners, I hope so too. We part ways, Blythe and I blending in with the crowd in our MP uniforms.

"We need to get off the street," she says, her voice low as we walk as quickly as we can without calling too much attention to ourselves. Even with a helmet on, I'm not sure if her eye is shielded from the scanners that can detect bionic equipment. Hopefully, no one will see the need to inspect the MPs on the street. Either way, she's right. I've seen what panic can do to crowds, and news of our escape from Stonehead is undoubtedly spreading like wildfire.

"Okay," I say, scanning our surroundings for a place to hide. There aren't a lot of options. Most of these buildings are filled with factory machinery and workers doing their jobs. "Keep your eyes open for an alleyway. We'll duck into one and maybe slip into a building's basement for a while."

We keep a steady pace for about half a mile before I find a darkened alleyway between two warehouses, one of which looks abandoned. Within moments, we are in the dark passageway with Blythe holding my gun and keeping watch as I pry wooden boards from across a doorway. By the time we get inside my palms are scratched and blistered, but we are alone, safe in a darkened warehouse that has been emptied of all equipment. Only stacked wooden crates and stray trash litter the floor, while a small beam of light trickles in through a few boarded-up windows.

I lower myself onto one of the crates and Blythe stands in front of me, removing her helmet before reaching for mine.

"You're hurt," she says, her eyebrows furrowing as she notices the nasty burn on my temple. Now that I'm sitting still and adrenaline has slowed, it stings like a bitch.

I shrug. "No big deal. I almost took you out with a grenade earlier. Compared to that, this is nothing. Sorry about that, by the way."

Blythe laughs as she starts unsnapping her armor, stretching her limbs as the heavy pieces clatter to the floor. I follow suit, glad to be free from the oppressive uniform.

"Luckily, the only part of me you broke is totally fixable."

I wince as I notice her bionic arm dangling uselessly at her side. "I could have killed you."

"I'm perfectly fine, see?"

I stand and grasp her waist, pulling her back up against my front and sinking into her softness and warmth. "Hmmm, yes," I say teasingly, burying my face in her hair. "Very fine."

She giggles and turns in my arms, only to jerk back when we're face to face. For a moment, I've forgotten that I'm not myself. Just my luck, I finally get her alone again and I'm wearing some other guy's lips when all I want to do is kiss her.

"Sorry," I say, dropping my hands from her waist. "I forgot."

She smiles. "It's weird," she says, her eyes tracing the contours of Jack Knightly's face. "I know it's you, but it's not you. You don't even sound like yourself."

"Unfortunately, you're stuck with Captain Jack Knightly until tonight when the serum wears off. I can't wait either; this guy is nowhere near as good looking as I am."

She smiles again and lowers her eyes shyly. "No, he's not."

Silence passes between us and, after a while, I become restless. My every nerve is on edge the longer we are inside of this building. I know it will be at least a few hours before we can move again and even longer before we hear from Jenica, but I've never been good at sitting still and waiting. Blythe has sunk down onto the crate I was on before I started pacing, her head lowered. She yawns and I can see how tired she is. We've been going nonstop since the Memphis hideout rescue mission and she has to be exhausted.

"You tired?" I ask.

She looks up and nods. "Been a long... couple of... well, hell, it's been a long couple of years, you know?"

I nod. I do know. Since those bombs dropped, nothing has been the same. "Why don't you sleep for a bit? I'll keep watch."

"Aren't you tired, too?"

"Yeah, but I'm too cranked up to sleep right now. I'll take the first watch and after you wake up you can take the second."

She was too tired to argue. After rifling around in the leftover crates for a while, I strike gold.

"Looks like this place used to produce military supplies," I say with a smile as I find a box full of canvas bags filled with survival gear. I open one and find a rolled-up sleeping mat, a few bags of dehydrated food rations, a bottle of water, a flashlight, a pocketknife, and a rain slicker. "Not sure how comfortable this bedroll is, but it's better than nothing."

"Right now it looks like a Dreamer."

"Wow, you really are tired." The Dreamer is a mattress filled with a viscous gel that molds to cradle your body's contours when you lay on it. It makes each one custom fit to the owner. To own one, I think you have to promise its manufacturers one of your firstborn. Blythe must be dead on her feet if she's comparing the flat, stiff bedroll to a Dreamer.

"Here, let me help."

I lower myself onto the bedroll first, near the top, and then pat the space beside me. Blythe is too tired to think twice and in a few moments, she's stretched out on the mat with her head resting in my lap. Her face is turned away, leaving me an obstructed view of the lovely nape of her neck. My fingers find her ponytail holder and I slip it free, watching cinnamon-colored hair cascade down to her shoulders. She sighs and nestles closer as I run my fingers through the strands. Within seconds she's asleep, but my fingers are still working, sliding through the locks of her hair, enjoying the contact for however long it may last, because I do not know when, or if, this will happen for us again.

TWENTY

GAGE BRONSON AND BLYTHE SOL
CITY INDUSTRIAL COMPLEX
WASHINGTON D.C.
AUGUST 18, 4010
2:00 PM

BLYTHE IS AWAKENED TO MY HAND OVER HER MOUTH.

"Shhh," I prompt her as the sounds of footsteps nearby caused my heart to thunder like racing horses. The MPs have arrived and are searching the warehouse. We've stayed too long. Eyes wide, Blythe nods that she understands and I lower my hand, putting one finger to my lips in warning before pushing her slowly into a seated position. We abandon everything except for water, flashlights, and our COMM devices. Even the armor is left behind, as we don't have time to put the heavy pieces back on. This will make Blythe especially vulnerable and my mind is already racing to our next move. My only mission for the moment is to keep her safe.

Wordlessly, our hands clasp and our fingers intertwine as we creep silently along the wall just as the glow of the officers' solar-powered armor shines in the doorway. We duck behind a massive crate just before they can spot us.

I feel as if they can hear my breathing, even the beating of my heart, so I hold my breath as the roaring of my own blood fills my ears. Blythe points to her left, indicating that they are coming around that side of the crate any second. Thank God she can see through things! We edge around the right side of the crate, keeping out of view but we are still sitting ducks. Any minute we're going to have to run for it and I'd rather it be before we are surrounded.

Pointing toward a shattered window a few feet away, I signal to Blythe that we are going to have to run. She looks like she's about ready to piss herself at the idea, but she nods anyway. A split second later, I shove her out in front of me, putting myself between her and the MPs.

And then we're running.

There's no way to do it quietly, so in seconds the officers are on our heels, their footsteps mingling and echoing with ours in the large, nearly empty space. With a boost from me, Blythe vaults through the window and I follow, trailing her as we take off down the alley. Blythe is cradling her bionic arm and I feel guilty for breaking it, because without the connections to her nerves working, I know it's nothing but a huge dead weight. If I didn't think she'd kill me later, I would toss her over my shoulder and run, but she's holding her own so I leave it alone. Shouts and gunfire follow us and every second I fear may be our last.

Yet, somehow, we survive, ducking and dodging through alleyways, a labyrinth of slender spaces that crawl between the factories like a venous system. I can tell by the echo of the MPs' footsteps, they've split up and are closing in on us from several different sides. I get a stitch in my side at the same time Blythe gets a cramp and we both slump behind a dumpster in an alley almost completely darkened by the tall buildings on either side of it blocking out the sun.

Fighting to slow my breathing, I pull her close, under my arm, and wait for them to find us and drag us back to Stonehead kicking and screaming. Hell, they'll probably just shoot us here and now and forget due process. We've led them on one hell of a chase today and I'm sure Jones is pissed. Olivia's battered face flashes through my mind and I decide that if I had a choice, I'd rather die here in this alley with Blythe then let them drag us back to that place. Just the thought of watching them tear her to pieces fills my mouth with bile.

I can hear their footsteps getting closer, feel Blythe shaking against me. To her credit, her face is set in stone, her jaw tightly resolute, as if she is ready for whatever is about to happen. A scraping sound nearby draws my eye to a manhole a few feet away. The heavy cover has been slid to the side and a gleaming, metal head and menacing, dark eyes appear in the darkened space. I recognize him instantly as Baron, the leader of the rebel sect known as the Rejects. I don't have time to wonder what the hell he's doing in D.C. When he whispers, 'Hey, over here! Hurry up, get in!' I don't care to analyze the situation. That hole in the ground is our only way out of this situation, even if we are literally hopping out of the frying pan and jumping into the fire.

I don't trust these Reject assholes. But now, they

are possibly the lesser of two evil, and so Blythe and I follow him down into the manhole without hesitation. Blythe scrambles down the ladder behind Baron and I follow, swiftly pulling the heavy metal plate back over the hole just before the MPs appear at the mouth of the alley we'd been hiding in.

"I know you have questions but there isn't a lot of time. Walk now, talk later."

Blythe and I exchange a look, but have no choice but to follow. The darkened tunnel we climbed down into led into the city's labyrinth of an underground railway. The lightning fast trains run beneath D.C. through a twisting maze of tunnels. We are walking along one of these tunnels now, on one side of the tracks, the meager light from our flashlights guiding the way.

I cringe as I stare at the back of the Aussie's head while he leads us through the tunnel at a near jog. The last time I saw him, the metal plate bolted to the top of his head like a helmet was freshly done, the skin around it angry and red. The skin looks better now, but it isn't pretty. In some places, it has puckered and wrinkled unattractively, warping an otherwise pleasant face. I wonder if he contracted an infection from his black-market parts, or the undoubtedly unsterile environment he received them in.

As we walk, I grab my COMM device, making sure I still have a good charge. This far down, I'm surprised to still have a good signal. Still no word from

Jenica and I'm starting to get worried.

We follow Baron quickly and quietly for God knows how long before he finally comes to a stop at the very end of a tunnel. It's the end of the line, running just a few yards past the turnoff for a nearby train station. Baron pauses in front of what appears to be a stone wall—a dead end.

"I'm taking a big risk bringing you here," he says, turning to stare at us both. "I know we have a difference of opinion but we are on the same side here. So, I hope you and your Resistance buddies don't come barging into our little hideout with your righteous indignation all fired up and aimed at your own kind."

It takes me a minute to realize that Baron has absolutely no idea who I am. Once again, I've forgotten that I'm wearing someone else's face. If he knew I was the same guy he'd gone toe to toe with in Tennessee not twenty-four hours ago, I doubt he'd help us. For some reason he's taken a liking to Blythe and it's for her that he helps now. Not that she returns the sentiment. In fact, she looks positively sick at the idea of going into a Reject hideout. But I know she's as curious as I am about a lot of things, and that wins out in the end. When Baron runs his hands along the seam in the round tunnel's end and it opens, we have no choice but to follow him deeper underground.

The panel slides back into place and, after a short walk down another tunnel, we enter the hideout. Several pairs of eyes are on us as we follow Baron into the very center of what appears to be a common hangout area. An old, bulky television is set up in the corner and surrounded by Bionics in various states of relaxation. On the screen, a newscast shows our faces—or, in my case, the face of Jack Knightly—as video footage plays of our escape from Stonehead. At least, the parts of the footage that can be twisted to make us look like the bad guys.

Couches and chairs litter the space and all around us are Bionics in various states of relaxation. Near the corner of the room, a group of teenagers are playing a simulation game, the helmets covering their faces pulling them into a world the rest of us can't see. Not far from them, a makeshift cooking area is set up where a woman with two bionic hands and a face full of piercings is slapping meat over a crudely made gas grill. The smell of cooking meat makes my stomach clench in hunger. Near the center of the room, a large group of them lingers over a table covered in what looks like schematics and maps.

One of them I recognize from Memphis. He's a surly-looking dude with two bionic arms. I remember him swinging through the Tennessee trees like a gorilla as he jumped on hover bikes and sent MPs flaming into the dirt. When he catches me watching him, he whispers something to his companions and they all glare at me while shifting to cover whatever it is they're looking at on the table.

"This way," Baron commands, gesturing toward one of several tunnels that branch out from the center room like the legs of a spider. "We can talk privately in here."

We are almost there, nearly out of the room

and away from the shocked stares, when a familiar sound stops me dead in my tracks. It's a laugh... more specifically, a girl's laugh. It wouldn't have seemed out of place, except for the fact that the sound is entirely too ethereal and pure to be trapped in a place like this, warming the hearts of people like these. It is a musical song, almost syrupy in its sweetness, and the sound sends a cold stone of anguish plunking down into my gut as I turn to find the source of the sound—the last face I would ever have expected to see.

My tongue is dry as my mouth falls open to form her name in a hoarse whisper.

"Tamryn."

The sound of her laugh taunts me, its innocence in the dark and grungy world of the Rejects jarringly out of place. She doesn't belong here, yet she looks for all the world like she does. Bionic legs peek out from under a leather miniskirt, the titanium gleaming proudly. The girl who was afraid of being a freak is gone. Her pose is provocative as she leans against a pool table, chatting up a dude in black who's covered in tattoos. She has one herself, a tiny red heart resting on her hipbone. Her blonde hair is in its usual pixie-cut style, but ebony streaks taint the nearly platinum locks, matching the dark eye shadow ringing her eyes. The eyes are still wide and blue but the innocence is gone and in its place is the gleam of a jaded girl, one who has seen and been through entirely too much to retain any sense of naiveté.

What she has become scares me. But more than that it fills me with guilt because I know it's all my fault for not saving her. It reminds me that what I'm seeing in front of me could be Agata in ten years if I don't protect her. It's too late for Tamryn but Agata... her, I can save.

When I spotted Tamryn and said her name aloud, Blythe's concern was evident. She glanced from me, to Tamryn, and back again, her brow wrinkled in confusion. Then understanding dawned in her eyes and she looked away, seemingly deciding not to comment on my obvious acquaintance with Tamryn. Instead, she reaches out to clasp my hand as Baron leads us to the first room off the tunnel we took away from the main area. Once inside, the door closed against the sounds of heavy metal and aroma of cooking meat, Baron takes a seat in a high-backed armchair and motions us toward a couch against the wall. The room is small and dimly lit, with old, beat-up furniture ringing its perimeter. A worn, faded rug covers the hard floor and a large, flat screen takes up nearly an entire wall. Expensive stereo equipment accompanies it, reminding me of how the Rejects operate. The state-of-the-art electronics are likely stolen, the theft justified by the Bionics' poor treatment.

Once Blythe and I are seated, I get right to the point. "Are you holding us prisoner?"

Baron studies me closely for a moment before answering. "No. At least, not as long as I feel you aren't a threat to us. I took a big risk, bringing you here."

"Then why did you?" Blythe asks, glaring venomously at Baron. She's doing nothing to hide her disdain for him or the other members of his extremist group.

Baron smiles and gives her body a once-over from head to toe, causing every muscle in my body to clench in reaction. I don't give a damn what kind of contraptions he's got coming out of that bionic arm of his, I won't hesitate to snap his neck like a twig.

"Because, love," he says, "I'd hate to see that pretty face of yours all bashed in like your blonde friend. If it weren't for me, you'd likely be dead."

Blythe arches an eyebrow. "You expecting a thank you card or something?"

Baron chuckles. "Nothing like that, but a little appreciation would be nice."

"Thank you," I offer, nudging Blythe with my elbow. We're going to have to play nice with these freaks if we want to get out of here alive.

Baron nods to acknowledge my thanks before using the slim remote at his side to turn the TV on. The news is showing security camera footage of Blythe, the Professor, Jenica, and me racing across the tarmac at Stonehead.

"You've caused quite a stir around here the last couple of days," he says. "For once, the heat isn't on my people."

"We're all the same to them," Blythe snaps, cutting her eyes at Baron. "Even though those of us on the side of peace know the true difference."

Baron shrugs. "Point taken. Either way, I hope it was worth it."

"Olivia McNabb and the others have been

rescued," I answer, even while hoping that Dax and Sayer managed to get them back to Headquarters safely. "It was more than worth it."

"I hope so, mate. I really do. Because now you're stuck here until the heat dies down. I can try to smuggle you back out to the city limits, but it's going to take a great deal of planning and resources on my end. I hope you intend to make it worth my while."

"We don't have anything to barter with," Blythe answers. "Even if I did, I'm not sure I'd give anything to you."

Baron folds his hands and rests them on his stomach. "See, there's where you're wrong. I have it on good authority that you have Professor Hinkley's ear. In fact, you are one of the Resistance's most dedicated soldiers. Which means you have plenty to barter with, love."

"You gonna tell me what the fuck you want?"

My fingers reach out to squeeze hers and I'm willing her to calm down. Her temper is getting the best of her and the last thing we need is to have to fight out way out of here, especially with her arm hanging like a lead weight at her side.

Baron continues, ignoring the venom her tone. I think he realizes that for all her bravado, he has the upper hand here. "As you can imagine, having a hideout here in D.C. is to our advantage, though it comes with its share of disadvantages as well. I've found that smuggling in food is the worst of our troubles and I happen to know that the Resistance has quite the underground exchange going."

"If you think for one second that I would agree to sharing our food with you, you must be crazier than I thought," Blythe answers.

Baron's lips tighten at the corners and I can tell that she's starting to annoy him. My grip on her hand grows tighter, almost painful by the glare she shoots me.

"Back down," I whisper, reminding her that in my own body I stand well over six feet tall and carry over two hundred pounds of muscle. I am not afraid of her and I'm not above throwing her over my shoulder and tossing her out into the hallway if she doesn't stop making negotiations with this jackass harder. As much as I admire her spunk, I can see where it's going to be a problem in this situation. "What exactly are you asking for?" I ask Baron.

"All I ask is that the Resistance considers sending a few packages a month our way. Bare essentials. We don't need much. Our organization is smaller than yours as we do not take on the... weaker of our kind."

"By weaker, you mean children," Blythe hisses. "Because you can't turn them into one of your deranged soldiers, can you? You'd rather leave them to die and take who you can use."

Baron shrugs. "I won't deny that. It's called survival of the fittest, love. It's natural selection. In time, a new society will emerge from this one. One in which our kind are the dominant species. We are a new race, a hybrid class deserving of respect and fear, not derision and prosecution."

"We are people," Blythe argues, her fingernails biting into the back of my hand as she holds on to it for dear life. I'm grateful her bionic hand is dead because if I were holding that thing, every bone in my hand would likely be shattered by now. "We are people, just like we were before."

Baron shakes his head. "This is where we disagree, and why we are on opposite sides of this fight. In the end, we will see whose methods win out, won't we? Don't worry, love, all the pretty girls get whatever they want once I establish the new world order. If you're nice enough, I'll make sure you never want for anything ever again."

"Enough." This guy's really starting to piss me off. "We will take your proposal concerning the food to Professor Hinkley and Miss Swan. It is the best I can offer you."

Baron considers this for a moment. "No. Not good enough. You have to do better."

"What do you expect me to do?" I argue. "Pull a crate of apples out of my ass? My word not good enough for you?"

"Not even a little bit," he answers without blinking an eyelash. "I know you have a COMM device on you, all Resistance soldiers carry them so don't try to tell me you don't. Call your people right now and tell them what I want. Once I have confirmation that they intend to play nice, I will do everything I can to get you safely out of the capital."

"There's only one problem with that," Blythe answers. "The Professor and Swan are on the run too. If we agree to make the deal, you have to promise you will help us get them out as well. They are the ones we have to convince, after all."

Baron doesn't bat an eyelash. "Done."

"We are supposed to be waiting on word from them," I tell him. "I don't want to risk calling them now and compromising their position. I don't know where they could be holed up."

Baron stands. "Fair enough. We'll put you up for the night and you can let me know when you've heard from them."

"Put us up where?" Blythe questions, standing as well. "In a cell?"

Baron laughs again, shaking his head as he eyes Blythe with admiration. "Kitten's got claws, doesn't she?" he says to me before turning back to her. "It's not so much a cell as a room that locks from the outside. No need to worry, the cots are comfortable enough and it even comes with a mechanic that can get that hunk of titanium hanging from your arm to start working again."

This pacifies Blythe and she stops giving Baron attitude. She wants that arm fixed bad.

After we are shown to the room we are to share for the night, Blythe is taken to a place Baron called 'the shop'. I assume that's where the Rejects turn themselves into freaks by outfitting their prosthetics with weapons and 'enhancements'. Hopefully, she won't come back with a gun on the end of her arm or some other crazy shit.

In our room are two narrow cots with a nightstand between them, a lamp, a stack of books, a notebook, some pencils, and a digital clock. Nearby there is a small, round table with two chairs. A shower stall closed off by a thin curtain and a sink with a mirror are in the other corner. After about an hour of trying to sleep, I just can't do it. Tamryn won't get out of my dreams. Every time I close my eyes, she is on the edge of my subconscious, asking me why I didn't come for her, why I couldn't have done more to save her. I give up on sleep and move over to the table, taking the notebook and a few pencils with me. It only takes me a few seconds to get caught up in sketching.

TWENTY-ONE

GAGE BRONSON AND BLYTHE SOL
REJECTS UNDERGROUND HIDEOUT
WASHINGTON D.C.
AUGUST 18, 4010
8:00 PM

BY THE TIME BLYTHE RETURNS, I'VE BEEN AT IT FOR HOURS AND have a stack of sketches at my side. When the door opens and she appears, the pencil drops from my fingers and I can feel the toll my long session has taken on my hand and wrist. I flex my fingers, wincing as I realize that I'd completely lost myself in my art as a way of outrunning the demons nipping at my heels and reminding me of things I'd rather forget. Like Tamryn, who I know is somewhere in this underground hole with me, close enough for me to have heard her laugh again.

"Hey," she says, holding her bionic arm up and flexing the fingers. "Good as new."

I nod and smile. "I'm glad."

"You should see the shop," she says as she comes into the room and closes the door before taking the seat on the other side of the table. "It's like nothing I've ever seen."

"They show you a selection of retractable knives for your arm?" I ask sarcastically.

Blythe smiles. "Knives, guns, grenade launchers... you name it. I could turn myself into a one-woman army if I wanted to." Her smile fades and she sighs. "That's what scares me about these people. They're outfitting themselves for war, Gage. Not everyone out there thinks like the President does. Most are just scared to stand up to the government. They don't deserve the wrath of the Rejects."

"We'll stop them," I say, trying to sound reassuring. Really, I'm not sure that we can. "The Resistance is large and growing every day. We can do it."

"Not if the Professor doesn't stand down on his whole 'peaceful revolution' bit. It's not helping us to keep running every time things get hairy."

She has a point. "So tell him what you saw today. He has to believe you; this has been brewing for a long time."

"I'll do better than that. I'll show him. I snapped a few pictures while I was in there. I don't think they noticed." At my confused look, she points to her left eye and smiles.

"Damn, is there anything that eye can't do?"

She shoots me a knowing glance. "It can't show me what you're thinking," she says, her voice low. "Or why you had such a strong reaction to that girl out there earlier. When you saw her, your heart rate spiked like crazy and your breathing sped up. And now you're drawing pictures of her."

I follow her gaze down to the sketch on top of my stack, a close up of Tamryn's face split down the middle by a jagged line. On one side of that line is the Tamryn

I remember, the fresh-faced, dewy, wide-eyed innocent. On the other is the black eye-shadow wearing, titanium leg-baring girl with dark streaks in her hair and tortured eyes. The difference is startling. I look back up at Blythe and see uncertainty in her expression.

"I know I don't have a right to ask when... I mean, there's Dax and all but..." She trails off and looks down. I can't help but smile.

She's jealous.

"Hey," I say, reaching for her hand. "Of course you have a right to ask. I know all about you and Dax, so it's unfair to leave you in the dark about Tamryn."

She nods and takes a deep breath. I guess she's bracing herself to hear that Tamryn is a long lost wife or that I'm still in love with her. I tell her the God's honest truth—the whole truth—for the first time since we met.

"Tamryn and I were high school sweethearts," I begin. "We grew up together and one day, it just clicked. Everyone—our family and friends—just knew we would get married someday. After I went to law school, of course. It was always expected for me to follow in my father's footsteps."

"Sounds serious."

I shrug. "It was, but it wasn't. I mean, I cared about Tamryn but our relationship was practical and comfortable. There wasn't a lot of heat or passion. I never wanted her the way..." I trail off and Blythe's sharp intake of breath tells me she knows what I was about to say. So I just lay it out there. My eyes meet hers and even though my gaze is not my own right now, I know she can see past it to what lies inside. She believes me, I know she does, when I say, "I don't think I've ever wanted anything or anyone as badly as I want you."

She swallows and I can hear it in the silence of the room. Her hands shake as she folds them on the table. She remains silent but I can see the war happening in her mind. Me versus Dax. The stranger versus the best friend. The spontaneous choice versus the expected, safe choice. This can't be easy for her.

"Anyway, things changed after the blasts."

And then I tell her all of it. About Tamryn getting hurt and about me talking her into registering for the Healing Hands initiative. I tell her about my guilt when Tamryn cried to me about feeling like a freak. I tell her about losing Tamryn when the government started targeting Bionics. I tell her everything I can without revealing the one final truth I'm not ready for her to know yet. I know if she finds out—learns the one last thing I am withholding—it will change everything and she will hate me. When I'm done, she is staring at the drawing of Tamryn silently, her face impassive. Not for the first time since we met, I find myself wondering just what she's thinking. Finally, she looks up at me.

"It's not your fault, what happened to her." Her statement catches me off guard. "That's what this picture is about, right?" she asks when I don't respond. "I'm not an artsy person, but I can see your perception here. Both sides of Tamryn; who she was and who she's become. The line down the middle represents you."

I smile. "Pretty close. The line down the middle of her face isn't just me. It's everything... everything that's happened to her, to all of us. Hey, you're artsier than you think—most people don't have an eye like yours."

She shrugs. "Just telling you what I see." She continues flipping through them and I clear my throat as she stops on the last one, which is actually the first thing I drew when I picked up the pencils. It's a picture of her in profile, the swell of her lips a beautiful temptation on a perfectly sculpted face. The shading of her cheekbones and brow are damn near perfect. The eye is void of all emotion because it is the bionic one I've drawn and, like the sketch of Agata I made not too long ago, it showcases the machinery inside of her head. Blythe traces the wires I've drawn running through her head and latching on to her optic nerve. She smiles. "This is amazing, Gage." She then fingers the symbol I've drawn on the corner of the page and frowns. "What's this?"

"I'm not sure, really," I say honestly as I glance at the little cog I doodled on the bottom of the page. It is round like a gear, with long spokes jutting out from the center like the rays of the sun. One side is like a typical, indented gear, the other smooth as if it's been polished. "I was drawing you and thinking about how you are everything the Resistance embodies," I say, watching as she traces the little cog with her fingertip, studying it closely. "To me the smooth side represents the humanity in you, the part of you that was in the before. The side that looks more like a gear represents what's inside, the changes."

"It's the Resistance," she says with a radiant smile as she looks up at me. The smile fades a bit and her eyes widen. "Umm, Gage..."

It's the only warning I have before a blinding pain grips me, taking me to my knees. The chair clatters to the floor beside me and Blythe is beside me instantly, chanting my name over and over as I thrash on the floor, my teeth gritted and my body jerking spasmodically. My eyes find the clock and I realize that twenty-four hours have passed since I was injected with the serum containing Jack Knightly's DNA and now I'm transforming back into myself. Somewhere out there, Dax is undergoing the same torture.

My teeth scrape together and I fight not to grind them as bones pop in and out of place and realign. Skin and muscle tear apart and reform, changing me from the inside out as Jack Knightly's DNA is stripped from mine. Blythe holds me as best she can, probably trying to keep me from bashing my head on the floor, but I just can't be still. Now I know why they strapped us to tables when we first underwent the transformation.

When it's over, the pain is gone instantly, but I'm still pretty shaken. Blythe rolls me onto my back, taking my head into her lap as her face appears in my line of sight. Her lips are quirked into a soft smile.

"Hi," she says gently. "Nice to see you again."

The way she's looking at me... I've been wanting her to look at me like that all day. The recognition in her eyes wasn't there when she looked into the eyes of Jack Knightly. I've never been more grateful to be myself than I am at this moment. My hand comes up to cup her cheek, my thumb tracing circles against her skin. She closes her eyes and nestles against my palm, turning her face inward to place a kiss there. A shudder wracks my body at the contact.

Her eyes meet mine again. "Everything is so uncertain," she says as her fingers run through my hair. My scalp tingles and the sensation is rapidly coursing over the rest of my body. I bite back a groan as she continues the soothing act. "I don't know what's going to happen. Hell, we could both be dead by tonight. We could have easily been killed this morning."

I'm not sure where she's going with this, so I just stare up at her. "Yes," I say.

"It makes you wonder... if you were to die today, could you say you went without regrets?"

"Oh, I'd have plenty of them," I answer. "Regrets for not standing up to my father sooner in life, for not being there when Tamryn needed me, for failing Agata and leaving her all alone in the world... for not ever having known you in the way I want to."

At that last bit, her eyes grow wide with fear, like they do any time someone mentions love or commitment around her. Blythe is afraid, whether she wants to admit it or not. And while I think Dax's feelings scare her, I know mine are a far greater threat. Dax is comfortable and familiar and I am virtually a stranger. A stranger she can't stop staring at because she's drawn to me the same way I'm drawn to her. A stranger who has the potential to smash her heart into smithereens... or love her beyond all reason. I know which of those guys I want to be, but I know in the end I may end up the first guy, the one who hurts her. As badly as she's been hurt before, I can't stand the thought of doing it again. But then, something in me just won't leave it alone.

One last kiss, I tell myself, as I grasp the ponytail at the nape of her neck and pull her down toward me. One last moment of weakness before I tell her I'm bowing out and that Dax is the better man. Because even if he isn't, he hasn't lied to her about his past. He isn't keeping a part of himself from her because he's afraid it will ruin everything. Unlike me, he is not a coward.

But then our lips touch and I know this won't be the last time, because kissing Blythe is unlike anything I've ever experienced. It's beautiful, painful, sweet, and terrifying all at once, like diving off a cliff. I know I can never willingly let go of this feeling. Electricity arcs between us as she settles herself over me, our chests mashing together as I wrap my free arm around her. Our breathing is heavy, filling the air between our lips with promises and desire as our tongues touch. The feeling is too much for me and I groan out loud, the sound bouncing and echoing from the walls and mingling with her own strangled cry. She trembles in my arms and I know that it's affecting her too, this feeling of being out of control but unable to stop.

I pull back for a second, my hands resting on her waist, my fingers curling and bunching the fabric of her shirt. My eyes ask for permission and she nods. It's all I need to strip her t-shirt off over her head, revealing a plain white bra. For some reason, the nondescript garment gets me even more jacked up and I touch her, cupping her and squeezing, filling my palms with swollen flesh. And then we're kissing again—dueling tongues, heated breath, and low, throaty groans. At some point, my shirt joins hers on the floor and flesh is against flesh, as I roll to switch our positions, my hips cradled by hers as I press her to the floor.

Before I lose myself in her completely, I pull back, propping myself up on my elbows and staring down at her. She makes a seductive picture with her lips swollen from my kisses, eyelids heavy and lowered over chocolate eyes, hair disheveled and framing her face. Her eyes are wide, and I see fear and uncertainty there along with desire and need. She is waging an inner war and I am watching it happen in her dark gaze.

"Blythe." I only say one word, but it's loaded. She knows what I'm doing as well as I do. As much as I want this—want her—I won't take it. I want her to give it to me and I need to know that she's sure.

Her hands come up to the back of my head and she pulls me down toward her, my name a sigh on her lips as she flexes her hips against mine in a gesture of surrender.

"Gage."

With that breathless whisper, I am hers completely. And I hope with all my might that she is mine. Because as I free her from the last layers of clothing separating us, it seems as if, even for this one moment, Blythe has chosen me.

TWENTY-TWO

GAGE BRONSON AND BLYTHE SOL
REJECTS UNDERGROUND HIDEOUT
WASHINGTON D.C.
AUGUST 19, 4010
6:00 AM

IT IS WITH RELUCTANCE THAT I TURN OVER IN THE NARROW COT where Blythe and I spent the night and open my eyes. I want to stay in limbo, in this tiny cell where only the two of us exist together—no Resistance, no government, no danger, no Dax. But I know that it won't last. Soon, I will have to contact Jenica and make arrangements with Baron to get us out of here. Then, if we aren't captured or killed, it's back to Headquarters where all the things I want to avoid are waiting for us. Including the truth. Now that we've been together, there's no way I can keep it from her now.

Blythe, who slept with her cheek against my shoulder, her arm around my waist, is staring up at me shyly, already awake. I smile and pull her up against my chest.

"Good morning," I murmur, my voice thick with the clinging remnants of drowsiness.

"It certainly is a good morning," she says. My body surges with heat at the sound of her voice first thing in the morning. It's husky and thick, like syrup. It makes me want to take her again, have her one last time before we have to leave. But I control myself because I don't want her to think it's all I want from her. Holding her, looking down at her after spending the night together, is more than I could have ever hoped for from her.

"Well," I say, giving her a light squeeze. "There's one thing I can scratch off my bucket list. One less regret."

She stares at me pensively and then nods. "Yeah, me too."

She has no idea what it does for me to hear her say that. "I should call Jenica. I was hoping to hear from her by now but... nothing."

"Hmmm," she mumbles, nestling beneath the scratchy blanket a bit further and burrowing into my side. "Not yet. Just a little longer."

I oblige her and we lay together in silence for a while before she speaks again. "The tattoo on your arm—why did you choose it? I've always wanted one, but never could decide what to get."

I glance down at the eagle taking flight on my right bicep and cringe. "At the time, it meant everything to me. Being a patriot, loving my country, hoping to serve one day as a lawyer and eventually a politician."

She glances up at me in surprise. "You wanted to be a politician?"

I nod. "I grew up here, remember? Politics is everything—it was a part of my life. I thought I could make a difference."

She sits up a bit, leaning over me with a wide

smile. "Senator Gage Bronson. I like the sound of it."

I frown. "Yeah, well, it's not going to happen. Even if making off with Agata hadn't made me a fugitive, I am no longer as naïve as I used to be. Our government is a joke and the people who run it are corrupt."

"True," she agrees. "But a guy like you could change all of that if he wanted to."

"I think it would take more than one person, Blythe."

She nods. "True. But it starts with one and that's all it takes. One voice. One spark. One person willing to stand up and declare that something is unjust. That's how a revolution is started. One spark and it grows like wildfire."

Her words fill me with hope for the future because I know that she is right. No matter how dark things might seem, as long as there is even one voice willing to be raised in protest against injustice, we can survive to see things get better.

"That's what I love about you," I say honestly, cupping her face in my hand. "You're so passionate, and I don't mean in a physical way." Then I smile, remembering last night. "Well, in that way too."

Her response is cut off by the sound of a key in the lock and I quickly cover her body with the blanket before the door is swung open. I feel as if a fist has been slammed into my gut as Tamryn appears in the doorway. She falters, tripping over the threshold as a ragged gasp tears from her throat.

"Gage?" My name sounds like a gunshot in the room. Blythe clings to my arm, seated a bit behind me on the bed with the sheet pulled up over her chest. I clutch at the sheet over my waist and stare back into the blue eyes meeting mine from the doorway.

"Tamryn."

Every possible emotion that exists flickers across her face. Confusion. Anger. Sadness. She looks as wrecked as I feel for a split second before she clears her throat, her expression stoic as she avoids my gaze.

"Baron sent me to wake you," she says, her voice still as soft and timid as I remember. It clashes wildly with her black leather getup, complete with corset-like top and platform boots. She runs her hand through her black-streaked hair. "He says he'd like you to join us in the main hall for breakfast so he can tell you the plan. He wants to know if you've contacted your people yet."

Finally, I find my voice. "Ah, no," I answer. "I'll do it now and be down as soon as I can."

She nods, once, before turning in the doorway to leave. A black line—a mascara-stained tear—runs down her face.

"Tamryn, wait!"

But she is already gone. Blythe grips my shoulders tightly as I lower my head into my hands with a deep sigh. "Shit."

"Go after her," Blythe says gently. "I'll put that call in to Jenica and meet you down there."

I turn to face her, shaking my head. "No, I should stay with you."

Blythe smiles. "Come on, Gage, I'm not going to be mad if you follow her. You guys have unfinished business and I think it'll make you feel better about the whole thing to talk to her. Get it over with and get some closure. I'll be fine."

I press a kiss to her forehead before standing and reaching for my clothes. I pull them on quickly before stroking a lock of her hair affectionately. "Thank you for understanding."

She nods and reaches for her own clothes. "We all have our baggage. Do what you have to do."

"Tamryn, wait!"

I just barely catch up with her before she enters the main hall. She pauses at the end of the tunnel, but doesn't turn, her body stiffening from head to toe.

"Please," I add, grasping her arm gently and turning her to face me. "Can we talk for a minute?"

She stares up at me as if unsure before sighing and gesturing toward a nearby door. "In there. Quickly. Baron is not a patient man."

We duck into what looks like a utility closet and Tamryn closes the door and flips on a light. "What do you want, Gage?"

Her venomous tone doesn't surprise me. She hates me for what I did to her, for what I talked her into.

"I just... I wanted..." What did I want? Blythe had told me to go get some closure and I guess that's what I need. To know that she's okay, and that she doesn't hate me for talking her into becoming something she didn't want to be.

"I'm glad you're all right," I say. "I thought you

were dead."

She smiles, but it is not a happy gesture. It is laced with sarcasm and irony. "Well, here I am, alive and well."

"Yeah, and hanging out with the Rejects. What's going on? Are you in some kind of trouble?"

Tamryn folds her arms over her chest and smirks at me. "Looks to me like you're the one in trouble. I never thought you'd be ballsy enough to join the Resistance. You're not even one of them, Gage."

"No, but my niece is. You know that."

"Do they know? Who you really are?"

"What does it matter?"

She laughs dryly. "That's my Gage, always avoiding confrontation."

She has me there and it stings like a bitch. "Look, Tamryn, I'm sorry, okay? I did what I could to help you. I thought that if you had another chance at life, you would be happy. But you just couldn't accept your new body and I'm sorry for that. If I'd known that you would hate it so much, I would have left it alone."

"Sure you would have. His Perfect Royal Highness wheeling around a crippled girlfriend? Not likely."

"That's not fair," I reply, my hand biting into her arm as I lean down over her, resisting the urge to give her a shake. "It was never about that for me. I loved you regardless."

"Loved? Has even that changed, then?"

"Of course not. It's just..." I trail off, trying to find the words.

She shrugs. "It's cool, okay? I get it. We loved

each other in a way that doesn't create passion and romance. We never were that kind of couple. And just so you know, I'm not mad about becoming a Bio. At least, not anymore. I was—I'll admit that. I was depressed and still adjusting to the changes. Then they started coming after us and I was scared. It was easy to blame you for all of it, but I made my own decisions. I couldn't bear to be a cripple, any more than you could have stood watching me live as one. I've accepted what I am now and I'm proud."

I cringe. "Proud enough to join an extremist group of terrorists?"

"Don't call us that!" she shouts, her voice shrill in her denial. "We are just trying to survive."

"By targeting everyone who is not like you? By killing mercilessly? Tamryn, I don't know how you came to be here, but you're not safe with these people. You need to leave."

"They saved me!" she insists. "When the MPs came and took me, Baron and his crew apprehended the craft holding me and several other prisoners before they could take us to Stonehead. They have done nothing but protect and shelter me."

"Have you even left this place since they brought you here? Don't you watch the news or know anything about these people? They're animals, Tamryn. They believe—"

"I know what they believe! I know, and I agree with them."

My jaw drops so hard I'm surprised it doesn't scrape the floor. "You've gotta be shitting me. You can't believe that!"

"Fuck you, Gage! I am so sick and tired of having my life controlled, of having people tell me how to act or what to think. Poor little Tamryn, too sweet and innocent for the realities of the world—let's shelter her and coddle her and pamper her like a perfect, spoiled princess."

"Look, I get it. We're from the same world and I understand how you feel."

"Maybe so, but that doesn't change the fact that you're one of the people who used to treat me like that. The blinders are off and I see the world just fine, thank you. I know what I've become a part of. This is a true revolution, a war, and in war there are casualties."

"Innocent people?"

"No one is innocent—can't you see that? Those people, those idiots out there who lap up the government's shit and call it chocolate ice cream, are the worst perpetrators. They stand idly by and watch the government terrorize us and take away our rights. They are no more innocent than the ones doing the killing."

I shake my head, backing away from her toward the door. "This is insane. I can't believe what I'm hearing."

She shrugs. "Sorry, honey. Things have changed and so have I."

I can't accept it. I won't. I can't accept that I had a hand in causing this new Tamryn to emerge. "Let me help you, Tamryn. Come with me."

She snorts sarcastically. "How would your little girlfriend feel about that?"

"She'd be happy," I answer, knowing I'm right.

"Because rescuing people like you is her mission. It's what she does."

"Thanks for the offer but I'm fine here," she answers, pushing past me and reaching for the door. "I hope that seeing me again has at least put your fears about my death to rest. But life has led us down different paths. Contrary to what you might think, I chose this path on my own." She goes to leave, but then turns, glancing back at me over her shoulder. "Oh, and take my advice. Your little girlfriend? Tell her the truth, Gage. Tell her before it's too late."

And with that, she is gone. I watch her leave, standing at the entrance to the main hall as others trickle in, taking turns in line at a counter lined with boxes of rationed protein bars and canned shakes. Just like that, Tamryn is really and truly gone, banished from my life forever.

Blythe reaches the main room just as I'm finishing up with Tamryn. The two of us find Baron at a table full of his cronies, including Monkey Arms and his girlfriend, a chick with retractable metal spikes that protrude from her body. He gestures for us to join him and we do, chewing slowly on rubbery protein bars. No wonder they're so hard up for food; this stuff's God-awful.

"I've talked with Swan," Blythe says to him, but also to me. I breathe a sigh of relief to know that Jenica and the Professor are all right. "They have agreed to a small share of the food goods in exchange for your helping us escape."

Baron smiles. "You people are smarter than I thought."

"She sent me her coordinates. They are closer to the center of the city, hiding out in a hotel room. Her DNA cloaking serum will wear off soon, so we'll need to get a move on. The disguise will help her get through the streets if they need to be out in the open to meet us."

"I assume this serum she speaks of is what you were wearing when you arrived yesterday," he says, staring at me. "You had me fooled until last night when Captain Jack Knightly and Officer Grayson Barnes were discovered in Memphis, tied up and gagged at the bottom of a ditch. It didn't take long for the authorities to discover that the two men they'd thought were traitors to their government were actually terrorists in disguise." He laughs. "I'd have hardly thought you capable of such a thing, human." He calls me human as if it's an epithet. He will never let me forget that he feels himself superior to me in every way. "At any rate," he continues when I only glare silently at him. "You and whoever was your accomplice in disguise should lay low for a while. It won't be long before they find your DNA at Stonehead. Now that Officer Knightly's is no longer attached to yours, they will be able to identify you. Besides Professor Hinkley and Miss Swan, you two will become America's Most Wanted."

I shrug. "We will take our chances."

Baron nods. "You do that. Now, get your friend on the horn and give her these coordinates." He slides

ALICIA MICHAELS

a scrap of paper across the table toward us. "We will rendezvous here in two hours. I am willing to part with one of my smaller crafts for you to use."

"We are grateful," Blythe says.

I shoot her a surprised glance as Baron and his companions stand to leave us.

"What?" she asks when she catches me staring, mouth hanging open.

"How'd that taste coming up?" I ask with a laugh.

She laughs too. "Like shit, but we have to play nice with these freaks if we're going to get out of here alive." Her face is suddenly serious again. "Did you find Tamryn? Is she okay?"

Remembering our confrontation in the utility room wipes the humor from my expression as well. "It was hard," I admit. "She's not the same."

Her hand covers mine on the table. "None of us are," she says. "It's not easy for any of us, life after the explosions. We're all doing the best we can."

"She's happy here," I confide. "She said as much to me herself."

"It's her defense mechanism," she replies, her fingers stroking mine soothingly. "She's been battered and broken, terrorized. We have all coped in different ways."

"I offered to take her with us but she refused."

Blythe smiles again. "I know you don't want to hear this, but you can't save everyone, Gage."

I lower my head. "I know that. But that doesn't stop me from wanting to try."

"You saved Agata. And you saved me back at

293

Stonehead. You're a hero, Gage. You're Agata's hero." I glance up and our eyes connect. "You're *my* hero."

Her words are everything I want to hear, but they settle in my gut like boiling acid because I know that I am no one's hero. I am certainly not worthy of the infatuation I see in her eyes when she looks at me. Telling her the truth has just become even harder. Damn near impossible.

TWENTY-THREE

GAGE BRONSON AND BLYTHE SOL
REJECTS UNDERGROUND HIDEOUT
WASHINGTON D.C.
AUGUST 19, 4010
9:00 AM

"WHERE ARE THEY? THEY'RE THIRTY MINUTES LATE."

I glance down at my watch, even though I know that Blythe is right. Jenica and the Professor are late. We are seated in a small, four-seater hovercraft with Barony and Monkey Arms—whose name I discovered is Ronnie—waiting for the other two members of our party to arrive. Baron was true to his word, navigating the small craft through the convoluted system of train tunnels before bringing us out on the very edge of the city, where we escaped to the wooded area on the edge of D.C. without being detected.

We arrived with five minutes to spare, but have been waiting far too long.

"Something's wrong," I say, staring out of the window and scanning the horizon for any sign of them. We are hovering just near the tops of the trees, concealed by branches, but still able to see quite far.

"Something is *very* wrong," Blythe agrees. "Jenica is never late for anything."

"It's your call, mate," Baron says.

"No," Blythe snaps, her eyes still locked on the distance for any sign of movement beyond the bustle of the city. There is none.

"We're not leaving without them," I add, putting an end to Baron's almost-suggestion. I'm sure he'd leave his own mother behind if it meant saving his own ass.

"Well, we can't sit here much longer without worrying about attracting attention," Ronnie argues. "So something's gotta give."

"Look, there!" Blythe cries, pointing in the distance at something we can't see. By the look on her face, it can't be good.

"What do you see?" I ask, trying to be patient as I remember that Blythe often forgets she can see miles farther than the rest of us. She's so used to the Bionic eye that it's now a part of her.

"Jenica and the Professor on a hover bike," she says, her hands shaking in her lap. "And about a dozen MP crafts in pursuit. They're coming in fast, too."

Just as she says this, I can see them, a black shape rising above the trees and hurtling toward us fast. Seconds later, twelve other black shapes rise up behind them like a swarm of wasps in pursuit.

"Goddamn it," I whisper under my breath as my mind races from thought to thought. What the hell are we supposed to do now?

From the corner of my eye, I see Baron smirk before exchanging glances with Ronnie. From behind me, another formation of dark shapes rises from the woods. At first, I think that we are surrounded and dead for sure now. Then, those shapes move past us, toward Jenica and the pursuing enemy. The top hatch of our craft is open and Baron and Ronnie are on the roof, flagging down one of the other small crafts passing by. One of them stops to pick them up and, just like that, they are gone.

Jenica and the Professor drop down from between the two groups as they hurtle toward each other, their intentions clear. For now, everyone has forgotten about America's most-wanted terrorists.

Chaos ensues.

Everything happens so quickly, yet later I know it will replay itself in my mind with slow-motion deliberateness. The MPs open fire first, their lasers whizzing in the open space between the Rejects. Blythe quickly grabs the controls of our craft—now abandoned by its original pilot—and steers us in the direction Jenica and the Professor took.

"What the hell is going on?" she screeches, her biceps and forearms tense as she grips the controls tightly, carefully steering us through the trees. She's not as good a pilot as Jenica, but she's certainly better than I am.

"Looks like Baron used us as bait to draw the MPs into a fight. Or he saw our meeting as a golden opportunity. Either way, it's just the distraction we need to get out of here."

"There they are!"

I follow Blythe's finger to where Jenica has set her bike down on the ground. She and the Professor have dismounted and are dashing toward us as Blythe lowers us to the ground. Before we are even completely landed, she lowers the bottom hatch. By the time the bottom of the small craft hits the ground, Jenica and the Professor are on board. Blythe quickly leaves the controls to Jenica and takes an empty seat behind me. The professor sits across from her, behind Jenica. Both look exhausted but are none the worse for wear.

"I take it our rebel friends are picking a fight," Jenica says as she takes off smoothly, pulling us back up above the trees. No one has to answer her, as we can all see what's happening clear as day. Instead of returning fire, the Rebels are concentrating on erecting and activating a single weapon.

The Annihilator.

"Shit!" Jenica hisses as we look on helplessly.. We can do nothing but watch. "We have to do something!"

"Fuck them," Blythe practically growls from her seat. "Are you kidding me, Jenica? The MPs have been using the Annihilator for years. It's about time they got a taste of their own medicine!"

Jenica turns, the right side of her face—the metal part—gleaming in the sunlight as her left eye narrows, zeroing in on Blythe. "That is *not* how we do things, Sol."

"No," Blythe agrees, "but we aren't exactly the ones doing it, are we?"

"All that aside," the Professor says softly, appearing grieved at the thought of watching this play out without intervening. "Short of crashing our vehicle into it, there is nothing we can do. You all know how I feel about violence but in this case, we can do nothing."

"We can do one thing," I say. "Get the hell out of here while they're focused on each other.

Jenica's jaw ticks in agitation and I can tell she doesn't like it, but we have no choice. She whips the craft around for a getaway, just as the Annihilator is activating, incinerating every MP within its sights, melting flesh from bone with the flip of a single switch. The Professor turns away from his window, hand pressed to his mouth as if he's going to be sick. Blythe is watching, though, her face unrecognizable to me. This is a part of her that I hate to see but know exists—the angry girl who lost everything and battles her own rage over it. I can see satisfaction gleaming in her eyes along with sadness. Sadness, because she knows that no matter how good it feels to watch those officers go up in flames, it won't bring her family back. It won't give her that normal life she lost back.

Not to mention the fact that even though the Rejects are responsible, the Resistance is going to get blamed. Jones and the Enforcers are going to be pissed, and that means dangerous repercussions are soon to come. The shit is really about to hit the fan and we are all about to get splattered.

Jenica takes the long way home, hoping to keep under the radar and shake off any pursuers as we make our way back to Resistance Headquarters. We are mostly silent during the flight, though at some point I let my hand fall back behind my seat and reach for Blythe. Wordlessly, she places her hand in mind and holds it tightly. We remain that way until our craft lowers over the Nevada dessert, its landscape set on fire by the setting sun. By the time we reach the tunnel that leads into the citadel, she has released my hand.

I try not to overthink things where Blythe and I are concerned. Something has happened, and I don't mean just in the physical sense. We made love physically, but there was more. A lot more. A lot of things unsaid. For now, though, so much has happened and there is more to come. Things will get worse before they get better, especially now that the Rejects are openly waging war with the rest of the country.

So for now, I am content with the knowledge that in the battle for Blythe's heart, I am now clearly the frontrunner. It's enough for me for now. Especially since I still have one last part of myself to reveal to her. As much as I know she won't like it, I hope that she can accept it. It has to be soon, before I let things go too far. Bruising her trust is the last thing I want to do when she already withholds it from most other people.

Once we are safe inside the refuge, Jenica lands us just outside the hangar where several members of our team are waiting for us. Dax is the first one we see as we disembark and he scoops Blythe up and hugs her so swiftly and intently that it take everything in me not to beat the shit out of him right then and there. I have to remind myself that they are best friends and that bond can't be broken no matter how she might feel about me.

Yasmine appears next, her arm around Agata. When she sees me, her face lights up like a city skyline and I imagine mine does the same. When she hurtles herself toward me and I swing her up into my arms, twirling her in circles, I am reminded of why I am here. I am fighting for her, for her future and the future of those like her. While things haven't been easy, and the fight is far from over, I count today as a win just for the simple fact that I've made it home to her safely. I've lived to fight for her another day.

Laura and Sayer Strom are there too, and everyone is accounted for. Sayer had to do some evasive flying to get away from D.C., we are told, but their return to headquarters was otherwise uneventful. Jenica exchanges a glance with the Professor before announcing that she's going to see to the welfare of our rescued prisoners.

"I'll go with you," he volunteers. The two disappear together across the landing strip just outside the small hangar where our Hovercrafts are stored, headed toward the main building. Somewhere in that building, a broken and battered Olivia lays recovering in the infirmary.

We all go our separate ways from there. Blythe to her room to shower, change, and rest, and me to tuck Agata in before doing the same.

"Talk later?" I mouth to her silently as she glances at me over her shoulder. She nods and smiles, heading across the artificial grass toward Mosley Hall.

I lead Agata toward Hexley Hall, listening to her excited chatter and watching her with a smile as she bounces and skips along the grass beside me. The Professor's weather simulator is imitating a balmy summer evening and the twinkling of false stars almost trick me into feeling as if I'm looking at real twilight overhead. It's wonderful, this safe haven the Professor has created for us with the help of so many, but it is also a prison, one that I hope Agata won't have to spend the rest of her life in.

"Hey, squirt," I say, pausing when we reach the park situated at the center of our hidden city. "Hold on for a sec, I want to talk to you about something."

"Okay," she answers as she joins me on a bench, blue eyes locked on me expectantly. She has so much of Trista in her and it reminds me of our encounter at Stonehead. I wonder if I will someday have to tell Agata that her mother has been killed. I want more than anything to go back for my sister, but keeping my word to her is more important. I can't very well keep Agata safe if I am killed or captured trying to rescue Trista. Now I wish I'd fought harder to get her to come with me when I made my first escape. At the time, she'd refused.

"I hope you're happy here," I begin slowly, trying to keep my tone conversational. "You making friends with the other kids?"

She nods and shrugs. "Yeah, everyone's nice, I guess. Although, none of the other kids know calculus."

I laugh, remembering Agata's first days out of surgery. After getting her bionic cerebrum, the kid had traded in her dolls for notepads and pencils, finding fun in equations that looked like hieroglyphics to me.

"Well, neither did you until you had a computer

for a brain."

"Only half my brain's a computer," she argues, shooting me a playful glare. "But it's okay because the scientists in the Professor's lab have promised to let me apprentice with them. If you say it's all right, I can study under them after my classes."

I mull it over for a moment and try to think of what Trista would want. "Okay," I answer, producing a smile from her. "But only if you keep up with your other schoolwork and take time once and a while to be a kid. Scuff your knees, beat up mean boys, and make mud pies or something. Deal?"

Agata smiles—showcasing a gap at the bottom where a tooth used to be—and points to a bandage over a red and bruised knee. "Way ahead of you."

I frown. "What the hell happened to you?"

"Dani Perkins pushed me down," she says as if it's no big deal. "He's bigger than me, twelve years old and a big bully."

"Want me to kick his ass for you?" I ask, only half serious. I'd at least pick the kid up by the back of his neck and shake him a few times.

"Already taken care of," she says slyly. That look has more of me in it than Trista. I know she's been up to no good.

"What did you do, you little demon?" I ask with a chuckle.

"Oh, just showed everyone in Hexley Hall that Dani is afraid of the dark. I shoved him through an open utility closet door and locked it. Used my EMP signal to turn the lights out. Left him in there until he started shrieking like a little girl. By then, everyone in the dorms had come out to see what the fuss was all about. Miss Milica let him out and, of course, Dani told on me."

My lips are twitching but somehow I manage to keep a straight face. Milica Brady, the Hexley Hall matron who watches over all the children, is a no-nonsense woman. "How much trouble did you get into?"

Agata shrugs. "Bathroom duty for a week. Nothing I can't handle."

"That's my girl." Seems like the kind of thing she'd have learned from me, anyway. After we sit in silence for a while longer, I speak up again. "I saw your mom yesterday."

Agata's smile fades and she looks up at me with tear-filled eyes. "Where?" she asks, her voice suddenly small. For all her intelligence, just then I am reminded that she is only a scared little girl.

"At the Stonehead facility." I decide not to insult her intelligence. She deserves to know the truth no matter how hard it is to hear. "She works there now. She didn't recognize me, though, because I was in disguise, but she asked about you. You should have seen her face when I told her that you were safe. She's happy about that."

"Is she going to be okay?" she asks, one tear spilling over and running down her cheek. I swipe at it with my thumb and fight tears of my own.

"I hope so, squirt. I really hope so. She could be in a lot of danger. She's been helping people like you escape. If they find out, it's not going to be pretty."

Agata smiles through her tears. "Mom's a hero,"

she says. "Like you."

I try to smile back but it's hard. "I'm not a hero, Agata. I'm just your uncle who loves you and wants you to be safe. No matter what happens, always remember that. I'll be here for you as long as I can but what I'm doing here is dangerous and I don't know... well, I may not always be around."

She swipes at her face with the back of her hand and sniffles before resting her head against my chest. I wrap my arm around her and pull her close.

"I pray for you," she whispers in the darkness. "I pray for you every day. When you went to Stonehead, and then when you went back again. I prayed."

I simply squeeze her tighter. "I know you do, squirt. I know you do."

And in the back of my mind, I wonder if the prayers of a child are enough.

TWENTY-FOUR

GAGE BRONSON
RESTORATION RESISTANCE HEADQUARTERS
AUGUST 20, 4010
1:00 AM

THE INFIRMARY IS NEARLY EMPTY WHEN I ARRIVE, BUT THEN, I planned it that way. I don't want a lot of witnesses or intruders during my visit. I pause at a makeshift nurse's station situated just outside the row of doors concealing recovering patients. Olivia McNabb is behind one of them.

After a lot of persuasion, the nurse lets me in to see her and I am grateful to find I am her only visitor.

"She is resting, though not peacefully," the nurse—who has two bionic arms—says, gazing into the room with concern as she opens the door for me.

I frown, seeing that Olivia is held down to the bed by a set of buckled straps. "What the hell is this?"

The nurse sighs, her face etched in sympathy. "The poor thing keeps trying to hurt herself. Can't sleep more than an hour before the nightmares start. She won't take her drugs because they make it hard for her to wake up from them, so she's in constant pain. She keeps ripping out her IV and won't let anyone touch her. We had to do it, especially after she broke a mirror and

306

tried to slit her wrists with the glass. They doctors have diagnosed her with Post Traumatic Stress Disorder, the poor thing. Keeps mumbling about what they did to her... awful things. It's no wonder..."

The nurse trails off as I open the door to the room, stepping inside slowly, afraid that any sudden movement might set Olivia off. As it is she looks exhausted, but I can tell she's fighting sleep. I close the door, shutting the nurse out, and step into the pristine, white room. White walls, white floors, and white sheets covering a pale and drawn Olivia. Even her eyes are washed out in the bright fluorescent lights, their depths empty and fathomless.

"Bronson," she croaks, her voice hoarse—likely from screaming.

"Hey," I say as gently as possible. She reminds me of a scared doe and I don't want to do anything to rattle her after the hell she's been through. Her hand rests at her side, now a bandaged stump. I sit by her bed and study her face, trying to decide where to start.

"I'm not dead, you know," she jokes.

I cringe. "I know."

"Then why are you looking at me as like you've just seen a ghost?"

I sigh and plunge ahead with what I've come to say. "I'm sorry, Olivia. For not protecting you at Stonehead. I should have done more to keep them from taking you."

"What the hell would you have done, Bronson?" she scoffs, rolling her eyes. "Sacrificed yourself? What a goddamn noble dude you are. Blythe's a lucky girl." She smiles when my eyes widen. "Oh, come on, if you guys haven't hooked up already, you will eventually. That girl's infatuated with you and any nitwit can see you feel the same way." I don't answer and Olivia keeps talking, her voice gaining strength with each word. "Look, you're brave, okay? You're hot and you have big muscles. You're sweet and you care about people enough to put yourself on the line for them. That makes you a hero, no matter what happened to me. Okay?"

I shake my head. "I don't feel that way, but thanks."

"Look at me." Our eyes connect. "You can't win all the battles. You can't save everyone. This is war, Gage. We are at war with our own government and there are casualties. The sooner you get that through your head, the better off you'll be. And while we're on the subject, that mission going wrong wasn't just your fault. The success of it rested on my shoulders too. We took the lead on that one together and one of us got caught and tortured. Don't go feeling sorry for me just because I'm a girl. I'm stronger than I look."

Hell yeah, she is. I know grown men who couldn't endure what Olivia has. And the worst is yet to come if her PTSD is as bad as the nurse let on.

"You're such a badass," I say with a laugh. "You're a true survivor, Olivia."

She tears up, but I pretend not to notice. "Get out of here, will you?" she says, her voice cracking. "I'm sure somewhere out there, there's a kitten up a tree that needs rescuing."

I laugh again and stand to do as she asks, not

wanting to intrude if she prefers to cry alone. "I'll come back to visit soon, okay?"

She nods. "I'd like that."

I turn to leave her, closing the door just as a sob rips from her throat. The sound stays with me, haunting me as I retreat back down the hall. I think I'm going to lose it myself when I turn the corner and come face to face with Blythe.

"Hey!" I say as I steady her after nearly knocking her over. My hands on her shoulders, I gaze down at her in relief. She is a sight for sore eyes. "What are you doing here?"

"Came to see Olivia," she says. "I couldn't sleep thinking about her. You?"

"Same," I answer. "She's in bad shape, Blythe. I would give her some time. I just left and she kind of hinted that she wanted to be alone right now."

Blythe nods. "I understand." Boy, does she ever. As I slowly get to know Blythe, I'm learning that she's the queen of wall building. Vulnerability is a weakness, one she detests in herself. "Can we talk for a minute?"

"Yeah."

She grabs my hand and pulls me into the first door we come to—a sterile and darkened procedure room. There is faint moonlight coming through the window, and we stand close to it, deciding to leave the light off so as not to alert anyone to our presence in the room.

The second we are alone, I grab her and pull her against me, pressing my lips to hers demandingly. She answers eagerly, coming up on her tiptoes to loop her arms around my neck, which presses her body neatly against mine from chest to hip. My tongue sweeps the inside of her mouth, tasting her, taking her in through all of my senses as my hands touch and I inhale her scent. The soft sounds from the back of her throat complete the sensory overload until I'm drowning in her, unable to come up for air even if I want to.

When I finally let her go, her breathing is harsh like mine, her mouth swollen and her eyes wide. She stares at me as if she is both afraid and enamored.

"What is this?" she asks breathlessly.

"I'm not sure," I answer as honestly as I can. "Blythe, there's something I need to tell you."

"Me first," she says. "I hope you won't be mad at me, but I think it's best that we keep this—whatever this is—just between us for now."

My eyebrows shoot up in surprise. "That's an excellent idea, actually. Why would think I'd be mad?"

She shrugs and then giggles. "I don't know, something tells me you'd like nothing better than to rub Dax's nose in this."

"As fun as that sounds, I agree with you about keeping it between us. So much is happening and things are uncertain all around. We should give ourselves time to decide just what this is before we go letting everybody in our business. Besides..." I pull her against me and bury my face in her neck. She gasps in surprise. "I like secrets."

"Hmm," she mumbles as I kiss her neck, working my way down the slender column to the slope of her shoulder before biting down there with just enough pressure to make her squeal.

"Secret kisses, secret touches," I stare at her pointedly, "secret sex in the infirmary."

Her eyes grow wide in shock but she laughs. "Here? Now?"

I shrug. "Why not? We're alone. This awesome bed-thing reclines. It's a sterile environment. Plus... I've always wanted to play doctor."

She shrieks and laughs as I grab her by the hips and lift her up on the table, laying her against the reclining back before stepping between her legs. My fingertip traces the seam of her jeans as she lays back, watching me with eyes gone dark with desire. I quirk one eyebrow up and grin as my finger trails up, lifting her shirt and exposing her beautiful stomach. Her ab muscles jump and bunch beneath golden skin. My touch skims back downward, circling around the button on her pants.

"Gage," she whispers, her voice heavy and thick, her breathing racing like a subway train.

My name on her lips sends a jolt of electricity down my spine and I make up my mind to have her saying it again, over and over, before the night is gone. I've just flicked the button at her waist open, when the sound of a key scraping a lock sends us into a panic. I rear up off her and she leaps to her feet, grabbing my hand and pulling me through another door on the far side of the room and closing it just as the other opens.

The room we've found ourselves in is on the other side of a one-way mirror, through which we can see Jenica and the Professor entering alone, looking just as we had a few moments before—as if they don't want to be seen.

"What is this place?" I whisper to Blythe as we watch them through the glass. Jenica steps behind a screen in the corner while the Professor starts preparing some sort of equipment. "What do you think they're doing here?"

"This room we're in is an observation room," she says. "Thus the one-way mirror. As far as what they're doing here... I'm not sure."

"They're a couple," I blurt out, needing to tell someone. "I overheard them on the hovercraft on the way to Stonehead. "He loves her. They're in love."

Blythe watches the Professor move around the room, collecting instruments and laying them on a tray near the table. Jenica emerges in a paper gown, naked beneath, and slowly walks over to the table.

"I always knew he loved her," Blythe said. "You'd have to be a fool not to see it. But Jenica..." she trails off.

"I know. She doesn't seem capable of love. She's so hard and cold."

But her eyes don't look cold. In fact, she looks downright scared and miserable as she lies back on the table, watching the Professor move around the room. The metal instruments rattle in his grasp as his hands shake, his eyes misty behind his glasses.

"Are you certain we are making the right decision?" he asks as he pauses, reaching out to grab her hand.

Jenica's voice wavers when she answers. "This world is dark," she says, clasping one of his hands in two of hers. "Too dark to bring an innocent life into it."

The Professor sniffles, his curly head bobbing as he nods. "You're right, of course. It's just..." he trails off and hangs his head.

"Neville," Jenica says gently—more gently than I would have ever thought her capable, "I want nothing more than to be a family. Me, you, and..." she pauses and I hear emotion creeping into her voice. Too much emotion to show outwardly. She clears her throat and schools her face into its emotionless mask. "But it's not the right time," she continues, once again herself. "It would be cruel to subject a child to our kind of life. Maybe someday but not now."

The Professor nods. "As long as you're sure, Jenica. I will do whatever you ask of me." A moment of silence passes between them. After a while, he gently lays her flat on the table and pulls a set of stirrups out of the table's sides. "Are you ready, my love?"

Jenica nodes silently, turning her face away from him and toward the mirror. I inhale sharply before I remember that she cannot see us. Blythe's hand is over her mouth and I turn my back, giving Jenica her privacy. The weight of what's happening on the other side of the glass causes acid to build up in my throat and anger to burn in my gut. Our world is so fucked up that a couple who love each other cannot even start a family together for fear that their child will live in a world where its parents are hunted and persecuted.

After another moment, Blythe turns her back as well, her shoulders shaking as she sobs silently, tears streaming down her face and neck. I pull her against me, burying her face in my chest to muffle her sobs. At some point, we sink to the floor together and I am holding her as tightly as I can, allowing her to get it all out, every bit of anguish she feels at having to be a witness to this moment.

I lose track of time, but it feels like hours before it's over and they leave, the Professor toting a bag of medical waste to be incinerated—what is left of their unborn child—and Jenica walking slowly beside him, her eyes glazed and unfocused as if she is in a trance. When we are alone again, Blythe turns to me with red-rimmed eyes, her voice hoarse from crying.

"It's not fair," she whispers. "They deserve to be happy. They deserved..."

I pull her back against me and rest my chin on top of her head. "I know. But maybe Jenica's right. Maybe it would be cruel to bring a child into the world at such a time."

"Then is it also wrong for us to be doing what we're doing? Starting a relationship during a revolution? Making room in our lives for love when there's so much hate in the world?"

"No," I answer vehemently. "Blythe, look at me." I tilt her chin up with my hand. "It is during times like these, when the night is its darkest and hate is at its strongest, that we are forced to remember love. We have to cling to it, to use it as a light against that hate, and as our anchor in the storm. It is the only thing that is constant and true, when everything else is falling apart."

She wraps her arms around my waist and clings to me as if for dear life. "Does that mean, if I were to tell you to let me go...?"

"Never. I would never let you go."

Blythe sleeps in my arms for what's left of the night. After her reaction to Jenica's abortion, I don't want her to be alone. Even though she won't say it out loud, I know she doesn't want to be. She sneaks out of my room at sunrise, promising to meet me downstairs for breakfast. I let her go reluctantly, wishing we could spend the rest of the day in solitude, much like we did back at the Rejects' hideout. It just feels right and everything outside of the moment when I turn to find her still next to me feels wrong.

Reluctantly, I let her go and then prepare to meet her downstairs to pretend in front of everyone that nothing has happened between us. When I get to the dining hall, the cleanup from breakfast is happening and there are only scraps leftover. I content myself with black coffee and some kind of pastry, scarfing it down as I go from the dining hall, to the second floor where the common gathering area is. I find Blythe already there along with Dax, Yasmine, Jenica, Laura, and Sayer, eyes glued to the news. Jenica shows no sign of her trauma the night before. She is her old self again: tight ponytail, tailored black clothes, stoic expression.

Dax sidles up beside me. "Looks like you made a splash in D.C.," he says, nudging me with his elbow.

He's laughing but a cold stone of dread just dropped into my gut as video footage of our escape from the Rejects' hideout flashes across the screen and a news anchor rambles on about dangerous, Bionic terrorists staging an attack on our nation's finest. They show the annihilator being used to incinerate the MPs, no doubt causing anger and shock throughout the nation, reminding everyone just how 'dangerous' the Bionics are. Naturally, there is no footage of the MPs mutilating Olivia or shooting at us first.

Then, my face is on screen again, and I know my secret is no more.

"Along with the most recognizable faces of the terrorist organization known as the Resistance, was this young man. His appearance on the wrong side of the fight against the Bionics may come as a shock to those who recognize him. He has been identified as Gage Drummond, who you may know as the son of President John Drummond. When contacted, the White House issued no statement and the president remains silent on the matter for now, but a source close to the family reveals that Drummond's son went missing months ago after repeatedly challenging his father on the issue of the Bionics. Close family friends reveal that Gage had become militant in his beliefs, bordering on extremism in his arguments, despite not having a Bionic prosthetic himself. He was said to have become violent in recent months before disappearing. He has now resurfaced and it would seem from this footage that he has chosen to align himself with terrorists against the very man—his father no less—who has worked so tirelessly to set our nation right after the horrific bombings of 4006. What does this mean for President Drummond—especially so close to reelection? Our political analysts will be debating the matter right here on Channel Twelve. Tune in at ten o'clock

pm Eastern. This is Channel Twelve News, Angela Kerney reporting."

Someone mutes the volume and several pairs of eyes are boring into me. My mouth is dry as I turn to face them, their expressions fixed in various degrees of shock, sadness, and anger. Blythe's eyes burn the hottest of all, like hot coals, as her mouth twists in disdain. And my worst fear since she and I first kissed is staring me in the face. The truth has come out before I had a chance to tell her, and now she cannot trust me anymore. Nausea churns in my gut as Jenica appears in my line of vision, her arms crossed over her chest.

"The Professor said he recognized you," she accuses, as everyone else watches me silently. "Now we know why."

"I..." I trail off, grasping for words. Really, what is there to say? I didn't reveal the truth from the beginning because I wanted them to accept Agata. Then, I figured if I could perform well on the first mission to Stonehead, they would trust me and believe that I truly wanted to be here to fight on the side of good. Then, everything went to shit and my window of opportunity passed me by. Now I'm going to pay for it and I'm not sure I'm ready to face the consequences. "I never meant to keep it from you this long," I finally say and it sounds pathetic, even to my ears.

"Dax, take him to lockup."

Dax does a double take as if even he doesn't believe his ears. "What?"

Jenica shoots him a glare that could melt titanium. "I said take him to lockup. He can't be trusted.

We need to keep him there until a decision can be made about what to do with him."

Dax stares back and forth from Jenica to me and back again before accepting a pair of the ionized handcuffs. He walks up to me, his face a mask of confusion and hurt. Damn, I actually feel sorry for lying to him now, too. Despite the Blythe situation, he and I seemed to be forming some sort of odd friendship. Men who fight together tend to find some sort of common ground, and Dax and I had finally found ours.

"Don't fight me," he warns as he advances on me. "Make this easy, okay?"

I can tell he doesn't want to do this anymore than I want to fight him. I turn and place my hands behind my back, surrendering without hesitation. As Dax cuffs me, my eyes meet Blythe's and see tears in her eye, though she's holding them in check. Anger is at the forefront as she seethes, glaring as if trying to burn a hole through me. When Dax guides me past her, I stop, bringing him up short and staring down in her gorgeous, chocolate eyes.

"Blythe." In that single word is a plea, a prayer. In that one word, I'm begging her to see me for who I really am and not just my name or who my father is. Willing her to see what's right in front of her—to see that I am who she thinks I am. The only thing that's changed is my name.

For a moment, she falters and looks as if she is softening. Then, as quickly as that vulnerability appeared, it is gone and anger appears once again. Before I can say anything else, her bionic hand comes up, swifter than a snake, and whips me across the face. Everything goes dark.

ABOUT THE AUTHOR

Ever since she first read books like *Chronicles of Narnia* or *Goosebumps*, Alicia has been a lover of mind-bending fiction. Wherever imagination takes her, she is more than happy to call that place her home. With seven Fantasy and Science Fiction titles under her belt, Alicia strives to write multicultural characters and stories that touch the heart.

The mother of three and wife to a soldier, she loves chocolate, coffee, and of course good books. When not writing, you can usually find her with her nose in a book, shopping for shoes and fabulous jewelry, or spending time with her loving family.

Alicia can be found on the web at any of the following links:

www.fantasybyalicia.com
www.facebook.com/fantasybyalicia
www.goodreads.com/alicia_michaels
www.pinterest.com/fantasybyalicia
Follow her at Twitter: @fantasybyalicia
Follow her on Instagram: @authoraliciamichaels

Sign up for Alicia's monthly newsletter for sneak peeks at upcoming works, insider news, and a special monthly giveaway for subscribers only: http://eepurl.com/pgwOz

More by Alicia Michaels

CPSIA information can be obtained at www.ICGtesting.com
Printed in the USA
LVOW12s0652180115

423243LV00006B/7/P